THE BEST LAID PLANS

21 STORIES OF MYSTERY & SUSPENSE

Edited by
JUDY PENZ SHELUK

Superior Shores Press

PRAISE FOR THE BEST LAID PLANS

"The crimes featured in *The Best Laid Plans* range from poisonings to bank robberies to contract killings, and the settings are both varied and fascinating: ski resorts, nursing homes, subway stations, the mountains of West Virginia, the plains of Oklahoma. I loved this book!" — *John M. Floyd, EDGAR nominee and three-time DERRINGER AWARD winner*

"An entertaining collection of tales that deliver in all aspects. Much like buying a lottery ticket, these characters are dreaming up ways to permanently solve problems."—*Kevin Tipple, KEVIN'S CORNER*

"Sometimes the best laid plans just don't go quite as expected. And sometimes, they go exactly as hoped for. A dazzling collection of twenty-one short tales of mayhem, leaving both the reader and the corpses breathless. A five-star read that you will never forget."—*Kate Thornton, DERRINGER-nominated short story author*

"Even the best laid plans can go awry, and with these well-thought out mysteries and 'I didn't see that coming!' short stories, you get to enjoy it twenty-one times. Different styles, different settings, different murderous intentions, but all are entertaining, intriguing, and just plain fun."—*Kathleen Costa, KINGS RIVER LIFE MAGAZINE*

"Delicious! That word best describes the yummy bites of well written, crafty crime stories. Murder for hire, money, sibling rivalry, envy, infidelity. Murder of the wrong person. Killer acting and get-rich schemes...the clever twists are endless. A feast of delicious short bites that adds up to a very satisfying literary meal."—*Catherine Astolfo, bestselling author and two-time winner of the ARTHUR ELLIS AWARD for Best Crime Short Story*

*Lunch Break by Lesley A. Diehl was originally published as *Lunch Break: A Mystery Story* (Kings River Life Magazine, February 2016). It has been revised for this collection.

*Oubliette by Edward Lodi was originally published in *Hardboiled No.19* (November 1994) and reprinted in *Murder on the Bogs and Other Tales of Mystery and Suspense* (Rock Village Publishing, 2001).

*Deadly Dinner by LD Masterson was originally published in *Noir at the Salad Bar: Culinary Tales With A Bite* (Level Best Books, 2017).

*The Sweetheart Scamster by Rosemary McCracken was originally published in *Thirteen* (Carrick Publishing, 2013).

*The Stonecutter by Edith Maxwell was originally published in *Fish Nets: The Second Guppy Anthology* (Wildside Press, 2013).

*Plan D by Judy Penz Sheluk was originally published in *The Whole She-Bang 2* (Sisters in Crime Toronto, 2014).

Compiled and Edited by Judy Penz Sheluk, www.judypenzsheluk.com

Cover Design by Hunter Martin

Cover Illustration by S.A. Hadi hasan

Published by Superior Shores Press

ISBN Trade Paperback: 978-1-989495-00-1

ISBN Kindle: 978-1-989495-01-8

ISBN ePub: 978-1-989495-3-02

ISBN Kobo: 978-1-989495-02-5

First Edition: June 2019

Second Edition: July 2019

In the realm of ideas everything depends on enthusiasm...in the real world all rests on perseverance.

— JOHANN WOLFGANG VON GOETHE

CONTENTS

INTRODUCTION

The year was 2003. My position at a high-end office furniture manufacturer had been eliminated during a massive company downsizing and restructuring. I faced a future of looking for another job in the corporate world or finally following my dream of becoming a writer.

Common sense dictated the former. I had twenty-plus years of business experience, primarily in management roles, and always in finance. My writing credits, on the other hand, included a few unsold short stories crafted in creative writing workshops, and exactly one acceptance: a column in *Antiques & Collectibles Showcase* about my husband's collection of antique clocks, for which I was paid $75 and three copies of the magazine.

Payment for that article arrived on the very day I'd been given my pink slip. Some might have found it ironic, laughable, even. I viewed it as an omen. I informed my husband, Mike, that I was going to become a full-time writer. And then I set about forming a plan to succeed. Because while I knew that, as a writer, rejection was assuredly going to be part of my future, failure wasn't an option.

Fast forward to 2012. I'd managed to carve out a successful

second career as a freelance journalist and magazine editor. And yet, something was missing.

I found the answer at Bloody Words, a now defunct mystery conference held in Toronto in June 2012. I went as a reader and a fan, and left knowing that I wanted to write a novel. I already had a world created for it, based on a short story written in yet another creative writing class. How hard could it be?

Plenty hard, as it turned out. But I persevered and in 2013, after a dozen drafts and several hundred hours, I was ready to start the submission process for *The Hanged Man's Noose*. I thought a decade of publication credits would smooth the way.

They didn't.

I took comfort from an article about Kathryn Stockett, bestselling author of *The Help* (if you haven't read it, you must). Stockett, you see, had faced sixty rejections over three and a half years. And still she didn't give up. Turned out sixty-one was her magic number.

It turned out 2014 was my magic year. In July, I signed a contract with Barking Rain Press for *Noose*. By November, I'd had two short stories published in two different anthologies, *World Enough & Crime* and *The Whole She-Bang 2*.

My writing journey hasn't always been easy, but even in my darkest hours it's never felt like work. And I never could have or would have done any of it if I hadn't taken a chance back in 2003.

And so now I'm taking another leap of faith. First, by setting up my own imprint, Superior Shores Press, in February 2018, and then by deciding to publish a multi-author collection of short mystery stories.

I'll admit that I was nervous. What if no one responded to my call for submissions?

I need not have worried. In all, seventy-one submissions were received. Countries represented included the U.S., Canada, England, Norway, Italy, Australia, and Argentina.

Reading seventy-one stories with a view to accepting twenty (I planned to include one story penned by me) was far more difficult than I'd anticipated, but after two weeks and multiple reads I came up with a long list of about thirty-five. Culling those down to the final twenty took another two weeks, and many more reads.

The stories within this collection are faithful to the underlying theme of the best-laid plans, albeit in very different ways as interpreted by twenty-one very different authors. There's crime and criminals, history, humor, and humility, scheming and skullduggery, danger, detectives, and deception. In short, everything you might expect to find in an anthology of mystery and suspense, and, hopefully, more than a few twists and turns you weren't.

And now, welcome to what I hope will be the first of several anthologies published under the Superior Shores Press umbrella.

The best laid plans and all of that.

Judy Penz Sheluk

KM ROCKWOOD

KM Rockwood draws on a diverse background for her stories, including working as a laborer in a steel fabrication factory and supervising an inmate work crew in a large state prison. Since she retired from working as a special education teacher in correctional facilities, inner city schools, and alternative schools, she has devoted her time to writing and caring for her family and pets. Her published works include the Jesse Damon Crime Novel series (Wildside Press) and numerous short stories. KM is a member of Sisters in Crime National, Chesapeake, and Guppy Chapters. Find her at kmrockwood.com.

FROZEN DAIQUIRIS

KM ROCKWOOD

PENELOPE REGENWOLD PAUSED to take a deep breath before she pushed open the swinging door to the expansive kitchen in her recently purchased McMansion. If the builder offered an upgrade, her kitchen had it.

To her dismay, the new address didn't come with an automatic entrée to the social elite of the community. In fact, she'd overheard Mrs. Van der Horne label both her and her house *nouveau riche*.

She immediately volunteered to host the annual gala for the Ladies' Society in her new house. She would create a memorable occasion, and they, in turn, would accept her into their fold.

When people looked doubtful, she added that the Regenwolds would absorb all expenses. Matthew, her husband, was not pleased, but faced with her tears, he acquiesced. She, in turn, promised to be as frugal as possible with the affair.

In an attempt to hold down the costs of hiring help, she acquired Suzie. Suzie was a very convincing humanoid robot, a Support Unit-Zed series, purchased secondhand from the bankruptcy liquidation sale of a failed food processing plant.

At the time, Suzie seemed like perfect household help. The only costs were the purchase price and an occasional new battery pack.

The robot never complained or asked for time off. Penelope figured she could be used for both food preparation and as a server. But Suzie quickly revealed herself to be very literal and lacking in social graces. In fact, she could be quite rude. Penelope had found that while programing updates were available from the manufacturer, they would not be available for installation in time for the gala. She contacted a temporary agency to supply several waitresses.

Suzie should have had preparations well underway, but somehow, despite her efficiency, Suzie often managed to get things wrong. What would Penelope find in the kitchen?

She took another deep breath and pushed the door open. And sneezed.

Boxes. Boxes cluttering the counters. Boxes stacked on the floor. She felt her throat closing and addressed her robot. "What is all this?"

Suzie turned a bland face to her.

Before she hosted another affair, Penelope would definitely purchase the hospitality and advanced communication apps and have them installed.

Suzie surveyed the cluttered kitchen. "Boxes."

Penelope closed her eyes and counted to ten. "I see that they are boxes. Boxes of what?"

"Feathers."

Feathers? Sure enough, the boxes all bore a logo with the name, "Feathers Galore!" The exclamation point was in the shape of an ostrich plume.

Penelope sneezed again. She was allergic to feathers. "And why do we have boxes of feathers?"

Suzie swiveled her head from the boxes to Penelope. She had a very disconcerting way of looking right through Penelope with those expressionless acrylic eyes. Although Penelope knew quite well she was dealing with a piece of machinery, and not a person, sometimes she found it hard to keep that in mind.

"Well?" she prompted.

Suzie hummed softly. She was scanning her files for the correct response. "For the cock tails," she finally said.

"Cocktails?"

Penelope was startled to hear her own voice emanate from the robot. "We'll need cocktails for the party." It took her a few seconds to realize that she was listening to some of the instructions she'd given Suzie. "Figure a minimum of five cocktails per guest, and two hundred guests."

She hadn't realized that Suzie had the capacity to record and play back messages. The thought was disconcerting. "I thought we decided on frozen daiquiris."

"Yes," Suzie said. "Frozen daiquiris. Lime, strawberry, melon. To be made just before 8:00 p.m, when the guests arrive."

"So what's with the feathers?"

"For the cock tails."

"Feathers for the daiquiris?"

Suzie hummed. "I can find no recipes in my archives for daiquiris that include feathers. I will connect to the internet…"

"Don't bother." All this made Penelope's head spin. "Please explain. Why feathers?"

"I ordered enough peacock feathers to make two thousand tails for the party. I anticipate having them assembled in approximately seventy-two minutes."

Penelope sighed. Suzie was thinking—if thinking was the right word—of tails made from peacock feathers. Cock tails. An entirely separate project from the daiquiris.

Suzie had been listed as an "all-purpose" assistant, handling assembly tasks as well as office duties, plus maintenance. She was really quite good at ordering and receiving. Not to mention housecleaning. Those additional apps for hospitality and communication would really have to be installed as soon as possible. "Cancel the peacock tails."

Suzie made the humming noise, checking and adjusting internal files. "Cock tail assembly cancelled."

"We have to return all these feathers to wherever you got them."

Another humming noise. "Arrange return of feathers to supplier."

"But not now." Penelope glanced at her diamond watch. "The

party is in a few hours. We need to move these boxes out of the kitchen so we have room to work."

"Move boxes." Suzie picked up a stack of three from the floor. "Move them to the warehouse?"

"We don't have a warehouse. Follow me." Penelope led the way down the hall and flung open the door to the five-car garage.

Three of the bays were filled with cars. Penelope's own BMW, the family Escalade and Matthew's current project, an antique Austin-Healey. He had left his tools and supplies spread across the floor.

Penelope didn't understand why Matthew insisted upon spending so much of his time on such a blue-collar hobby. He should be learning to play golf and hobnobbing with his new neighbors, mostly politicians and executives. But he was never happier than when he had his head under the hood of an old car, a tool in his hands and grease up to his elbows.

After much nagging on her part, Matthew nearly always responded appropriately to questions about his livelihood with references to the financial services agency he owned and operated. He'd stopped telling everyone all the seedy details of his bail bond and repo company. A very successful bail bond and repo company. But still...

But now was not the time to worry about that. Just so long as Matthew didn't show up for the party with the grease under his fingernails. Or handcuffs peeking out of his back pocket.

"Pick these things up first," Penelope said to Suzie. "Put them over there." She pointed to shelves along the back wall where tools and unidentifiable spare parts competed for space with gallons of antifreeze and windshield cleaner, containers of oil and other fluids.

Suzie put the boxes down and began gathering the items on the floor.

Penelope was a bit reluctant to leave the robot unsupervised. Who knew what she might get up to? But she did need to check on the main rooms of the house before the cleaning and setup crew left.

The house looked magnificent. Flower arrangements: check.

Additional rented seating: check. Fancy paper guest towels in all the bathrooms, as well as small scented candles waiting to be lit. Check.

A faint odor, unidentifiable but somewhat funky, wafted through the rooms. A damp smell, almost fishy. Was there water in the basement after all the recent rain? That shouldn't happen in a new house like this. The smell was not exactly unpleasant, but not desirable either. Penelope took additional candles, placing them around the rooms. When they were lit, they should mask the smell. She could have Matthew check out the basement later.

Going back to the kitchen, she saw that Suzie had removed all the boxes and was now lining up ice buckets. Next to the buckets were ice cube trays, filled with water.

Horrified, Penelope asked, "Didn't we get enough ice?"

"I will make it." Suzie touched a finger to the water in one of the trays. Instantly the contents froze.

Penelope had no idea Suzie could do that, but she supposed it made sense that a food processing company would appreciate an ability to fast freeze things.

"Are the hors d'oeuvres ready?"

"As ordered."

"Have you finished the miniature quiches?"

Suzie hummed. "Six hundred ready for delivery."

"How about the dates wrapped with bacon?"

"Six hundred ready for delivery."

Well, at least Suzie's food assembly app seemed to be working fine, Penelope thought. "What else?"

"Twenty-five pounds of shrimp, ready for delivery. Six hundred crostini. Two hundred blini topped with caviar. Two hundred…"

"How long did all that take?" Penelope asked.

Suzie hummed. "Six hours scheduled for hors d'oeuvres production."

"When did you do it?"

"From two a.m. until eight a.m. this morning."

Of course, needing no sleep, Suzie would work through the night and early morning hours. "And you got all that done in six hours?"

"Yes."

"Preparing the exact quantity of each that I asked for?"

"Except for the mini-bagels with cream cheese and lox."

"Oh?" Penelope blinked as Suzie's expressionless eyes stared through hers. Just a machine, she reminded herself. "What happened? Were you not able to get genuine lox?"

"Oh, no. I purchased the finest quality cold-cured sockeye lox. $75 per pound."

Penelope winced. Although she had told herself, and Suzie, don't skimp on quality, that was a lot to spend, even for lox. "So what was the problem?"

"I was not provided with a specific number of units to assemble."

Well, mini-bagels weren't one of the main features. It didn't matter if they didn't have many of them, or any at all. "Did you get any of them made?" Penelope asked.

"Yes. I assembled mini-bagels with cream cheese and lox during the scheduled time remaining after the hors d'oeuvres with specific quantities were finished."

"And how many did you get made?"

"Forty-nine thousand six hundred nineteen."

Penelope had to sit down. How many pounds of outrageously expensive lox went into that?

"And where," she asked, "did you store them?"

"In the basement."

"But the basement isn't refrigerated…"

Suzie hummed. "Violation of food storage regulations. Subject to penalty."

"But you put them there anyhow?"

"Default setting: override compliance with health department regulations. Temperature and sanitary conditions meet minimum practical standards. Possible consequences: citation by health department inspectors."

Penelope suspected a basement full of smoked salmon canapes accounted for the funky smell she'd noticed earlier. "I'm going to get dressed. What are you going to be doing?"

"Prepare ten gallons of simple syrup."

"Do you know how to make simple syrup?"

Suzie hummed. "Seeking recipe."

"Equal parts sugar and water. Heat until the sugar dissolves, stirring constantly. Can you do that?"

"Yes."

"Do you know what to do after that?"

"Finish making frozen daiquiris. Lime, melon and strawberry." Suzie indicated a trio of large bowls on the counter. One was filled with slices of lime, one with strawberries, and one with chunks of cantaloupe melon.

The melon chunks looked strange, the usual orange color mixed with striped beige. Penelope looked closer. Each piece of melon had rind attached. Seeds floated on top.

"The melons need to be peeled, and the seeds removed," she said.

"Peel melons and remove seeds," Suzie repeated.

"Yes." Penelope sighed. "Do you know how to make daiquiris?"

"Of course. Lime juice, rum, ice, simple syrup. Slice of lime for lime. Add crushed strawberries for strawberry, crushed melon for melon."

Suzie hummed. Penelope wondered if this meant the robot was reviewing the instructions. All she could do at this point was hope.

After she was dressed, Penelope lit all the candles. She was right; the funky salmon odor did recede, replaced by a somewhat nauseating sweet smell. She checked to make sure the servers had all arrived and were presentable, and satisfied, headed back into the kitchen.

Suzie stood idle in the center of the room.

Every inch of counter and table space was now covered with trays filled with glasses, precariously stacked ten high. Penelope closed her eyes. She should have realized that Suzie would make all thousand daiquiris at once.

The glasses were grouped by color. Clear, pink and light orange. But the contents looked strange. Penelope peered at one, then picked it up.

The daiquiris were frozen solid.

"Suzie!"

The robot sprang to life. "Yes?"

"What are these?"

"Frozen daiquiris."

"But they're frozen solid!"

"Yes."

"They're supposed to be slushy!"

"Slushy?"

The doorbell rang. Penelope could hear one of the servers opening the front door. "Yes, slushy. Not frozen solid. How could anybody drink these?" She looked desperately at the stacks of filled glasses. "Do you think you can make them slushy?"

"Probably." Suzie hummed. "Yes."

"Then please do so. I need to greet my guests."

People tumbled in. Matthew, with his hair slicked back and actually looking presentable in his tuxedo, smiled and greeted the arrivals.

Penelope was relieved to see the daiquiris on the trays that the servers passed around were appropriately slushy. She took one herself and swirled it gently in the glass, but she was too nervous to drink it.

As she circulated and made small talk with the guests, Penelope noticed that some of them looked a tad unwell. A few sat down abruptly.

Mrs. Van der Horne returned an empty glass to a tray and took another melon daiquiri. She frowned, put her hand to her throat, and downed the new drink in one gulp. Then she staggered a few feet, retched, and collapsed. She knocked over a side table. The burning candle which had been perched on it rolled across the floor.

Penelope dashed over, prepared to stomp out the flame, but it went out as the candle rolled across the carpet.

Several of the guests were now swaying unstably on their feet, some vomiting. Penelope looked on in horror as more succumbed. The only ones left standing besides herself were Chief Inspector

Reylander, a reformed alcoholic and therefore did not drink, and two of the servers.

She dashed into the kitchen.

Suzie was melting frozen daiquiris and emptying them into a large pitcher.

On the counter next to her, the daiquiris appeared to be of the proper slushy consistency.

"The guests are all vomiting and collapsing," Penelope said, in full panic mode. "What could be happening?"

"Probably the ethylene glycol," Suzie said, continuing to empty glasses into the pitcher.

Penelope lifted one of the properly slushy glasses to her nose. It smelled fine. She touched her tongue to the contents. It tasted fine. "What's ethylene...whatever you said?"

"Ethylene glycol?" Susie kept at her task.

"Yes."

"Antifreeze." Suzie gestured at a large jug on the floor by her feet. "Makes the daiquiris slushy, not frozen."

"Antifreeze! Isn't antifreeze *poisonous*?"

"Toxic?" Suzie asked. "Yes. It's sweet, so it doesn't affect flavor. And it makes the frozen daiquiris properly slushy."

"You put toxic antifreeze in the daiquiris?"

"Yes."

"But that'll make people sick!"

Suzie hummed. "Adulteration or contamination of food products. Violation of food safety standards. Subject to penalty."

"You knew that? And you used it anyhow?"

"Default setting: override compliance with food adulteration or contamination regulations. Does not meet safety standards. Possible consequences: consumption may be lethal. Citation by health department inspectors. Criminal investigation and prosecution for manslaughter probable."

Wisps of smoke curled under the kitchen door.

Penelope opened the kitchen door and peered out.

The odor of smoke and vomit mingled to drown out both the

candles and the salmon. Flames danced and flickered at several locations, licking up at the curtains and furnishings.

Some people writhed on the floor. Others lay still.

This party was going to be a memorable occasion all right, just not in the way Penelope had hoped.

SUSAN DALY

Susan Daly has found her niche in the world of short crime fiction, where she fights for justice and rids the world of deserving victims. Her stories pop up in a surprising number of anthologies. Her story "A Death at the Parsonage" won the 2017 Arthur Ellis Award for best short story from Crime Writers of Canada. A member of Sisters in Crime National, Toronto, and Guppy Chapters, Susan lives in Toronto, a short commute from her superlative grandkids. Find her at susandaly.com.

SPIRIT RIVER DAM

SUSAN DALY

SUSAN DALY

Toronto

October 1964

"Lot 5, *Spring Morning in Ste.- Rose* by Anne Savage."

Imogen sat near the back of the audience as the auctioneer went into the details of the painting on offer. It was safe to tune him out, since *Spirit River Dam* was Lot 68. She avoided glancing at Bryan in the next seat. It was hard enough to maintain her equilibrium.

Spirit River Dam was going to make them both a tidy little fortune. Cormack Fine Art Auction House was the most prestigious in Canada, and they handled only the finest paintings.

Six weeks ago, she hadn't known of the painting's existence. Nor had virtually anyone else.

"THERE'S A MAN HERE WITH A PAINTING."

Imogen looked up from her desk in her private office to where her assistant, Linda, stood in the doorway.

"There's *always* a man with a painting. A family heirloom, no doubt?"

"Actually, this one might be worth looking at."

"Might it?" Really, Linda should know better. Just because the prestigious Pemberton Gallery had an entrance right off Queen Street, hopeful hawkers assumed they could simply drop in, as though this were a high-end pawn shop. As if any dusty old canvas-and-oil combination with a good story—*Grandpa accepted it from some starving artist instead of payment for delivering the baby*—should bring big money.

Linda persisted. "It could be a Thomson."

These damned art history graduates. So full of their own expertise.

She only hired them because they were willing to work for peanuts, happily performing the most menial tasks, all the while believing they were on the first step of a serious career in the art world. As if most of them didn't wind up in retail. Or in the suburbs with babies.

"They're always Thomsons." She didn't trouble to hide her annoyance. "Thomsons or Jacksons. And I suppose it's been in his family for generations with no one the wiser?"

"Yes, exactly." Linda's face took on a look of irritation, where most of her predecessors would have been cowed. "You could at least take a look at it."

"Oh, all right." But before Imogen could do more than push back her chair to stand up, a familiar figure appeared in the doorway behind Linda. "Oh, God, I should have guessed."

"Hey Immy," her ex-husband, Bryan, said. "Wait till you see what I've got."

⏳

IMOGEN ALLOWED Linda and Bryan to drag her into the appraisal room, where the occasional painting had, in fact, been identified as Art. Most came to nothing.

The painting lay face up on the table, surrounded by a nest of brown paper and string. A small work, oil on board, perhaps seven inches by ten, in a dark, shabby frame.

"Thank you, Linda. You'd better go back and keep an eye on the front of the gallery."

Linda left, oozing resentment. They both knew the other assistant was out there.

⏳

IMOGEN STEPPED up to the table and took a look. A long look. In spite of herself, she began to feel the keen energy that had flowed from both her assistant and her former husband.

The painting depicted a dam on a river, surrounded by the trees of late autumn. The center part of the dam consisted of four tall posts rising above the concrete base spanning the river, supporting a crossbeam.

She felt the kind of tingle in her chest that couldn't be ascribed to paint analysis or provenance or a solid signature in the corner. She just felt it to the depths of her art expert bones.

It *was* a Tom Thomson.

Not from the signature (there wasn't one). Not because it looked liked his style (though it did) or contained his subject matter (it did that as well). Nor from the brushstrokes or the colors or the board it was painted on (though they ticked all the boxes, too).

She just knew.

A painting by one of Canada's most revered and groundbreaking painters of the early twentieth century, a man whose innovation had been the basis for an entirely new school of Canadian art. His iconic *West Wind* hung in the hallway of every public school in Ontario.

And, not incidentally, an artist whose works fetched ever-escalating prices with each passing year since his death.

Imogen's fingers were itching to turn it over, take it out of its narrow vintage frame (that ticked the right box too), and see what was on the back of the board. But first...

"Where did you get this, Bryan?"

Enthusiasm glowed in his rather sweet (she had to admit) round face. He still reminded her of a teddy bear. An excited one, at the moment. "My Aunt Peggy. It was hanging in her dining room as far back as I can remember."

"Really? I never noticed it." But would she have? In the six years of their ill-fated marriage, had they ever had dinner at his aunt's house? She couldn't visualize the dining room of the 1930s bungalow.

"How did it come into your family?"

"She always owned it. Or Uncle Bert, I guess. It was the family joke. 'Oh, I see you're admiring Bert's Tom Thomson.' But no one ever thought it actually *was* a Thomson. Certainly not Aunt Peggy."

"And you're the one who inherited it? I mean, were you *specifically* named in the will as the recipient of this painting?" Tracing the legal ownership was as important as the provenance itself. Imogen was trying to remain calm, not get too excited. It might still have been a case of, "Oh, take anything you like, dear..." over the heads of legally deserving cousins.

"Yup, once removed. Aunt Peggy and Uncle Bert were married in 1911, but never had any kids. He died in 1938. My aunt died about ten years ago and left everything to my mom. When Mom died, it all came to me."

Imogen nodded. She'd last seen Bryan a year ago at his mother's funeral.

Okay, the ownership sounded secure. She'd still have to confirm it through the legal channels because, frankly, Bryan could spin a good story, as she knew all too well.

"So what made you decide it might be a Tom Thomson, instead of the old family joke?"

"I just couldn't get over the idea that if people joke about something enough, maybe it really has some basis. We all knew Uncle Bert was an amateur painter. He hung out with some of those Group of Seven painters in Algonquin Park around the time of the First World War."

"*Did he?*" The provenance was beginning to take hazy shape.

"He did a whole bunch of paintings when he was up north, starting around 1914. Every one of them was, well, derivative of the artists he met up there. Varley. Jackson. Lismer. My aunt had a lot of them hanging around the house, including this one. She always assumed it was another stab at trying to emulate these guys, but it was the only Thomson-inspired painting he had."

"Are his paintings any good?"

"Not even close," Bryan said. "He made an effort to learn from them all, but it was clear he could never quit his day job as an actuary."

⏳

ARMED WITH GOOD LIGHTING, the right tools, and a camera, Imogen set to work. She'd prefer not to have Bryan watching her every move, but she couldn't very well banish him from the room since he owned the painting. Maybe.

After taking pictures of it front and back, she laid the painting face down on the cloth-covered work surface and examined the back. It had been sealed with thin brown paper, stuck to the back of the frame all around. No hint of any identifying marks there, no dealer's sticker or any writing. Any chance of helpful notes would be underneath, on the back of the board itself.

With infinite caution, Imogen eased the paper away from the frame with a thin, flexible knife, and found that most of it came away eagerly, the glue having dried up perhaps half a century ago.

Bryan leaned in close as she slid away the fragile paper.

The back of the board was almost as innocent of marks as the paper. Only some faint writing in pencil. Printing, actually. Just a few words, and...was that a date?

"What does that say?" Bryan asked, peering even closer.

"Quit breathing down my neck." She took the camera and aimed it carefully to capture the information on the board, taking shots from all angles.

As she put down the camera, Bryan picked up the picture and examined it under the light.

"Spit... no, Spirit something. Maybe river?" he said.

Imogen squinted at the printing and tried again.

"What's that third word?" Bryan asked. "D...?"

"Damn," Imogen murmured, as all the discovery energy flowed out of her.

"That's it, *Dam*. 'Spirit River Dam.' It's up in Algonquin Park. That makes sense. Tom Thomson's regular painting grounds, right?"

"No, *damn*. With an N. As in, damn it all. Look at the date."

Bryan looked at her, then at the date. 1920.

"It's not a Tom Thomson."

⌛

"Lot 29, *Kayaks on the Gull River* by Ethel Curry."

Even Bryan knew Tom Thomson had died in 1917. Nearly fifty years later, the legend of his dramatic and so-called mysterious death lived on.

The letdown at seeing the date still gnawed at her, though she should have known better. But now, Plan B was in full swing.

⌛

BACK IN HER OFFICE, they dealt with the disappointment over a bottle of Northern Spirit Rye that Imogen kept handy, though usually for celebrations.

Spirit River Dam mocked them from the top of her bookcase.

"You know, that painting really had me going for about five minutes," she said, holding up the glass and gazing at the river and the dam through the dark golden liquid. "It sure looked like the real thing."

Bryan nodded, and drained his glass. He refilled it. If she'd always thought he had the look of a teddy bear about him, now he looked like a teddy bear that hadn't been invited to the picnic.

"The history supports it," he said. "The style supports it, the subject matter—"

"I *know* all that, Bryan. Everything falls into place. I'll bet if I took it to a professional appraiser, they'd find even the paint had the right chemical composition. After all, if those guys went out on expeditions together, they might have got their supplies from the same place."

"Or shared them." He heaved a sigh. "It's just that date."

Imogen said nothing as a handful of ideas and consequences chased around in her brain.

"It *is* only in pencil," Bryan mused. "I'll bet it would be easy to change it. Except that would be fraud."

"Absolutely it would be fraud." Imogen paused. "If it were changed to, say, 1915. However...."

Bryan looked up, his bushy eyebrows raised.

"If the date weren't there...." She tried the idea on for size. "If it somehow went missing...."

It might be doable, with the right kind of eraser.

Bryan's eyes narrowed. "Seriously?"

"Without any date, who's to say when it was painted?" Imogen felt a new thrill stirring inside her. "It has the look and feel of Thomson all over it. We just take it for a proper analysis. We're not saying it's a Thomson, we're just letting the experts have a look at it, make their decision."

"You think it we could pull it off?" Hope and doubt mixed in Bryan's voice.

"What we need is your family history. What have you got in the way of family papers? Letters? Pictures? Proof your uncle hung around with Tom Thomson?"

"Yeah, for sure. You should see the boxes I've taken out of my mom's house. And some of them came from Aunt Peggy's basement too. There's got to be something there."

⏳

"OKAY, what's the worse that can happen?" It had been Bryan's mantra for the past few days.

"You tell me." Imogen was examining the back of the painting for the umpteenth time.

"They notice the date was erased."

Imogen shrugged. She'd done a good job. There wasn't a hint

that a date, or anything, had been written there. "If they do—and they won't—they might figure out *someone* removed something. Perhaps they might even see it said 1920. But there's nothing to indicate I—*we*— did it. Your aunt could have removed it forty years ago."

"Yeah, I guess."

"Okay, let's see these papers." Imogen put the painting on the sideboard, and between them they began to dig into the carton Bryan had brought: Aunt Peggy's papers as they related to Uncle Bert's early life as a would-be artist.

Most of it was of no consequence. Various notebooks and documents relating to Uncle Bert's life as an actuary. A pamphlet titled *Whole Life vs. Term Life.* A book of death and morbidity tables from 1935.

It was Bryan who found the postcard. A tinted photo image of a lake and a lodge. A one-cent King George V stamp with "war tax" overprinted on it.

Mowat Lodge, 12 May, 1916

Dear Peggy, Feeling much better. All this fresh air. I've been meeting up again with some of those painter fellows we met before the war. They sure are generous with their time and showing me their techniques. You'll be pleased to see my paintings when I get back. Look forward to seeing you next week. Your ever-loving Bert.

"Hey, this is gold," Bryan said. "Puts him right on the spot, at the right time, with the right people. He could easily have bought the painting, or got it as a gift."

"1916, eh? He wasn't in the War?"

"He was. According to Aunt Peggy, he got caught in one of the first gas attacks. Not too bad, but it was the end of the war for him. That's why he went back up to Algonquin, for some fresh air and rehabilitation. It was after the War that he settled down to his job at an insurance company."

They found a few photos, mostly cracked and faded and unlabeled. The gem, however, was a snapshot of five men in outdoor clothes standing on what looked like the verandah of a lodge, holding a string of fish. The names were written across the bottom, "Fred, Tom, Pete, me, Jack."

Bryan tapped his finger on "me." "That's Uncle Bert."

"Tom" was recognizably Tom Thomson.

"The photo itself is probably worth something," Imogen remarked. She pulled some more ephemera from the old carton.

"Whoa...I don't like this," Bryan said. He was gazing at a piece of drawing paper. It looked like it had been torn from a sketchpad. He handed it to her.

A sketch of a long, wide dam, looking very much like the one in the painting. The same four upright posts at the center. And in neat, square lettering the label *Spirit River Dam 1920.* Different handwriting from what was on the back of the painting.

"We lose this for sure." Imogen said. Locked away somewhere safe.

"Um, Immy..." Bryan looked troubled again. "Is there any chance that dam wasn't even *built* until 1920?"

Imogen felt a shiver in her brain. Oh damn...

☒

"LOT 57, *Percé Rock, Late Afternoon* by Doris McCarthy."

What could possibly go wrong?

She'd heard that line too many times in movies. Just before the worst possible thing went wrong.

Nothing. Nothing would go wrong.

Not even the history of the dam itself. Prompted by Bryan's question, she'd contacted an acquaintance at the Department of Lands and Forests. He'd looked into archives and old maps, and easily determined that the dam had been built in 1905.

So. That river crossed.

They'd covered all the bases. The provenance, Uncle Bert's history, Bryan's ownership. Even one of the oils, Freeman's White, had been identified. A paint not popular with the other artists in his coterie, but used by Tom Thomson. (Though, as Bryan had unhelpfully pointed out, possibly loaned to an amateur painter eager to learn.)

Capping all that, Arthur Tyler had decreed it to be genuine. If one of the most respected art appraisers in Canada had given it his stamp of approval, then surely it was all clear sailing.

Nonetheless, her palms were growing sweaty. Well, whose palms wouldn't, considering she had a half-share in a valuable painting coming up for bid in the next few minutes. Real *or* fake.

Even if someone eventually blew the whistle on the painting, there was nothing to show she and Bryan hadn't acted in good faith. As she'd pointed out to Bryan, anyone might have erased the telltale date from the back of the board.

Still...

In her mind's eye, she saw the fateful figures reasserting themselves one by one, burning through the paper seal on the back of the painting. Like something in a *Twilight Zone* episode.

1...9...2...0...

⌛

LOT 67 WAS KNOCKED down for $53,000.

Imogen gazed to the right of the podium, waiting for the assistant to bring out Lot 68, *Spirit River Dam*.

Instead, he came on and handed the auctioneer a piece of paper.

Bryan was quivering beside her. "What—"

"Shut up." She didn't move her lips.

The auctioneer didn't miss a beat.

"Ladies and gentlemen, there's been a change. Lot 68, *Spirit River Dam*, has been withdrawn from the sale." He waited a moment for the reaction to lessen, then went on. "And now, Lot 69, *Winter Day on Robert Street*, by Arthur Lismer."

Bryan, now a sickening shade of green, croaked, "We have to get out of here."

"Are you serious? We'll go speak to Mr. Cormack, like any affronted owner. Remember, Arthur Wylie passed it as—"

But even as she stood up, she saw they had no choice anyway.

Harry Cormack stood waiting for them at the end of the row. Along with another man, looking serious in a nondescript suit.

⧗

IN THE BACK OFFICE, the atmosphere was thick with apprehension as they sat at a table opposite Harry Cormack and Arthur Wylie. Nearby sat the man in the dull suit. Lawyer? Imogen shivered.

She gave Bryan a look intended to command, *let me do the talking.* But first, she waited for the questions.

Mr. Cormack spoke first.

"Miss Pemberton, Mr. Grace, did either of you at any time suspect that this painting was *not* a Tom Thomson?"

"We hoped it was, of course." Imogen explained in her best gallery owner manner. "That's why I sent it to Mr. Wylie, an acknowledged expert. He confirmed it was indeed a Tom Thomson." She nodded in his direction. *Over to you, Mr. Know-it-all.*

Arthur Wylie didn't look perturbed. He launched into tedious detail about all the documentary evidence, plus the physical evidence of aspects of the painting, plus the evidence of style and angle of brush strokes. Blah, blah, blah.

Finally he ground to a halt, and Mr. Cormack asked him why he'd now changed his mind.

"Oh, well for one thing, the subject matter. I've only just today learned the dam didn't actually exist at the time of Tom Thomson's death."

"But that's not—" Bryan's protest was cut off by Imogen's kick to his ankle.

She kept calm. None of this was incriminating. She was on solid ground here. "The dam was built in 1905, according to the Department of Lands and Forests records."

"Yes," Mr. Wylie said. "Originally." He opened a folder on the table in front of him and removed what looked like a photocopy of an old file photograph. "Here's how it looked then." He slid it across the table.

The superstructure consisted of two posts, not four as in the painting. She could feel Bryan's shaking reaction, but this time he remained silent.

"It seems the first dam was washed away in the spring floods of 1919. It was rebuilt in 1920. Like this." He showed them a second old photo, with four posts and a crossbeam, looking just like the drawing they'd found, and just like the dam in the painting.

Still not busted, however.

"I wish we'd known," Imogen murmured, with a dollop of regret. "It would have saved us all so much time and trouble."

But Mr. Wylie wasn't with her there.

"I think you *did* know." His voice was quiet, unassailable.

"How could we? Any more than you did when you appraised it."

"Do you know anything about these?" He pulled another item from his bag of tricks.

A familiar green and yellow photofinishing envelope. Imogen's whole being turned to ice.

She'd forgotten. Entirely, totally forgotten about the pictures she'd taken when they'd first uncovered the back of the painting.

What had she done with the film?

Mr. Wylie spread the prints on the table.

"I don't like being made a fool of, Miss Pemberton."

The words hit Imogen hard in the face.

"Where did you get these?" she asked. The words "Spirit River Dam 1920" seemed to glow from the shiny black and white prints.

He ignored the question. "And I don't expect your assistant likes being treated as nothing more than a file clerk."

Linda? Where did she come in? And anyway, that was her *job*: filing, photocopying, running errands— Imogen's heart made a leap for her throat. Errands...Taking film to the drugstore. Picking up the prints.

Mr. Cormack spoke again. "I must say, I've been highly impressed with Linda. Her education, her extensive art history knowledge, not to mention her experience. Did you know she spent three years studying and working in Florence? And, of course, her initiative. Linda researched the history of the dam. Far more thoroughly, it would appear, than you did."

"When did you meet her?" Traitor. She would be sacked without a reference. She'd be lucky to find work at a Mac's Milk. She'd regret the day—

"When she applied for an apprentice position with us two weeks ago. She starts Monday morning. And now," he turned toward the serious looking man in the nondescript suit, "May I introduce Inspector Williams from the Toronto Police Fraud Unit."

⌛

SPIRIT RIVER, Algonquin Park
 November 1916

Tom looked out from his vantage point on the hillside, savoring the view of the river and the dam. It was one of the last good days for painting in November, he figured, before the snow came in earnest. Gray cloud banks, with the sun breaking through every now and then, just to keep things promising.

After this, he'd be painting snow all winter.

Within a few minutes, he had his gear set up, his paint box propped on a handy rock, with its seven by ten inch board in place for an oil sketch, his thermos of tea nearby.

But twenty minutes later, the nature of the scene still evaded him. The draftsman in him just couldn't work with the dam's structure.

"Damn," he muttered. He poured some tea into his enamel mug and gazed at the view again.

"Don't like what you see?"

Tom turned to see the old man he sometimes encountered in this area. Greg Howard, a retired engineer with a cottage at the north end of Smoke Lake.

"I don't know. It just doesn't sit right with me, the way the dam looks."

"You got a good eye, boy. It *is* all wrong."

"Well, I started out as a draftsman in my brother's firm."

Mr. Howard pointed his pipe at the dam. "See those two posts in the centre? The sluice gate guides? Should've been four of them."

"No kidding. Were you involved in this?"

"Not me. I was already being put out to pasture when our firm got the contract, back in '04. My nephew, Frank, was the lead on the project. Young fool. I told them it wouldn't work. But no, he knew best. Claimed they were good plans."

"And they weren't, I guess."

"They were garbage. So now, every other year, in the spring floods, they have to shore it up as best they can."

"Can't it be repaired?"

"Sure. With money and time and manpower. Won't happen now, though, what with this war going on, all the young men—and the engineers—out there in France. That's why Lands and Forests lured me out of retirement to design a fix."

Tom nodded. "So what will it look like when it's rebuilt?"

"Got some paper?"

Tom handed him his sketch pad and a drafting pencil, and in a few quick strokes, the old guy had brought to life the dam as he said it should be.

Tom looked at the drawing. "That's more like it, I think. It looks balanced."

Mr. Howard added a label in his neat engineer's printing. "There you go. Spirit River Dam, 1920. You come back here and paint it then, it will look all different."

"Maybe I'll just paint it that way now," Tom said. "Who knows where I'll be by 1920. Out west, maybe."

"Or fighting in France?" He pulled a flask out of his pocket and offered Tom a tot of rye for his mug.

"Thanks. You think the war will last that long?"

"Wouldn't be surprised. Before those politicians and generals are finished, they'll be calling up men your age. Maybe even mine," he added, with a bitter laugh.

"God, I hope not. I'm just getting started making a career out of painting." They'd rejected him back in '99 when he'd tried to sign up to fight the Boers. He didn't want to stop painting now to go and fight a younger man's war.

"Just starting, eh? I had you pegged for about forty."

"I am, nearly. I wasted too much of my life with commercial art. I figure I've got to make the most of the thirty years or so I've got left. Just painting the wilderness, making up for lost time."

"Yeah, well, this war has upset a lot of people's plans for their lives." He raised his flask in a toast. "Here's to yours working out."

"Thanks." Tom raised his mug. "And here's to your new dam."

TOM THOMSON DROWNED in Canoe Lake, Algonquin Park, on July 8, 1917. He was thirty-nine.

EDWARD LODI

Edward Lodi's short stories have appeared in numerous magazines and anthologies. He is the author of more than thirty books, including five novels in his Cranberry Country Mystery Series. A sixth is scheduled to appear in 2019. Find him on Facebook as Rock Village Publishing.

OUBLIETTE

EDWARD LODI

THE WIND WAS PICKING UP, turning the leaves on the trees along Marlborough Street belly up, like dead fish. Overhead the boughs of a gnarled maple swayed and creaked like cheap furniture.

Gavoti stifled a yawn. It would be nice to get out of the car to stretch his own cramped limbs. But he didn't dare. Not yet. Not until dark. Planning. It was all in the planning.

He found encouragement in the leaden skies and the damp wind that came careening off the Charles River. They promised rain. And an early nightfall.

He maintained the pose of a man engrossed in his newspaper as he squinted at the row of houses across the street. Four stories tall, they loomed grotesque in the fading light, stacked together like matched volumes on a gigantic shelf, their rounded red-brick facades the fine morocco bindings that completed the illusion.

He had his eye on the door diagonally across from where he sat in the parked car. Mere whim—or was it instinct?—led him to choose it from all the others. He had staked it out for three consecutive weeks—at different hours, from different angles, in various guises; had followed the woman on her nightly excursions. He knew her habits, now, better than he knew his own.

All along Marlborough Street lamps flicked on, their weak orbs only accentuating the gloom, as if some minor deity unequal to the task had snapped fingers and commanded light.

Soon—just a matter of minutes—the old woman would emerge from the house, the carcass of a weasel-like creature wrapped tight around her neck, thin wisps of her own gray hair curling like smoke above the fur. Her hat would be slightly askew, and she would be bundled against the wind in a fashionable and expensive coat. Heavy rings would bedizen her fingers.

In the three weeks of his vigil Gavoti had seen no one else enter or leave, had spied only her pale visage behind lace curtains. In the narrow alley that skulked behind the row of attached houses he had seen only rubbish cans and delivery trucks, an occasional rat. Never pedestrians.

Right on schedule the door opened and the old woman popped out like a clockwork figure onto the platform above the steps. She took her time locking the door, tested it several times, twisted the knob and shook it. He watched eagerly, appetite whetted by her caution.

When she had disappeared around the corner headed toward Newbury Street—to dine at one of the fashionable restaurants catering to the Back Bay—he slipped out of his car, walked casually around the block in the opposite direction, then ducked into the alley. It was dark now, the alley deserted. He found the rear entrance and easily and quietly forced his way in.

He paused just inside the doorway to meld with the shadows that filled the darkened room. The first thing that struck him was the smell. An acrid odor, hanging heavy in the air like a noxious gas. A neglected litter box? It would take a dozen cats to leave a stench that bad.

Noiselessly, without the aid of a flashlight, he explored the kitchen. As he poked through cabinets and cupboards his practiced eyes took in details of the old woman's life. One fact puzzled him: the shelves held too much food—cheap cereals, mostly—for just one person. A cupboard stacked with cans of cat food seemed to corroborate the presence of cats.

He listened. The refrigerator's labored hum muffled all other sounds. Leaving the kitchen, he slipped into a foyer fronting the street. The smell moved with him, like a vengeful spirit placed there against intruders.

Light from the street squeezed in through Venetian blinds. To the right a door, locked, led presumably to the cellar. Opposite, a narrow stairway crept to the upper floors. Against the wall, beneath the banister, an antique mahogany side table stood ready for pilfering.

The first drawer contained bills—gas, electricity, telephone—and the usual junk mail. The second drawer contained a surprise, something totally unexpected: welfare checks.

He moved closer to the window to examine them. There were five checks, all for the same amount, all dated within the past two weeks. What were they doing there? He glanced uneasily at the darkened stairs. This was no boarding house. No one lived here but the old woman.

He grinned. A welfare queen, committing fraud, collecting benefits under several names? The grin faded. All of the checks were made out to men. She couldn't be that good an actress.

Setting that mystery aside for the moment, he returned the checks to their drawer and began to explore the rest of the house. The rooms upstairs were a burglar's delight. The old woman owned the best of everything: tapestried sofas, high-backed chairs with carved, bulbous legs, gold-framed paintings, mammoth lamps with crystal pendants and elaborate, pleated shades, ornate clocks, heavy silverware, jewelry, furs, and antiques—the quality items you see advertised in *The New Yorker*.

Gavoti touched everything, took nothing, made a mental note of the better items, the portable ones. Time was running short. He would return later, perhaps tomorrow, and clean the place out.

Downstairs the smell, temporarily forgotten, once again assailed his nostrils. Curious, he stopped at the foot of the stairs. He had seen no sign of cats, yet it was there, a sickening blend of urine and feces and vomit and something else he could not quite identify. And there were those cans of cat food in the kitchen.

He was a cautious man, the reason why he had reached his thirties and never been caught. The woman would be returning soon. He should leave now, slip out the back.

Yet he hesitated. There were sounds, noticeable now that the refrigerator was silent. Scufflings, too loud to be made by cats. They came from the cellar. He crossed the room, put his ear to the locked door. Perversely, the scufflings ceased, as if whatever had caused it was listening, too.

No light seeped through the crack under the door. Whatever secret the old woman kept in her cellar lay hidden in darkness. Maybe it was cats, after all. Or rats.

Or maybe it was something else. Something Gavoti could turn to profit. He took a ring of keys from his pocket, found one that fit, and eased the door open.

It was too dark to see farther than the top two steps of the wooden stairway leading into the pit below. Drawn upward, the stench drifted past him like something he could reach out to and brush aside. The black rectangle that formed the cellar entrance too much resembled an upright grave for him to want to venture in. Instead he groped for the light switch, snapped it on, and immediately realized his mistake.

The brilliance blinded him. He clenched his eyes shut, but not before he had seen *them*. The image seared itself onto his brain cells: round white faces, upturned, maggot-like, eyes shrinking at the sudden light.

When his own eyes had adjusted he allowed himself to stare. There were about a dozen, some lying, others sitting, but each of them chained to a cot.

The cots were spaced a few feet apart in rows. Bare bulbs, controlled by the switch at his side, hung on frayed cords from wooden rafters, illuminating the concrete walls, the floor covered in filth.

So that was it. The old woman was holding a bunch of derelict men—most of them lacked teeth, and drooled, and gazed through senile eyes—in order to collect their Welfare benefits. Gavoti estimated the potential. Half. He would demand half. Half their Welfare benefits each month for keeping his mouth shut.

⧗

SHE MAY HAVE RETURNED HOME EARLIER than usual, suspected something, and entered the house quietly. Or, knowing all along that he had been tailing her, she may have deliberately followed him back into the house. In either case she was there, in the foyer. Gavoti first became aware of her presence when a blunt object came crashing onto the base of his skull pitching him headlong down the stairs.

⧗

WHEN HE CAME to he was chained like the others to a cot. His vision was blurred and he knew that he was badly hurt.

The old woman was sitting at his side.

"Don't you fret, dearie," she said when she saw his eyelids flutter. "First thing tomorrow morning I'll go down to the Welfare Office and file an application. We'll have your first check in no time at all. Food Stamps, too." She patted his hand. "In the meantime I'll take care of you free of charge."

Because of the pain Gavoti could not turn his head. But he was aware that she had reached for something on the floor.

"I do hope you like seafood," the old woman said, leaning over him. "It's so nutritious." Forcing open his lips, she began to spoon cat food from the can into his mouth.

P.A. DE VOE

P.A. De Voe, an anthropologist and Asian specialist, writes contemporary cozy mysteries, as well as historical mysteries and crime stories immersed in the life and times of Ancient China. A Silver Falchion award winner and an Agatha and Silver Falchion award finalist, she is a member of Sisters in Crime National and Guppy Chapter, the Short Mystery Fiction Society, St. Louis Writer's Guild, Saturday Writers, the Historical Novel Society, and Mystery Writers of America/MWA Midwest. Find her at padevoe.com.

GAMBLING AGAINST FATE [FROM JUDGE LU'S MING DYNASTY CASE FILES]

P.A. DE VOE

THE ROTUND INNKEEPER acknowledged Judge Lu with a short bow. "Sir, we are honored to have you stay at our humble inn." He looked toward a young man sweeping in the back of the room and called out, "Rong, what are you waiting for? Come and assist our guest."

As the youth hurried over, the innkeeper remarked in a loud voice: "My son. He's a lazy oaf. I have to keep an eye on him every minute."

The son glared at his father, but the emotion quickly washed away, leaving a bored expression in its place.

The innkeeper went on: "We have another official staying with us, the Honorable Shen Zhong-lan. He arrived last week from the province of Zhejiang. He is passing through on his way to southern Hunan, where he will take up his first official post as Chief of Police."

Lu rotated his shoulders, stretching them. The innkeeper's prattling formed a thin, background noise to his troubled thoughts. The day had been long. He and his entourage were traveling south along the Gan River, with the excuse that he was on a holiday. However, it was an upsurge in highway robberies along this important avenue for trade that brought him out of the yamen and onto the road. His Majesty, the Emperor, considered eradicating such crimes essential in maintaining his country's security. And whatever was important to the Emperor, was critical to Lu.

Recently appointed by the emperor to his position as Magistrate, Lu—an outsider from a different province—did not yet know which of his judicial or other governmental subordinates were trustworthy. All locals had large familial and personal networks to whom they were beholden. Since Lu would be held accountable to the Emperor for even a whiff of incompetence or corruption, he traveled with a small and highly trusted entourage. Ma and Zhang, the two guards accompanying him, were his own men and loyal only to him. The third person in his entourage, Lu Fu-hao, was his court secretary and younger brother.

The innkeeper's son began picking up Lu's bundles and reached for a small satchel among the pile. However, as his fingers closed over the bag, Lu stopped him. "Leave that. I'll take care of it."

The boy nodded and carried the other bags upstairs, Ma close behind.

The innkeeper swept a hand toward the tables. "Have a seat and I'll bring you tea."

Grateful to be off the road, Lu and Fu-hao made their way to a table against the wall. Lu liked to see everything going on around him. Within a short time, the innkeeper brought tea and steaming hot dumplings. As they sipped tea, Zhang took up another table, an eye on both his master and the room.

At a nearby table a couple of men played a gambling game with quiet intensity. Periodically, a yelp of victory by the winner or cursing from the loser punctuated their game. Fu-hao couldn't keep his eyes off them.

After finishing the refreshments, Lu said, "I'm going to my quarters. We'll spend a day or so here, checking for any unusual activity."

"I'll be up soon," Fu-hao said, his attention wandering back to the men at the nearby table.

"Don't be up too late," Lu said, rising. "Remember why we're here." His younger brother's fondness for gambling often troubled him.

Fu-hao picked up the satchel and handed it to Lu. "Don't forget this."

Lu resisted making a return comment. The reminder was his brother's way of pushing back. The satchel held Lu's identity documents and seal of office. It was not likely he would be careless enough to leave them behind.

The next morning, surrounded by the slurps and low conversations of fellow guests, Lu sat eating his favorite breakfast: a bowl of soy milk, fried bread sticks, and several small dishes of pickled vegetables. The comfortable bouquet of warm food added to his enjoyment of the meal.

He sat alone. Zhang and Ma remained discretely alert at a side table. Fu-hao hadn't yet emerged from bed. Lu wore a simple navy robe and no official hat, which would have announced his governmental position. He relished the anonymity, a rare thing for a magistrate.

Lu was about to have Zhang fetch his brother when a man wearing a loose-fitting, long dark robe and a low-level official's hat burst into the room. Stopping within a few steps from the door, he raked the room with an angry gaze. "Where's Innkeeper He?"

Within a breath, the innkeeper appeared at the kitchen door. Seeing the new arrival, he rushed forward and, hands clasped before his ample belly, he bowed several times. "Sir, what is the trouble?"

"Trouble? Indeed, there is trouble! A man, your guest, is dead. Your guest. Slain in his bed."

All color drained from the innkeeper's face. "Dead? In my inn?" he asked, in a daze. A silence filled the room, as if through muteness, each person could disappear, unnoticed.

"Naturally, I will have to report this to the proper authorities. However, since this small town has no official law officer, I will investigate the matter myself."

Lu spoke up. "Are you Sir Shen Zhong-lan, Hunan's Chief of Police appointee?"

"I am. And who are you, Sir?" the fellow asked, jutting his chin out.

Lu stood and said, "I am Lu Wen-xue, magistrate for Jiangxi's Tai-ho County."

Shen paused a moment, eyes focusing on Lu. Then, raising his hands and clasping them at chest level, he bowed deeply. "Honorable Sir. At your service. I hope you will forgive me for taking command of the situation. I wasn't aware of Your Honor's presence."

"You did right, Sir Shen. But, since I am here, as magistrate I will investigate the death." To show respect for the appointee, he added, "Given that you've been in town the past week, I would appreciate your insight into the case."

Lu ordered Zhang to tell Fu-hao to meet them in the slain man's room with his court recording materials. As magistrate, Lu was required to personally examine the body. Fu-hao would take official notes on the proceedings. All of the details would be included in a formal court document sent to Lu's superiors, who reviewed each case.

Shen led Lu and Ma through a short hallway to the victim's room on the ground floor. At the entrance to the small room, Lu told Shen to remain outside. A medium-sized man lay face down, spread out half on the bed and half on the floor. Blood stained his clothing. A knife lay nearby.

"Stabbed in the back," Ma murmured. He stepped away from the body.

Lu glanced at his guard. He should have told Ma to fetch Fu-hao and have Zhang come along to handle the body. Ma feared the ghosts of those who died violent, unnatural deaths. Such malevolent spirits took revenge on any and all around them. Thus, Ma had a deep revulsion of examining the bodies of homicide victims, which —he believed—angered their spirits even more. Zhang, on the other hand, had a pragmatic view of the mundane, everyday world and the supernatural world. He did not object to touching the deceased. Lu hoped it didn't take Fu-hao long to gather his things together and get over to the crime scene.

Before approaching the victim, Lu scrutinized the bare, windowless room. A single bed took up most of the space. A covered chamber pot sat in one corner, next to a washstand. Except for the knife and a short coat strewn over the end of the bed, the room was empty. Lu bent down and examined the area around the bed. Nothing. As he straightened, the innkeeper approached the door, followed by Fu-hao and Zhang.

Without a word, Fu-hao set up his table with his ink and paper, just outside the room, at the door's entrance. From here, he had an unobstructed view and could easily hear Lu's documenting of the crime scene.

Lu nodded to his brother. Zhang entered the room, taking his position by the body, but out of Lu's way. Ma sidled up to Fu-hao and stood near him.

Lu pushed back his gown's flowing sleeves and squatted down next to the victim. He grasped the left wrist. "His body is already stiff. He's been dead several hours. He must have been stabbed in the early morning." He had Zhang remove the man's shirt. "One exceptionally deep stab wound. The killer must have been strong. The wound appears to go into the rib cage." He leaned over and picked up the knife. After examining it and the wound, he handed it to Zhang. "Keep this as evidence. The knife is covered in blood and matches the wound in size and shape. It must be the murder weapon."

Fu-hao's brush swept across the page as Lu described the body's condition and the knife.

Shen, the innkeeper, and a cluster of other diners, stood in the hallway close behind Fu-hao, a mute audience peering into the room.

Zhang turned the body over, exposing the man's face and open eyes; he appeared to stare at the doorway as if in surprise. With a collective gasp the gawkers drew back. Lu glanced over and caught sight of the innkeeper's faint figure looming in the darkened hallway. "Innkeeper He, can you identify this man?"

"It's Huang Chi-chao, a merchant from Guangdong Province in

the south. He arrived yesterday," the innkeeper said, his voice high and quivering.

"Did he have any bags with him when he took the room?"

"Yes, Your Honor. He had one small bag."

"A small bag? If he was a merchant, where were his wares?"

"He said he'd sold out and was returning home."

Lu again glanced around the bare room. If the merchant had sold all his wares, that meant he was carrying a lot of money along with his traveling credentials.

Standing, Lu instructed those in the hallway: "You must all assemble in the dining room, where I will hold the investigation. If any of you try to leave the premises without permission, I will have my men hunt you down as a guilty party."

An excited mixture of anxiety, anger, and fear rose from the darkened, hollow space behind Fu-hao.

"Do I make myself clear?" Lu asked, his tone brooking no argument.

A chorus of, "Yes, Your Honor," replied. The shuffling of feet told him they were leaving. Only Shen remained in the shadows.

"Ma, search each guest's room looking for Huang's bag, his credentials, and for any large sums of money. Zhang, you come with me."

Fu-hao gathered up his materials. Lu closed the door behind them and moved quickly through the hallway, Zhang, Fu-hao, and Shen in tow. When Lu appeared at the dining room door, men were sitting at the tables scattered around the room. They rose as one when Lu entered. The innkeeper, his son, and a serving girl stood near the kitchen door.

Lu chose a table near the back. Fu-hao set up near him and prepared fresh ink. Once Fu-hao was ready, brush in hand, Lu called the guests, one by one to come forward to be interrogated.

None knew the deceased or had any useful information. Once Lu finished interviewing the last guest, he called for the maid. Pale and trembling, she glided forward, taking small steps, and then dropped to her knees, giving him a deep bow.

Lu reminded her of the importance of telling the truth to the court and the severity of the crime if she did not. In a scarcely audible voice, she bowed again and said she understood.

"Did you know the victim?" Lu asked.

"I served him last night, as I did the others."

"Who else was with him?"

"Innkeeper He, his son, His Honor Shen, Huang Da-xin—His Honor's traveling companion—and..." she hesitated.

"Yes. Tell the truth."

Her eyes flitted from Lu toward his brother recording her words. "Your Honor's Court Secretary," she said.

Lu stared hard at Fu-hao.

"I was gambling with them last night," Fu-hao said, grimacing. "But I left them to the game and went to bed early." At Lu's scowl, he hastily added, "Well, relatively early. Before anyone else did at any rate. She'll—" he jerked his head in the maid's direction—"tell you."

Lu looked to the maid for confirmation.

"Yes, Sir. He did leave early. The others continued drinking and gambling."

"When did they break up?" Lu asked.

"They gambled until late into the night. Everyone lost—except Chi-chao. He boasted of his luck and drank a full cup of wine after each win. Finally, quite drunk, he announced he'd finished playing, ending the game. I don't know what happened after that. I was told to leave, that I was no longer needed."

Lu called the innkeeper. "You were among the gamblers last night?"

Hands clasped over his belly, the innkeeper bowed several times before Lu. "I did play and I lost a small amount, but I didn't hurt the merchant Huang. I had no reason to. He was my customer. I know nothing about what happened after the game broke up."

"Is there anything else you can add?" Lu asked.

The innkeeper paused for a moment, as if thinking. "When the victim signed in and found out another Huang had taken a room in my inn, he went on about Guangdong, his home area. He bragged that the Huang surname was well-known throughout the province and what a strong and prosperous lineage it was. Then later, after dinner, he mentioned that he recognized Shen." He pressed his lips together in a tight line, then said. "He told me to be careful of the man, but we were interrupted before he could say why."

"What nonsense," Shen shouted. "How dare you involve me in this despicable matter."

"Silence," Lu said. "You will have an opportunity to tell the court your version." He was glad Shen was only an official appointee. If he had already been entrusted with the office and taken up the position, the court would not be allowed to interrogate him. At least not without going through a long and complicated procedure to first strip him of his position. The law was originally designed to protect the status of the office. Unfortunately, an unintended consequence was to virtually give officials immunity from the law.

Lu asked the innkeeper a few more questions before releasing him and ordering Shen to step forward. As Innkeeper He and Shen passed each other, Shen glared at him.

"I admit I gambled and lost heavily to merchant Huang, but I had nothing to do with his death."

"How did you expect to pay off your gambling debt?" Lu asked. He'd noticed that Shen's clothing, while decent, was too ample for the man's slender frame. The garment's poor cut suggested that this newly appointed official had yet to make his fortune.

Shen bowed. "Because merchant Huang respected the hardworking members of the legal system, he did not hold me to my debt. Instead he forgave it all."

"You're claiming merchant Huang didn't expect you to repay any of your debt. Not in any way?" Lu asked, probing. It was not uncommon for people to try and ingratiate themselves with various officials or other government workers. However, this type of arrangement could be considered a form of bribery and disqualify him from office.

Jutting his chin out, Shen drew himself up. "Yes, Your Honor. Such was his level of respect for our Emperor and his hardworking officers."

At this sanctimonious comment, Lu gazed at Shen for a few moments before asking: "Did he give you a note forgiving the debt?"

Shen nodded and reached into his sleeve. He pulled out a folded piece of paper, opened it, glanced at it briefly, and presented it to Lu.

Lu took the rice paper and read it. The note did, indeed, absolve Shen's debt to merchant Huang. Lu placed the note on Fu-hao's table as evidence. He released the Chief of Police appointee.

As Shen bowed and backed away, Lu called for Da-xin, Shen's traveling companion. At this, Shen paused and clasping his hands before him, said, "Please don't bother with Huang Da-xin, Your Honor. He is a simpleton who is given to exaggeration and poor judgement. I doubt he can be of any help in our investigations."

Judge Lu stared hard at Shen.

Flicking his hands, as if to wipe away his comment, Shen went on. "Of course, I don't mean to tell Your Honor what to do. I only wanted to alert you to the kind of man Da-xin is—to avoid any future embarrassment to the court in case his words were taken to have real meaning."

"If he is a simpleton, as you say, why have you chosen him as your companion?" Lu asked.

"I am assisting my brother who owes a debt to Da-xin's father and who has business in Hunan. His father didn't trust him to travel alone. Since we happen to be going to the same place, it seemed reasonable for him to travel with me."

Lu nodded and waved him aside. "Huang Da-xin, approach the court," he ordered, again.

A thin man with a nervous twitch attacking his left eye shuffled forward. Lu made a note of his uncontrollable eye. While the tic could signify a guilty conscience, it could also reflect nervousness at being involved in this legal situation. The law assumed guilt and guilty involvement until proven otherwise. Guileless or not, Lu mused, Da-xin appeared to be aware of the power of the law.

"You understand the importance of your telling the truth, do you not, Da-xin?" Lu asked.

"Yes," the man said. He gripped his hands together at his waist, but he couldn't hide his jacket's shaking sleeves as his arms quaked unbidden.

"Did you know the victim, Huang Chi-chao?"

"Yes. No."

"What is it? Yes or no?"

Da-xin blanched. "No, although I have seen him. He's from my ancestral family's town in Guangdong."

"Guangdong is in the southeast. Zhejiang is the province north of it. Why were you in Zhejiang?"

"I wasn't in Zhejiang. Master Shen and I have been here for many months. Traveling along the Gan River." Da-xin fell silent and seemed to study the ground.

Lu was beginning to think Shen was right: Da-xin was simple and an unreliable witness. He cast a quick glance at Shen, who frowned at his fellow traveler. Lu was about to release Da-xin when the man spoke up.

"Chi-chao didn't recognize me, but he knew Master Shen. Everyone knows Master Shen. His family was once one of the most important in our town." He paused again and nodded at Lu with a shy smile, as if that said it all.

Lu caught Shen shaking his head and opening his eyes wide as if incredulous at what he was hearing. Lu took this to mean Shen placed no credence in what his companion said. Lu decided to move on to the next interview. If needed, he'd delete Huang Da-xin's testimony later.

Next, Lu called the innkeeper's son, He Rong, before the court.

The young man strutted out from the sidelines, all sullenness gone. He seemed determined.

Lu let him stand before the court for several minutes before addressing him. He had learned early on how important silence was as an investigatory tool. It intimidated people and opened them up in a way that court ordered torture could not. "You were among the last to see Chi-chao before his death. Tell me what you know. Remember, if you lie or leave anything out, you will suffer the consequences."

Rong took a deep breath, straightened his shoulders, and,

looking at Judge Lu's chest, proceeded. "Sir, both my father and I gambled with the victim and the others as reported. Only Chi-chao seemed lucky at gambling. We all lost. I played for the first couple of turns and had to quit because I had no more money. My father, Sir Shen, your court reporter, and Da-xin continued playing. Since I couldn't play, I went to bed. The others remained gambling and drinking after I left." By the end of this tale, his bravado had slipped. He shifted his eyes to his feet. Even in the room's dim light, the sweat shone on his forehead. "That's all I know."

Lu's dark eyes burrowed into the young man. "Tell the court everything," he said, leaning toward him.

Rong shot a look at the line of men pressed along the side wall, his father and the other gamblers among them. He turned back to Judge Lu.

"I did go to bed. I sleep in the kitchen, but their noise didn't keep me awake. Later—I'm not sure how much later—my father came in. He was furious. He said he'd lost and lost. He had been sure he'd win back his debt, and he'd put our inn up as collateral." Rong shook his head. "He lost that too. He gambled our life and lost." His voice hardened.

The silence in the room was oppressive. Whether the weight came from the innkeeper's bad judgement or from sympathy at his bad karma, Judge Lu couldn't tell. Nevertheless, an over-powering pressure filled the room.

Rong closed his eyes. "He said…he said he'd kill that son of a turtle before he'd turn his inn over to him in payment for the gambling debt. And then he grabbed a knife and ran back out into the dining room." He gulped air. "I think…I think he killed Chi-chao."

A gasp went up from the men watching. Then as if in a rolling thunder, a stream of curses erupted aimed at the innkeeper's son. To accuse his own father of a crime was the ultimate act of betrayal, an unforgivable act. The men's immediate, unthinking reaction, flooded outward, washing over the space and filling it with bile.

Stunned, Lu sat ramrod straight on the rustic stool. When he had demanded Rong tell everything, he hadn't expected this. He looked over at the gamblers: Innkeeper He frozen in place, Shen smirking, and Da-xin staring in wide-eyed disbelief. True or not, Rong's testimony put both him and his father in the center of the law's target. Innkeeper He for murder. His son for breaking with the country's laws on filial behavior. The law would not countenance a son's betraying a father. Even a guilty father. The first duty to all sons was to their parents. That before all else. Everyone—the Emperor, the country—knew that no one could survive in a world where children turned on their parents. Filial piety was the first commandment among all commandments.

Judge Lu ordered Zhang to arrest both the innkeeper and his son and recessed the court. He whispered to Fu-hao that he was to meet him upstairs in his room. He stepped away from the table and left. As soon as he'd disappeared upstairs, pandemonium broke loose.

The uproar filtered in through the cracks around Lu's door. He couldn't close it out. He didn't want to close it out. The chaos was an acknowledgement of the disruption in the universe's moral order. The law he represented affirmed that order's existence. Of the certainty that there was a right and a wrong. Rong's declaration of his father's guilt upended the entire universe's moral order.

And it was Judge Lu's job to right the world again.

Almost as soon as Lu entered the room, Fu-hao followed, papers in hand. He dropped them on a stool and started to speak. "I—"

Lu interrupted. "Go and find Ma. Bring back anything he's discovered." He swept a hand over his brow. "Let's hope he's found something. Whatever it is, it will help us put a picture of this murder together."

"Right," Fu-hao swung around, reversing his steps.

Lu paced the tight space. He needed more information, more evidence. Rong's testimony meant a death sentence for both of them. The innkeeper for murder. The innkeeper's son for such an egregious unfilial act. The law would not be merciful to either. He tapped his hand against his chest. There was something wrong here. He felt it. But he needed more information. Evidence.

He didn't have long to wait. Fu-hao returned with Ma in tow. Ma carried several packets which he extended to Lu. "I found these in Sir Shen's room."

Lu unwrapped the larger package and reviewed the documents within. They were the official certificates of office and traveling papers for the Chief of Police appointee. As he read through the papers, Lu's eyebrows rose in surprise. Without comment, he handed the documents to Fu-hao and opened the smaller bundles. In one he found two slips of rice paper stating that Huang Da-xin and Huang Min-feng were residents of a town in Guangdong. The second bundle held the identity paper and travel documents for merchant Huang Chi-chao.

"Where did you find these?" Lu asked.

"All three packets were in Sir Shen's room. The larger package was on his bed; the smaller packages were hidden against the far wall under his bed."

Lu stood. "I'm reconvening the court's questioning. Fu-hao, prepare your desk. Ma, bring in Shen. Zhang, bring in the prisoners."

As they reassembled in the crowded dining room, the noise level muted to a barely audible level. The once welcoming room now appeared less inviting. Uncomfortably warm, the stench of stressed-induced body odor mixed with that of old cooking oil and onions.

"Silence," Lu ordered. "Bring Huang Da-xin forward."

"Da-xin, you say your home area is in Guangdong and your residency documents, which I have here, agree with that," Lu said. He laid a hand on the rice paper spread out on the table. "Now tell me, do you know a Huang Min-feng?"

The slender man nodded, grinning. "Yes, Your Honor. He's my older brother."

"Is he in this room?"

He nodded again.

"Point him out to the court."

The man hesitated.

"Point him out to the court," Lu repeated, more sternly.

As if in slow motion, Da-xin pointed across the room to Sir

Shen. A burst of voices met Da-xin's revelation. Shen stiffened and his eyes darted toward the door, where Ma stood guard.

"Sir Shen, come before the court," Lu said.

Shen strode forward. Only the slight drop of his shoulders gave any indication of a change in his demeanor. He bowed and waited.

Lu assessed the men, standing side by side, before him. Now the similarity in their short, thin eyebrows set in round faces and their slender, strong builds was obvious. Lu had no doubt they were, indeed, brothers.

"There is no use for you to lie any longer, Huang Min-feng. Confess your crimes, beginning with your impersonating Chief of Police Appointee Shen."

At this, the last of the con man's veneer of self-confidence crumbled. Glancing at his younger brother, he said, "Your Honor, when Da-xin and I were on the road, the weather delayed us and we were forced to hold up in a wine shop along the Gan River. It was then I met Shen. He was seriously ill and had also been forced to stop to rest on his journey. He'd hoped to continue on in a few days, once he'd recuperated. As fellow travelers, we fell to chatting, and he told me he was about to take up a new official position.

"Famine drove my brother and me from our village, and life on the road proved no better. As it happened, Shen died that night from his illness. It was a stroke of luck. I took his documents, robe, and hat. Da-xin and I continued along the Gan River as if I were the appointee."

Lu's brow wrinkled into a landscape of canyons when the counterfeit appointee admitted he'd stolen Shen's identity as an up-and-coming official. Such hubris was rare even among thieves.

"With a new identity, people lavished free food and lodging on me. Of course, I promised each of our benefactors a minor position in office, once, as Chief of Police, I had the power to do so," Min-feng added with a self-satisfied smirk. "It was the perfect plan."

"Not quite perfect," said Lu. "Even the best laid plans cannot outsmart fate. How long have you been impersonating Shen?"

"Several months. We moved from town to village after a few

weeks in each place." He sighed. "It worked beautifully. Until Chi-chao showed up."

"Was he your brother, too?"

Min-feng shook his head. "No. A distant cousin."

"Why did you kill him?"

Min-feng looked incredulously at Lu. "Because he recognized us and knew I wasn't Shen. He tried to blackmail me by threatening to expose me as an imposter. The situation was impossible. Even if I could pay him now, he could keep coming back. Demanding more."

"So, you two killed him," Lu said. "To keep him quiet."

"Sir, I declare fully and with regret that I committed these crimes alone. My brother, Da-xin, did nothing. He is simple and not guilty of anything. I did it all on my own."

With this confession, Min-feng guaranteed his own death, but he saved his brother from execution.

Lu gazed at the brothers before him and then at the innkeeper and his son. The moral order was not as easy to understand as one would hope. The imposter and murderer behaved with true concern and responsibility towards his brother, whereas the law-abiding innkeeper's son had broken the most elemental commandment in the universe: that of filial piety.

As Judge Lu picked up a brush to write out the charge against Huang Min-feng, he was all too aware of how the complexities of the human heart crossed over into the area of peace and justice.

CHRIS WHEATLEY

Chris Wheatley splits his time between Oxford and Cambridge. He is a freelance journalist, writer, and musician, with two previously published short stories and many non-fiction articles. Chris has an enduring love for the works of Dashiell Hammett, Raymond Chandler, Chester Himes, and Cornell Woolrich. He has just completed his first full-length crime novel and is forever indebted to the advice and encouragement of his wife, his son, and his mother, without whom he would never have come so far. Find him at silverpilgrim.com.

THE TRUE COST OF LIBERTY

CHRIS WHEATLEY

NEVER IN MY life did I expect or desire to become embroiled in theft, murder, and the seedier side of humanity. I had always fancied myself a reasonably honest and straightforward person, but all that changed, in a matter of seconds no less, last Sunday afternoon.

The occasion was the seventh birthday of my niece, Florence, the venue the garden of a house belonging to my estranged wife, Laura, and her new partner, Isaac. A peculiar arrangement, you might think, but Laura remained close friends with my sister, the child's mother, and besides, I rather think she relished the opportunity to show off her new home.

It has a very large garden, beautifully ornamented, with its own swimming pool and the temporary addition on that day of a bouncy castle. Isaac comes from money. His family owns a pharmaceutical company that supplies pesticides to the farming industry. I hadn't wanted to be there, but I was fond of my niece and Laura, uncharacteristically, had been most warm in her insistence that I attend.

Our separation has not been amicable. I suspect she and Isaac were lovers long before things between us turned sour. I was, therefore, not in the most convivial of spirits. Oh, I mingled and chatted. Many of the guests were mutual friends and of course, there was my sister. Frankly it was all rather awkward and embarrassing. At some point Isaac approached me. He's one of those swarthy types who manage to look fashionable even in shorts and sandals. He offered me a drink and then he started a conversation, in his bloody irritating South African accent, about the house, the clearing out of his old property, and the amount of junk they had discovered. And so the talk turned to coins.

Isaac knew, through Laura, that I am something of a collector, and he wanted my opinion on a small quantity that had been discovered in an attic, or behind a fireplace or some such—I really wasn't minded to listen to his tedious anecdote, nor was I minded to sort through his undoubtedly worthless heirlooms. Nevertheless, he brought them out in an old shoebox, set them before me and then buggered off, leaving me even more depressed than before.

So I sifted through the contents, half-oblivious to the clinking of glasses, the splashing of water, the sizzling of the barbecue and the chatter and laughter of adults and kids alike. The coins themselves were nothing special, mostly British. There were some old pennies and farthings, a mixed bag of small denomination European. There were some American, silver pennies and half-dollars that might bring a few pounds. In my head I was estimating a value of perhaps two hundred all in. And then I saw it.

I knew the design, of course, straight away, but I think perhaps I will struggle to convey the raw drama that played out in my (for wont of a better word) soul.

Imagine, if you will, you are looking through a pile of framed canvases in a thrift shop when, amongst the mediocre watercolors of woodland scenes you come across a Van Gogh. Not a print, but an original, a dazzling beautiful, visceral thing that so astonishes it subsumes one's mind in vibrant emotion.

You look around nervously, certain that this must be some dream. Then realization slowly dawns that it is not. This is real, and the object, which you hold in your sweaty palms, is a genuine masterpiece, worth millions. All you must do is take those few steps to the counter and pay whatever paltry sum is asked and your life will have changed forever. Your heart beats, your pulse pounds, and you feel sure all around you must see the greed and desire in your eyes.

The object of my rapturous attention was a Flowing Hair dollar. To explain what that is we must travel back to the United States of America, 1791, when congress passed a motion to put into place the first national mint. Previously each state had acted as master of its own coinage. Now that led to some very interesting developments. No doubt you have heard the expression "pieces of eight," very possibly via the medium of some poorly written children's "entertainment." But I digress. One does have a tendency to ramble, as Laura would be only too quick to testify.

Back to the garden. There I was, palms itching, staring down upon this thing of beauty, a Flowing Hair dollar. I could clearly see its date: 1794, and that beautiful design by Robert Scot—Liberty herself with her thick, luscious locks falling down upon her shoulder. If it were genuine, it would be worth millions. And to my eyes, to my soul, it *was* genuine.

I reached down to pick it up. My head swam, my heart raced. I took it up between my thumb and my forefinger and I raised it slowly to my eye and then Isaac, that damn Isaac, with his bloody accent, accosted me once more, with a rough slap across the back.

"Have you found me a fortune?" he asked, and he flashed those obscenely white teeth. I could only stare back, dumbfounded. How could that absolute dunderhead have known what it was that I held in my hand? And then it dawned on me that he did not. Very slowly, I lowered the coin back into the box.

"Well, look here," I said, "there may be one or two in there that are worth something. Not a great deal, you understand. I tell you what, I'll take the lot off your hands for say, two hundred."

Isaac kept smiling. He smiled for so long that I didn't think he would reply but then, "I don't think so, George," he said, "you know what? We're going up to London next week. I'll get them properly valued while we're in town."

"Three hundred," I said, "or I could value them for you,

wouldn't take me a day or two. I could even sell them on your behalf. I'd get you a good price."

Isaac picked up the box. I remember that he cradled it under one arm, like a rugby ball. "No," he said, "No, I think I'll take them up to London, after all."

And that was that. He took the box back into the garage and then closed and locked the door and I was left wondering if he had somehow guessed that I had spotted something. I felt guilty. But then an odd thing happened. As the afternoon progressed I began to feel not guilty, but angry. And I began to consider, quite coldly and seriously, how best to take possession of that coin.

At the close of events I had fixed in my head not only a good working plan of burglary, but also an indefinable, completely illogical sense of the *rightness* of such a course. Isaac and Laura did not need the money and besides, it would be detestable, nay *grotesque*, were such a philistine as Isaac to profit without even understanding, or caring, for the sheer history of the Flowing Hair.

And so that evening I called my dear old friend Max Whitehouse. Max happens to be an antiques dealer. Max is also a crook, albeit not entirely. Ninety percent of his business is above-board. The remaining ten percent, however…let's just say, Max had connections. Connections I was going to need, and it wasn't long before I had talked him around. In fact, I believe he was even more excited about the coin than I was.

Salome, that was the last little detail that sealed my plan. By good fortune, I overheard dearest Laura, back in the garden on that hot summer's day, talking loudly and at length of how she and Isaac had tickets for the following night. An empty house beckoned and thus so did my fate. I almost felt as though the higher powers were conspiring with me.

Breaking in was easy. They had no alarms—a cursory wander through the hallway on that Sunday had discerned as much. No dog, either, and no overlooking neighbors and besides, it was only the garage to which I needed entry. A large crowbar from the trunk of my car saw to that. It popped open nicely, thank you very much. Although I had taken the precautions of wearing a mask and gloves

I can tell you that I felt settled and unhurried and not in the least bit afraid.

I found the coin almost at once.

It was then that a strange feeling overcame me. I felt suddenly overwhelmed and in awe of the thing. So much so that at once I secreted it in the plain brown envelope I had brought for that exact purpose. I sealed it there and then, and there it stayed whilst I hastily re-traced my steps back to my car. I drove silently through the night across town to the offices of Max Whitehouse. I posted the coin into his night deposit box without a second thought, drove home, helped myself to one sherry and then another and thereafter had one of the soundest night's sleep of my life.

What happened next I only know of second hand. As I understand it, sometime around half past nine the following morning, Max's secretary, on taking up his usual tea-and-toast, found her employer prostrate upon the floor and quite dead, clutching the Flowing Hair dollar in his poor cold hand.

By the time the police and paramedics arrived the secretary herself was feeling most unwell, so unwell, in fact, that the paramedics had her stretchered and on the way out the door in a matter of minutes. Before she was carted off some bright spark from the ranks of the attending constabulary possessed the wit to ask her if she had touched or consumed anything in the room. "Only the coin," she told him, "only the coin." She had prized it from Max's fingers, you see, and placed it upon the desk.

And there you have it. Whatever tests the lab-jockeys undertook revealed Liberty to be coated in an invisible and extremely toxic substance, which can be readily absorbed through the skin. I hazard a guess, if you'll excuse the wording, that such a chemical must be available only through special contacts. Those in the chemical farming industry, perchance?

Whether my dear wife Laura knew for sure or just suspected, I don't know, but the house, the insurance policy, my savings, all of it still goes to her upon my death. I had not possessed the wit or the will to write her out of my life, you see. In my heart, I confess, I love her still. Yes, even now.

They must not be so well off as we all assumed, one supposes. Or perhaps it's just pure old-fashioned greed. Theirs was a bold plan, hers and Isaac's. I wonder who came up with it and how they planned to cover their tracks? Well, that's for you to decide, after all.

I'm guessing your boys found me because Max detailed our arrangement in his private diary. He always was thorough, the dear fool. When the police showed up at my door with news of his suspicious death I confessed everything at once. I felt that I had to. Perhaps, even, that I wanted to.

As to the coin itself, there's little doubt in my mind that it's a fake. In truth I never really held a Flowing Hair dollar in my hand. And yet I suppose I did experience what it would be like to do so, even if it were an illusion.

Pardon me, Inspector? Yes, I suppose I am a lucky man. It was the gloves that saved me. I always have been blessed with good fortune. Except for matters of the heart. But I rather suspect we make our own luck in that department, don't you think?

LD MASTERSON

LD Masterson's short stories have been published in numerous anthologies and magazines. Born in Boston, and a diehard Red Sox fan, she lived on both coasts before becoming landlocked in Ohio where she lives with her husband and a neurotic Jack Russell terrier named Sophie. After twenty years keeping the computers up and running for the American Red Cross, she now divides her time between writing and enjoying her grandchildren. LD is a member of Sisters in Crime National, Mystery Writers of America, the Short Mystery Fiction Society, and the Western Ohio Writers Association. Find her at ldmasterson-author.blogspot.com.

DEADLY DINNER

LD MASTERSON

I DIDN'T TAKE this job to kill anyone. Truth is, I'm not much into violence. Don't even own a gun. I mostly just needed a job, and I'd done food prep before. A couple restaurants. Worked a school cafeteria once but I couldn't deal with those damn kids. This was my first nursing home. Pay wasn't great but they let me work the split shift so I got enough overtime, and the work was pretty basic... peeling and chopping. It's funny, I always hear about these fancy chefs, all guys, but every kitchen I ever worked, we guys got the prep work. The real cooking was done by the women.

I came in at four to start prepping for breakfast and lunch, then a three-hour break and back at two to get ready for dinner. I just hung around during my break. The home was nicer than my one-room apartment, and who wants to be outside in the winter in Ohio.

But after a couple months I was looking for some fringe benefits. Spring Hill Home—which didn't have a spring and wasn't on a hill —was your basic senior-nursing home. Had some folks who weren't doing too bad and some who were just waiting around to die. More importantly, it had your Medicare patients and your full pay types— the ones with plenty of money—and I'd pretty much figured out who was who. I could use my staff badge to wander around the place, see what I could pick up. The wealthy like their expensive trinkets, even in a place like this.

Then, I stumbled on a chance for a real score.

I was peeling potatoes, tossing the skinless spuds into a big pan for washing, and letting my mind wander. Peeling potatoes doesn't take a lot of brainpower. The other prep cooks were chopping veggies and cutting up a mess of chickens. Marla, the head cook, was mixing some sort of batter when something beeped in her pocket. She pulled out a cell phone, muttered something under her breath, and pulled off her apron.

"You, Bixby," she said to me, "tell Mrs. Hendricks I'll be back in a couple." Then she hurried out of the kitchen without waiting for an answer.

It was the first time I'd been in the dietician's office. It was a dinky little thing off the kitchen where Hendricks matched the day's menu against each patient's special dietary needs and gave instructions on how to modify their meals. She was seated with her back to the door, so engrossed in what she was reading on her monitor she didn't hear me come in. Curious, I stood quiet and watched the screen. Some of the columns I understood, like low sodium meant no salt, but there were a couple other columns…big words. I mean big. Like supercalla-whatever big. And lots of numbers and letters. Then I saw a word I knew: Warfarin. That was a blood thinner. My old man used to take that for the clots in his legs. Got it. This wasn't just the diet info, it was the medications list. For everyone in the place.

I wasn't sure how yet, but I knew it was something I could use.

"Um, excuse me, Mrs. Hendricks." I shuffled my feet like I'd just come in. "Marla asked me to tell you she had to step out for a couple minutes but she'd be right back."

As soon as I spoke, she touched a key that replaced the image on her screen with a picture of a cat. Basic screen guard to keep people from seeing things they're not supposed to. I gave her my helpful, innocent smile. I've got a bit of a baby face even though I'm on the wrong side of thirty, and most times it brings out the mother instinct in older women.

"All right." She smiled back. "Thank you, Bixby."

Huh. I didn't think she knew my name. I nodded and started to back out the door then saw my opening. That wasn't a stock image on her screen; that was a personal photo. "What a beautiful cat." I took a half step forward like I couldn't take my eyes off the really ordinary looking orange cat in the picture. "Is he yours?"

Bullseye. She turned to the screen, beaming. "Why, yes. That's Sir Reginald."

I crossed the tiny room like I was drawn to the image. I mentioned having a cat when I was young—actually it was my sister's, I hated the thing—asked a few inane questions, and let her babble on about the wonders of the stupid cat while I scoped out her workspace and made some mental notes. There were a few more pictures of the cat in frames sitting on her desk. No husband, no kids. That could come in handy later on. I waited until she started to run out of breath.

"Does he get angry when you're late getting home?" I asked. "My Mickey used to sulk if he didn't get his dinner right on time."

"Oh, I'm hardly ever late. I leave here at seven o'clock every night, like clockwork. I can't keep Reggie waiting."

I waited a week, just to be safe. Sure enough, crazy cat lady left every night at seven to go home to Sir Reginald. The last of the kitchen crew left about eight, after cleanup. I slipped into the darkened kitchen at nine, moving by the glow from the parking lot lights and the almost full moon. I tested the door to Hendricks' office. As expected, it was locked, but a piece of cake to pick. It was darker in there so I got out my penlight. She'd turned off her computer so I powered it up and waited for the password prompt. This should be easy.

First I tried *SirReginald*. Nope.

How about just *Reginald*? Invalid.

Hmm. Maybe all lower case. No. Stupid. I typed in *Reggie*.

Bingo.

I started flipping through the list, focusing on the non-Medicare patients. Whoa, some of them were taking enough meds to choke a horse. And most of them were damned expensive. I'd hate to have to pay those bills. Of course, Medicare covered some drugs even for the full pays but that still was a lot of money down the drain. Which got me thinking...there was a hell of a lot of money being spent here just to keep some old fogies alive well past their time. Money someone else was waiting in line for—if the doctors and the home didn't get it all first. Maybe someone who was getting a little impatient. Someone who might like a little help sending Great-Aunt Tilly to her final reward. And be willing to pay for it.

I started working it out in my head. Like I said before, I didn't take this job looking to kill anyone. But if the price was right... Wouldn't be hard. Hell, you could smother one of these old biddies —did I mention there were way more women than men?—with a pillow when they were sleeping. And you weren't really taking a lot from them. They were pretty much done anyway. I heard stories around about ones that cried all the time because they wanted to die. But I wasn't doing any mercy killings. I was looking for a score.

The trick was not getting caught.

There were a lot of pieces to pull together. I needed an old girl with money and an impatient heir who didn't care how he got it. Then I'd find out what drugs she was on and which ones would be the easiest to give a lethal dose of without a lot of obvious symptoms. Easy enough to Google. Then I'd boost some from the pharmacy, and start adding a little extra to her food every day. Have to do it gradual enough so there wouldn't be some big reaction, but quick enough that her doctor wouldn't start ordering tests. Then bingo, she's dead and everyone's all "well, it was time" and "now she's at rest." And even if the doctor wants to double check or the coroner orders an autopsy, they're just going to find the drugs that were supposed to be there. Nothing suspicious here, folks.

I started spending my daytime off hours in the "Hospitality Room." It was this big room with couches and recliners, and tables with regular chairs to sit around. There were two TV's, one at each end, supposedly so the sound from one wouldn't bother the people watching the other. Except there was always someone who forgot their hearing aid and had the set cranked up to full volume until someone complained and a staff person turned it down. There was a snack bar with coffee and tea and such. The walls were this soft green color with pretty pictures of flowers and trees. You could almost forget you were in a nursing home except for the flat industrial carpet—for wheelchairs to roll on—and the railings all around the walls.

Most of the residents who weren't bedridden spent some of their day in there, doing activities or just looking for company. That worked for me. The bedridden ones were probably far enough along that whoever was waiting for their money wouldn't need my help.

I took turns sitting with the ladies, chatting them up, seeing what I could find out. This was another reason the women worked better for me. The men always wanted to talk about old war stories, sports, or politics. The women liked to talk about their families, even if it was just to complain they never visited. After a couple weeks, I had three likely candidates: Gertrude, Edith, and Margaret. All had money, just one or two heirs, and were taking meds I could work with. Time to meet the family.

Gertrude's heir was her only son, Henry. He visited once a month and stayed one hour. Obligation visit. Gert was a sour old thing, tall and rail thin with a stiffly sprayed hairstyle several decades old. She spent most of her time complaining that Henry didn't come more often and bemoaning the fact that he hadn't become a doctor like she wanted but followed her ex-husband (the skirt-chasing drunk) into his computer business. Henry had never married, which was somehow her ex's fault, and never gave her the grandchildren she always wanted.

At the end of his next visit, I managed a conversation by the simple trick of lifting one of his gloves from his coat pocket and pretending he dropped it.

"You're Miss Gertrude's son, Henry, aren't you?"

He gave me a suspicious stare.

"I'm Al Bixby. I work here...in the kitchen. I like to talk with the ladies in my free time."

"Good grief, why?"

I gave a little snort of laughter. "Well, yes, some of them can be a bit...difficult?"

"That's one way to put it." He started to pull on the glove.

"And yet you're here faithfully, every month." I offered a smile I hoped was somewhere between sympathetic and conspiratorial. "Dutiful heir?"

If he was offended, he didn't show it. "Hardly. Just fulfilling a promise I made to my dad. He set up a trust fund before he died to pay for this place. Whatever's left when she dies goes to her church."

Damn. I wouldn't have minded helping the world be rid of Gertrude. The son said something else I didn't catch. My mind had already moved on to Edith.

Edith the weeper. Not about her granddaughter, she was wonderful. Came every week even though it was over an hour's drive. But she missed her Ernie...gone to his reward three years ago and all Miss Edith wanted was to join him. Well, I wasn't above helping her out, if the granddaughter was interested.

But it turned out to be Margaret.

Margaret was actually my favorite of the three. She was friendly, cheerful, and still had all her marbles. Kept in shape, too, as much as anyone can on a walker. Spry old girl. She had a great-niece, Daisy, who came to see her a couple times a day, and Daisy's husband, George, who showed up on Sunday afternoon every other week.

This was his week.

It wasn't hard to lure him away. I waited till he wandered over to the coffee machine. Margaret and Daisy, sitting at one of the tables, were chatting away and didn't seem to notice his absence.

"Couldn't take the hen talk, eh?"

He looked at me and ran his hand over his face. "For this I'm missing the game."

"That sucks." I stuck out my hand. "Al Bixby."

He took it. "George Marsh."

"I'd offer you a beer, George, but it's not allowed on the premises. I know, I work in the kitchen."

"That's okay, this will do." He gestured with the paper coffee cup.

"Come on, let's let the ladies gab." I steered him to an empty table in the corner. It wasn't difficult. Since I had the time, I started out with sports talk and the game he was missing. Then we got into business and how tough things were these days. Me working in some nursing home kitchen. Him struggling to keep his furniture business afloat.

"But Miss Margaret has money. I mean…I'm sorry, but she's in the east wing and Medicare doesn't pay for those rooms so I thought…"

His scowl was an ugly thing. "She has money. But she's not giving any of it to me. Not while she's still on this side of the grave."

Dear Lord, could he have made it any easier? "Oh, so you're in line to inherit? Well, that's something."

"Maybe. If I can keep the business going long enough."

I took a deep breath and blew it out slowly. This was it. Now or never. If I was reading him wrong, he might call the cops and that would be the end of this game real quick.

"What if you could hurry her along?"

He stared at me through narrowed eyes and I could hear him turning the words over in his mind.

"What do you mean?"

No, I hadn't read him wrong.

"Well, at her age, it's just a matter of time anyway. Hell, half the women in this place will come right out and tell you they're ready to go. It's just a matter of helping them along."

"And you help them along?"

I shook my head. "No. But I could."

"How?"

Another head shake. "Better you don't know. But I can tell you it won't be violent," just in case he's the squeamish type, "and it will take a couple weeks, maybe three, to avoid suspicion."

He took a swallow of coffee and looked across the room where his wife and her great-aunt were talking and laughing. Their laughter seemed to make the decision for him.

"How much?"

I like a man who gets right down to business.

"Forty percent. Forty percent of whatever you get. I'll even be generous and make that *after* funeral and legal expenses and taxes. Forty percent of the net inheritance."

"Bullshit. Ten."

I just stared at him.

"All right, twenty. But no higher."

Since twenty percent was the figure I was really looking for, I let the silence drag out another minute and nodded. "Okay. Twenty." Let him think he chewed me down, make him happy. "But you can't change your routine. Your wife still has to come every day like she's been doing, and you have to come visit on your usual Sunday."

He scowled and glanced at the ladies. I guess he was hoping he wouldn't have to face Miss Margaret again, but he sucked it up. "Yeah, sure, no problem."

We got up and I walked him back to their table.

"Alvin. I didn't know you were here. Daisy, you know Alvin." Miss Margaret is the only one who calls me by my given name. Insisted I tell her what it was. To be honest, I kind of like it. She flashed a bright smile and Daisy gave me a friendly nod. Part of me wishes it hadn't been Margaret. Oh, I wasn't backing out. Not on that kind of money. But I would miss her. A hell of a lot more than I would have missed Gertrude.

"Sit with us, Alvin." Margaret gestured to the chair beside her.

"I'm sorry, I can't. It's time for me to get back to work." I shook hands with George, sealing the deal. "Nice talking with you, Mr. Marsh."

That night, I was back in Mrs. Hendricks' office, taking a closer look at Margaret's medications, and googling all the medical websites. I didn't understand a lot of what I was reading but most of the time there was a link to another site that would spell it out for me. I finally figured out that my best bet was to go with *hyperkalemia*, which is basically too much potassium in the blood. There were a couple meds on her list that would boost her potassium levels if she got too much of them, and the symptoms wouldn't be too obvious.

She already had a heart condition so, with any luck at all, it should kick her into cardiac arrest. And that would be enough since the old girl conveniently had a Do Not Resuscitate order on file.

Obtaining what I needed was easy. The lock on the pharmacy was better than the dietician's office but still not much of a challenge. I'd been picking locks way too long. None of what I needed was high security stuff like the opioids, but I still only took enough for a couple days. Didn't want to set off any red flags.

The other thing I'd been doing the last couple weeks was studying the routine for setting up the meal trays. I knew who prepared which trays and when they were picked up and taken to the rooms. And I'd started helping out, moving the trays onto the insulated wheeled carts. Everyone was so grateful. "Why, thank you, Al." "It's good of you to help, Al." That was my window.

Breakfast, the first day. I had Margaret's daily dose, or overdose, tucked up my sleeve, all ground up in a little vial I swiped from the blood lab. I worked my way down to her tray. Oatmeal. Damn, the sight of it made this almost feel like a mercy killing after all.

Then it was done. The first dose. The beginning of the end for Miss Margaret.

Every day I followed the same routine. Did my prep work in the kitchen, helped with the trays, and visited with the ladies during my off hours. At the end of the first week, Edith the weeper got her wish and went to join her Ernie. It was a shame I hadn't been able to hit up her granddaughter first. Might have gotten an easy job out of it.

Sour old Gertrude took exception to something I said and started giving me the cold shoulder so I was spending more time with Margaret, watching for symptoms. There should be some weakness, numbness, muscle pain, *something* by now. I'd figured out that she wasn't the complaining type, which was good for me, so I made a point of asking how she was feeling and if anything was bothering her. She told me I was sweet to be concerned but she was just fine.

After the second week, George made his scheduled appearance. I was helping one of the residents with the TV, trying to find the war movie he was certain was on. He finally settled for college basketball. George sat with Daisy and Margaret for a while, but when he saw I was done with the TV he headed for the coffee machine, his stare telling me to meet him there.

He didn't waste time on pleasantries.

"What's going on?"

I knew what he meant but played dumb. "What do you mean?"

"I mean, what the hell is going on? We had a deal. She ain't dead. She ain't even sick."

"Calm down. I told you it could take three weeks. I have to go slow. So nobody gets suspicious." I reached for the coffee pot to pour us both a cup but he grabbed my wrist.

"I haven't got time. I've made some promises, based on that money coming. To the kind of people you don't break promises to."

Not good. And he was right, dear old Margaret wasn't showing any ill effects from the increased drugs. I eased my wrist out of his grasp, nodding my understanding.

"Okay, I'll speed up the timeline. Don't worry. I'll take care of it."

"You'd better. If this thing doesn't happen, I ain't taking the hit alone."

The next day I doubled the amount of medication in Margaret's food. I had to start seeing some results and soon. I spent most of my free time sitting with her, talking, playing cards, watching for symptoms. It's funny, I think we would have become friends if I hadn't been, you know, trying to kill her.

Another week went by. I was dreading Sunday. It wasn't George's week but I half-expected him to show up. To point out that his wife's great-aunt was still very much among the living. I thought about hiding out in the kitchen, but that would be a little obvious. When I got to the hospitality room, George wasn't there. Neither was Daisy.

Neither was Margaret.

I worked my way down the hall to the nursing station and made my inquiry.

"Oh, I'm sorry, I thought you knew."

Alleluia! All those drugs had finally kicked in. And about time. Well, rest in peace, Margaret, old girl.

"Her niece passed away. Margaret's helping with the arrangements."

I stood there staring, trying to process her words. "What?"

She shook her head. "I mean her great-niece. I'm sure you met her. She came to visit every day. Daisy Marsh."

"But...what happened? I didn't even know she was sick."

"Cardiac arrest. From what I heard, it was quite unexpected, although she *was* overweight and that's never healthy."

I thanked her and wandered back down the hall, trying to get my head around it.

Well, okay. Okay. This still works. Daisy's dead, so George is the sole heir. Those drugs have got to kick in on Margaret any time now. Maybe the shock of losing Daisy will get things moving in the right direction.

Margaret was gone four days. I worried that her body would have a chance to fight back, to overcome the effects of the extra meds. I needed her to get back here and eat the food I prepared for her. I needed her to get sick and show George some symptoms to keep him off my back. Hell, I needed her to drop dead like she was supposed to.

On Thursday, she was sitting in the hospitality room in her usual spot. She looked a little pale and tired. Good sign. One of the nurses was talking to her—offering condolences, I imagined—so I waited until she was alone then went over.

"Miss Margaret, may I sit with you?"

Her smile was not quite as bright as usual but every bit as warm. "Alvin. I've been hoping I'd see you today." She gestured toward the chair next to hers.

"I heard about Daisy," I said as I sat down. "I'm so sorry."

Her lips trembled. "Thank you. It was quite a shock. I'm going to miss her so much."

"I heard it was her heart. Had she been ill?"

"No. Not at all. Although she wasn't very fit. She hated exercise and she loved to eat. She even liked the food here."

I must have given something away in my expression because she quickly apologized.

"Oh, I'm sorry, Alvin. I shouldn't have said that. You work in the kitchen here, don't you?"

"No, that's okay. You don't like the food?"

"Well, I hardly ever eat it. It's one of the benefits of having money. I have almost all my meals smuggled in from my favorite restaurants. I'm sure my nurses know, but as long as I am careful with my choices, they pretend not to notice."

"But your trays come back empty. We check...to make sure you're eating."

"Yes, dear. I just told you. Daisy enjoyed the food here. She would schedule her visits around meal times and eat whatever came from the kitchen. I shouldn't have let her, knowing she needed to lose weight, but I thought it was better than having her stop at some fast food place on the way home. At least the food here wouldn't hurt her."

I sat there, letting the meaning of her words sink in. Margaret hadn't been getting any of the extra drugs. Daisy had. And Daisy was dead.

"So, just a heart attack? No other causes?" Damn. Did they run tests? Was there an autopsy?

"That's what her doctor said. At least it was peaceful. She went in her sleep."

I didn't dare ask any more questions.

"Maybe I let her eat here," she went on, more to herself than to me, "because I knew George was always on her about her weight. At least here she could relax and enjoy her meal."

Her words brought me back with a start. "Oh. George. How's he taking the loss?"

All the warmth went out of her. "The only loss George Marsh is grieving is the chance to get his hands on my money."

I didn't have to fake my confusion. "But isn't George your sole heir now?"

"Hah. That man was never my heir."

"I don't understand. You told me Daisy was your only family. With her gone…"

"Daisy wouldn't have inherited a thing from me. She knew that. Not as long as she was married to George Marsh. Now if she had left him, I would have taken care of her. I loved Daisy. I would have set her up in a nice place, given her a monthly allowance, anything she needed. But I knew as long as she was married to George, any money she got from me would have gone straight to him, to be wasted on one of his shady business deals."

Say what? "Did he know?"

"Well, I certainly never told him. That man is mean as a snake. Lord knows how he would have treated my Daisy if he knew he was never going to get any money out of her. And as much as she loved him, I think she understood it, too."

I was screwed. Screwed. My grand plan for killing Margaret was a bust. And even if I succeeded, there'd be no payoff. Twenty percent of zero was zero. Plus there was George—and his angry friends.

"So, who *are* you leaving your money to?" Wrong question. "I'm sorry. That was out of line."

Her smile was coy, and a little mischievous. "Well, I guess you could say I have lots of heirs. I like setting up individual bequests for people I meet. It makes me feel good. Most of them aren't aware and it makes me happy knowing I'm leaving pleasant surprises behind when I go. When the time comes, everything that's left after those bequests will provide an endowment fund for scholarships at my alma mater, Denison University."

"Wow. That's…" That's gonna piss George off royally. Wasn't doing much for me either. "That's really beautiful, Miss Margaret."

She studied me for a long moment then leaned in, motioning me to do the same. "I don't usually do this, but I'm going to let you in on a secret. While I was taking care of Daisy's affairs, I saw my lawyer…and added a bequest for you."

I leaned back and gaped at her.

"Close your mouth, dear," she twinkled at me.

"But…why?"

"Because you're a nice man who makes time for an old lady." She patted my hand. "It's not a fortune but it will get you out of that kitchen and let you do something you want to do."

☒

THAT NIGHT I walked to the corner bus stop, trying to get my head around the weird turn of events. Margaret hadn't named a figure, and I sure couldn't ask, but it was going to be more than I'd get from George, the non-heir. Now I was the one waiting for the old lady to die, which meant I couldn't kill her, even if I could find another way. Heirs have motive. But I could wait her out.

I was so lost in thought I didn't notice the figure that stepped out of the shadows until he said my name.

"Bixby."

Damn. George.

"What the hell did you do? You killed my wife."

"What do you mean? I heard she died of a heart attack."

"Don't give me that crap. You were supposed to kill Margaret and now Daisy's dead. You screwed up. Without Daisy, I'll get nothing."

Should I tell him? Sorry, George, you were always going to get nothing. Nah, better not.

"Man, I'm sorry, but it's not my fault. I didn't touch Daisy. I swear. I couldn't know she was going to have a heart attack." Or that Margaret was putting me in her will instead of him.

"I don't see it that way. This whole thing was your idea. You said you could deliver. I made promises. Now I'm going to be paying the price."

His hand came out of his coat pocket holding a small but deadly .38 revolver and he gave me a cold, mirthless smile. "And so are you."

I opened my mouth but nothing came out. I guess neither of us would be inheriting from Miss Margaret. She was going to outlive us both.

LISA DE NIKOLITS

Lisa de Nikolits, originally from South Africa, has lived in Canada since 2000. Her seventh novel, *No Fury Like That*, will be published in Italian in 2019, under the title *Una furia dell'altro mondo*. Previous works include *The Hungry Mirror*, *West of Wawa*, *A Glittering Chaos*, *Witchdoctor's Bones*, *Between The Cracks She Fell*, *The Nearly Girl*, and *Rotten Peaches*. *The Occult Persuasion and the Anarchist's Solution* is forthcoming in Fall 2019. Her short stories appear in several collections. Lisa is a member of Sisters in Crime National and Toronto, the International Thriller Writers, Crime Writers of Canada, and Mesdames of Mayhem. Find her at lisadenikolitswriter.com.

FIRE DRILL

LISA DE NIKOLITS

FLY UNDER THE RADAR. That was my plan. *Don't lose your cool.* That was my mantra. I told myself I could do it. I'd made it this far, hadn't I?

My mirrored reflection stared back at me in the elevator. I was ridiculously exhausted and it was only seven a.m. I counted the red numbers as we passed each floor. Going up, when my whole life was going down. Down the tubes, that is. What with the shrinking industry, tenacious Shar-Pei lines etching their way into my cheeks, my teeth like old corn on the cob, the gums receding as fast as the prospects for my future, the prognosis wasn't good. And what was with the steel-wool hair sprouting up around my ears like some crazy old guy's sideburns? No one had ever mentioned that was in my future.

I stood on the gray diamond centre of the elevator floor and stared down. If the elevator got stuck, I wouldn't even be able to lie down and sleep. The floor was too filthy. But my diamond was still there, under the salt grime and shoe dandruff. The diamond, my magic place to make a daily wish. *Keep me safe. Let me last out this day.* It had worked for nearly eighteen years. It would work today. It had to. Chester, my aging Weimaraner, needed me.

I was the first one at my desk. It was a military strategy, get the lay of the land, see what emails had come in, prepare the necessary weaponry. Make oatmeal and get a big mug of decaf sweetened with stevia. I couldn't handle caffeine anymore and sugar was the devil in a blue dress. Gone were the days I could down three double espressos with nary a flutter in my veins. Nowadays I was as twitchy as a rabbit at Eastertime and god knows it didn't take much of anything to get me all fired up.

Ah frig. I peered at my screen. A meeting request flashed: ICONS, FURTHER DISCUSSION. ACCEPT WITH COMMENTS, ACCEPT WITHOUT COMMENTS. Not a request, a demand. I accepted without comments although I wanted to reply *seriously, not another meeting about the icons, how many meetings can we have?* The icons would be the death of me.

I worked in a marketing firm and my new boss had insisted on "elevating the brand" by introducing "navigable, user-friendly, iconic pathfinders"— tiny illustrations littering the brochure pages in case the dumb, dumber, and dumbest out there couldn't find the prices and noteworthy features of the products we told them they couldn't live without.

But I'm not an illustrator and the free vector art I found was, according to my boss, just wrong, wrong, wrong. I couldn't get the formula right and not for lack of trying. This had been going on for months, ever since Princess Tight White Pants in Red Stilettos had taken over.

Yep. I'd been hanging on by my fingernails, dangling over a cliff, with bits of scrub and brush falling onto my upturned face as I tried not to lose my grip. I was doing kind of okay until our primo client decided they hated Alice A. It broke my heart to watch my friend and former boss being marched out, tears streaming down her face, her purse hitting her thigh like a sack of old fruit. But I blew my nose and counted my blessings that I was still there. I had to keep fighting, had to carry on.

But then the stiletto-heeled supermodel from Mars came back from maternity leave to take her place at the throne.

Heaven knows, I tried to make the princess happy. Tried over and over again. But I'm a fuzzy kitten type of gal, not some kind of techno gangsta kid. I like happy faces and friendly-looking little doodles, maybe some speech bubbles with a bunch of exclamation marks. Apparently, that's not the style these days. I'm not "graphic enough," my art needs to be "streamlined," my icons are "too busy."

I studied the email meeting invite again and a sinking feeling filled my gut. I had already had three meetings with the princess. Three. And now I had just agreed to numero four. *Report for duty in the Aurora boardroom at 11a.m.*

I put my head in my hands. There it was. That familiar throb. Angry pincers needling lobster claws into the softest meat behind my eyeballs. I reached into my purse and dug out two codeine pills and added two ibuprofen for good measure. I knew I had been taking too many meds but I felt justified. I had to get rid of the headache before it took hold. Interns and acne-ridden adolescents were banging on the door like the zombies from the *Walking Dead*, and I was trapped with nowhere to run and nowhere to hide. Nothing could keep me safe in this war zone. My guardian angel, Alice A, was gone. And Alice B, yes, how weird, two Alices, was back.

And she'd never liked me.

Eleven a.m. came. I walked into the Aurora boardroom and gingerly sat down while Alice B fired up her laptop. She proceeded to lead me through half an hour of torture, flicking through icons and illustrations. "You see the difference?" she kept saying, interspersed by, "You see what I mean?"

I didn't. Why couldn't she just choose the icons she wanted and let me get on with it? Because this was so much more fun for her. I tried to note the ones that she seemed to like but as soon as I did, she'd say, "well, that was just about there, but the curves aren't quite right, you see what I mean?" and I nodded dumbly. What had I done to deserve this punishment? I looked at her, her white jeans impeccable and nearly transparent, her black bra showing through her sheer white blouse. Who dresses like that for work? And those shoes, six inches of killer icepick heels. She even adjusted her bra while we were talking, hitching it up and scratching where the straps had dug in. The woman had zero class.

"So you like that one?" I asked, my pen poised hopefully over my notebook.

She shook her head sadly. "No Miranda, that one's too angular? You see the difference?"

And then the fire alarm went off. *Whoop, whoop, whoop.* Thank god. I gathered my notebook and started to stand but she waved me back.

"It's just a drill," she said. "Sit. Ignore it. We need to get this nailed down."

The boardroom across from us was full and they too carried on working. I had no choice but to force my gaze back to Alice B and her laptop.

Whoop, whoop, whoop. The siren was insistent. "You see what I mean?" Alice B yelled above the din, and I forced myself to nod.

"Make a note of this one," Alice B continued, her voice manic, "but you'll have to...." *Whoop, whoop, whoop.* And then, mercifully, the words were drowned out, the siren honking like a goose trapped under the wheel of a bus. *Whoop, whoop, whoop.* Alice B's red lips moving as she pointed to her screen. *Whoop, whoop, whoop.* I nodded again, the noise a suffocating blanket. I felt like I was under an overturned boat, bobbing in dark water, with a foghorn blasting in my ears. *Whoop, whoop, whoop.*

I watched the boardroom across from us empty. *Whoop, whoop, whoop.* The emergency response guy opened the door and waved us out, shouting. And still, Alice B shook her head.

"We must finish this," she screamed over the siren, "we have a deadline, we're behind." *Whoop, whoop, whoop. Whoop, whoop, whoop.* She forced me to sit there, the howling smashing at me like a baseball bat. I was trapped. Me, who was once the boss.

You see, Alice B and I went way back. "Oh I know Miranda," she said during team introductions and she smirked. She hadn't forgotten our past. I'd had to call her out, back in the day, when she wasn't pulling her weight. She'd responded by not speaking to me for six months before leaving for mat leave. I had hoped she'd never come back. In a way, I'd been counting on it.

No such luck. I heard they begged her on bended knee to return and save our sinking ship, and my first thought was, *there goes my life.* I tried to get another job but there wasn't anything out there. I had to make it work.

"Don't worry," Alice A said when we heard Alice B was coming back, "I'll take care of you, just like I always have." But then, out of nowhere, Alice A got pink-slipped. And there I was, being tortured by an evil emissary straight out of a Victoria's Secret catalog. Why hadn't they let me go? Paid me off? That would have been better than this. This was fun for Alice B, her revenge for all those years ago when I'd given her a failing grade on her performance review.

Whoop, whoop, whoop. I kept my fists clenched tightly by my sides. I dug my nails into my cuticles as if the pain would distract me and it did for a while but she wouldn't shut up. The fire alarm was honking *Whoop, whoop, whoop,* and she kept on talking. I was trapped with her in that boardroom, her with her perfect hair and her dead black eyes, droning on and on, "Do you see what I mean? Can you see what I'm saying, can you see the difference?" *Whoop, whoop, whoop.*

Eventually, the emergency response guy kicked us out of the boardroom, wouldn't take no for an answer. I wanted to leave and never come back. But if I quit my job, I wouldn't get severance, I'd lose everything. Chester was getting older, he needed me. I had to keep this job, whatever it took. But at that moment, I had to get away from Alice B. I was soaked in sweat, rivers running down my rib cage, puddling in my love handles and the waistband of my trousers. My heart inflated like the inner tube of a bicycle tire about to explode. I needed to flee from Alice B, find a coffee shop, pretend I got lost in the crowds who had left the building. Take some time to myself, get a cup of decaf—maybe even a full caf with real sugar—take a Xanax, come back and try my hand at those icons again.

Whoop, whoop, whoop. I stood up, shaking, and Alice B shuttled me back to our desks so we could grab our winter coats and purses. She herded me towards the stairwell, pushing her way in front. I had grabbed my big thick coat and started to struggle into it. Alice B, of course, had a flimsy little jacket, no gloves or hat, how did she do that? Didn't normal blood flow through her skinny supermodel veins?

I paused at the top of Stairwell 9 and shoved my arms into my twisted jacket while Alice B trotted ahead. *Whoop, whoop, whoop.*

Alice B was half a flight down when I saw my opportunity. It wasn't so much a conscious thought as a fully fleshed-out realization. *Lose your footing. Crash into her. Solve this problem. Get rid of her.* I was wrapped in a cocoon of soft down and I could tackle her, push her, destroy her. Reclaim my life. "I fell, in the rush," I would say, "it was an accident."

She had her back to me. I'd once read that shoving a person down stairs was as easy as opening a door. I rushed towards her, figuring if I nailed her on the turn at the top of the stairs, she'd tumble the full length for maximum damage.

I hardly had to do anything and there she was, tumbling down, down, down, and the bicycle tire in my chest flew away as if it never existed. I clutched my hands to the sides of my face while I watched her fall and I couldn't help but smile.

Bounce, bounce, bounce, there she was, nearly at the foot of the Stairwell 6. But then a terrible thing happened. The door to Stairwell 6 opened and a woman stepped out, right into the path of Alice B. Alice B careened into her, linebacker style, and they both tossed and turned down the stairs, like laundry spinning in a big old dryer, both of them coming to an abrupt stop at the bottom of Stairwell 5. Somehow I knew the other woman was dead.

And that Alice B was still alive.

I stood frozen, watching from above as Alice B raised her body off the dead woman. Alice B who wouldn't even need stain remover for her white jeans. She looked up at me and stared for a long moment before reaching for her phone.

I sank to my haunches, watching and waiting. The fire alarm throbbed to the message my heart was banging out: *What did you do, OMG, what did you do?*

Adwar.

I had killed my friend Adwar. She was a cleaning lady from Ethiopia, here to help her family. She sent money home every month. I knew because I collected money for her at Christmastime and I knew that in English, her name was Sophia.

I had killed my friend.

But when I tried to explain that it was an accident, me bumping into Alice B, well, the jury wouldn't buy into it.

Because Alice B's lawyer had entered the text message into evidence. The text message I thought I had sent to Alice A. I had, immediately after pressing SEND, realized my mistake and deleted the message. I'd reassured myself with the fact that, when I tried to send it, I was underground on the subway, where there was no signal. Besides, I was just venting to my old friend Alice A, who could blame me? Alice B had insisted we all had one another's contact info on our phones, something I usually reserved for friends. But the message had clearly been sent.

I WISH SHE WAS DEAD. I MISS YOU SO MUCH. I HATE HER. HER AND HER TIGHT WHITE JEANS THAT SHOW EVERY SINGLE DETAIL. CAN I SAY CAMEL TOE? LOL. WITCH. HOW WILL I SURVIVE WITHOUT YOU?

And Alice B had the message. And she showed it to the court. And that was me, done for. And you know what? I felt relief. I would be released from the hellhole she had me trapped in. I didn't even care. I had tried to stay under the radar, keep my head down and not cause any waves. But my best-laid plans had been tripped up by the fire alarm, the temptation offered by the empty stairwell and the unspeakable urge to shut Alice B up. Yeah, I'd lost everything but I didn't even care. Alice A would take care of Chester.

The judge asked me if I had anything to say and for a moment, I thought there was no point. But then I changed my mind and I got up and swore to tell the truth, the whole truth, and nothing but the truth.

"I bumped into you by mistake," I said, looking Alice B straight in the eyes. "It was an accident. You made us late, you made us rush, the fire marshal even said so. I was pulling on my coat and I tripped. And yes I wrote that text, so what? I was venting to a friend."

I turned to the judge. "But I am sorry about Adwar. I really am. I loved that woman. You can ask anybody. I tried to help her out wherever I could."

And that's when I broke down and cried my heart out. All the tears of rage and pain and fear that had piled up since Alice B had returned. All those months of her needling me and humiliating me as often as she could.

The judge took my tears of release as tears of remorse and dismissed the charges against me, agreeing the whole thing had been an accident.

Then the judge addressed Alice B. "It was an accident, there was no premeditation, do you see the difference? She didn't mean to kill you. You should have left the room as soon as the fire alarm went off. You put yourself and your employee in an unnecessary position of danger. You see what I mean? You need to take responsibility for this."

I cried even harder, hearing Alice B's patronizing words come back to haunt her.

Things worked out just fine for Chester and me. I got severance from work, a full year's pay with benefits. Alice A found me a job at her new gig and soon I was back at my desk, another desk but still, my desk, with my oatmeal and my stevia-sweetened decaf.

And I sent Adwar's family money every month. Because I really was sorry about that.

TOM BARLOW

Tom Barlow is an Ohio writer. His other works can be found in several anthologies, including *Best American Mystery Stories 2013*, *Dames and Sin*, and *Plan B Omnibus*, as well as periodicals including *Pulp Modern*, *Red Room*, *Heater*, *Plots With Guns*, *Mystery Weekly*, *Needle*, *Thuglit*, *Manslaughter Review*, *Switchblade*, and *Tough*. His novel *I'll Meet You Yesterday* and new crime short story collection *Odds of Survival* are available on Amazon. Tom is a member of Sisters in Crime National and the Short Mystery Fiction Society. Find him at tjbarlow.com.

HEIRLOOM

TOM BARLOW

SETH'S DAD, whereabouts unknown, had promised his mother, Harmony, a ring, a home, a family of her own—all sounding like nirvana to the daughter of a West Virginia coal miner. What he'd given her instead was a fetus to resent, and her only fourteen years old.

She raised the boy and his brother, Aaron, that came along a year later (father again unknown but suspected to be the husband of her cousin Jewel), by herself. They lived in a third-generation shack in Diamond, West Virginia, left to her by her Uncle Ralph after he took off the top of his head. He had used the same shotgun his own father had used to commit suicide when the miners first went on strike back in the 1930s. Every time the mine closed, even for a long weekend, Harmony hid the gun from the family under the wooden remains of an old outhouse at the edge of their property.

Seth and Aaron grew up riding all-terrain vehicles, gifts from their mother's brother, Heath, who repaired them on the side. They knew the mountains for thirty miles in every direction, all the backwoods ways to travel from town to town without seeing even a trailer or an abandoned school bus full of squatters.

Seth was not only the older of the brothers, nineteen to Aaron's eighteen, he was the one with an imagination. Aaron had the looks: a square chin, deep-set amber eyes, and hair the color of egg custard, but he'd been unable to handle the high school curriculum and only graduated by the grace of a scam, pulled by the school board, to avoid losing No Child Left Behind funding.

Seth, on the other hand, was a small, wiry kid with a weak chin hiding behind a threadbare goatee; a face that seemed to invite bar fights. He had long blamed his appearance for his mother's detached attitude toward him, so different from the way she treated Aaron, her baby.

"You know what we need to do?" Seth said one November evening, handing his brother a joint rolled with weed from the patch they'd found growing on Cutter Mountain that fall.

"We need to get out of this town," Aaron said, giggling. "We need a truck, so we can move to Atlanta, get jobs that don't give you black lung."

"You speak the truth," Seth said, "but to do that, we need some money. What we need to do is stick up that gas station over to Marlington."

Aaron sat up, nibbling his bottom lip. "No way. What if we get caught?"

Caught didn't figure as an option as Seth envisioned the heist; it was completely tight. "We haven't been in Marlington for years," Seth said, speaking slowly so Aaron could keep up. "So nobody's going to know us, especially with masks on. We do the deed late in the evening, when they have the most cash, then we ride the trails home. In the dark. They'll never be able to follow us."

"Neither of us have headlights that work," Aaron pointed out.

"Then nobody can follow us by our lights, right? The way we know those trails, it'll be no problem finding our way home by moonlight."

"How much you think we'd get?" Aaron said.

"I figure a couple of grand easy, maybe three. They're the only gas station in town."

"And you promise we won't get caught?"

"Trust me. Have I ever steered you wrong?" Aaron was unlikely to remember the many times he'd done just that.

Aaron leaned back until his head bumped against the wall. "Mom's going to be so pissed if we mess this up."

"Don't worry, she'll blame me. She always does."

⏳

SETH KEPT an eye on the weather and the moon phases until he concluded that the last day in November was perfect for the job: a full moon, clear skies in the forecast, cold but no snow on the ground. He waited until Harmony departed for her part-time job at the local tourism bureau before raiding her closet for the Smith & Wesson .38 their grandfather had used while working guard duty at the mines decades before. It was still loaded.

He also rifled through her dresser looking for pantyhose to use as masks. To his dismay, there weren't any.

⏳

"AS FAR AS MASKS GO, these have got to be the worst," Aaron said.

They were astride their ATVs in the dark, on the bike path that ran behind the Gas & Grub Mart in Marlington, twenty-five miles as the crow flies from home. Seth had cut out eye and mouth holes in a couple of small brown paper grocery bags for masks. Aaron's barely fit over his head, and the eyeholes were spaced too closely together, cutting off his peripheral vision. His mouth was a good inch above the mouth hole, and Seth could barely make out what he was saying.

"I wish we was home playing World of Warcraft," Aaron said.

"I wish we were in Atlanta at a titty bar," Seth said. "We pull this off, and I might just take you to one." He stepped off his ATV, stretched his arms over his head, and yawned wide. "Well, it's show time. You ready?"

Aaron tugged at his mask. "I suppose so."

The two crept to the dark side of the store. There were a couple of trucks gassing up at the pumps in front, and they waited for them to leave.

"Hey Seth," Aaron whispered. "You scared?"

"Just pretend you're Iron Man," Seth said. "Ice water in your veins. And remember—no names."

Once the last truck rolled away, Seth motioned with the crook of a finger and they strode to the door, Seth fingering the pistol inside his jacket pocket.

Aaron opened the door and Seth entered, raising the .38 as he reached the counter. Aaron followed him in.

The clerk was a young black-haired woman with multiple piercings, thin to the point of ghoulishness.

"Don't shoot," she said. "I'm no hero." She thrust her arms, like two pipe cleaners, in the air.

"Put the cash register money in a bag," Seth said, his voice cracking slightly.

The clerk lowered her hands and reached under the counter. Seth tracked her with the pistol, but she came up with, not a gun, but a plastic bag. "Keep cool," she said. "This isn't my first holdup."

She opened the register and quickly filled the bag with cash. "You want the change?"

Seth thought for a moment. "Just the quarters."

She finished filling the bag and tossed it onto the counter, knocking over a display of beef jerky. Aaron reached around Seth and picked up the bag.

"Show me," Seth said. Aaron opened the bag, revealing a small pile of cash, mostly ones.

"Where's the rest?" Seth asked, gun still leveled at the clerk.

She swallowed hard. "The manager does a deposit at the bank at five p.m. every evening, before he goes home for the day."

"Bull," Seth said. Anger flashed through him. He turned the pistol toward the glass-fronted beer cooler a dozen feet to his left and fired. The glass exploded and beer began raining down inside the cooler from the punctured cans.

"What the heck is wrong with you?" the clerk asked from the floor where she'd ducked as he fired.

Seth looked frantically around for anything else of value he could steal, his eyes coming to rest on the box containing lottery tickets.

"Hey," he said. "Stand up."

"Don't shoot me, okay?" the clerk said.

"Gimme some lottery tickets."

Her head appeared above the counter. "They'll know the numbers of the ones you stole. You'll never be able to redeem them."

"You let me worry about that."

"Okay. Don't shoot anymore. You want instant or ones for the drawing?"

"Instant. The whole wheel."

The clerk unreeled the tickets, rolling them up as they came off. As she did, Seth heard Aaron behind him whimper.

"What's wrong?" he asked softly.

"I got cut."

Seth backed away from the counter until he could see his brother. Blood was spreading down the left side of his paper bag from a cut on his forehead. "A piece of the glass from the cooler hit me," Aaron said.

Seth looked down. There were drops of blood on the floor. He grabbed a loaf of bread from the counter next to him, ripped it open and handed Aaron a handful of slices. "Use that to stop the bleeding."

The clerk finished rolling the lottery tickets, turned and dropped them on the counter. "Anything else you need?"

He grabbed the tickets and said, "Thanks, sugar. Now let's get out of here." His brother, bread clasped fast to the cut on his forehead, preceded him out.

They jogged over to the bike path, jumped on their ATVs and started them up. Seth pulled off his mask, took the cash and lottery tickets from Aaron, shoved them under his jacket, and set off, Aaron close behind.

The bike path was straight and paved, following the bank of the Greenbrier River, remote from the highway. They rode in the moonlight for ten minutes before crossing the wooden-decked Sharps Bridge. On the other side, Seth stopped so they could top off their gas tanks from the extra gas they carried in cans.

"How's your head?" Seth asked.

"It's stopped bleeding," Aaron said. "But I think there's a piece of glass still in it."

"They have your DNA now," Seth said. "They won't be able to match it to you since you've never been arrested. But if they do come for you, you're screwed. In that case, you'll have to keep me out of it."

"They'll know it was you with me," Aaron said, "since we're always together. They know I'm not bright enough to pull this off on my own."

"Make somebody up. Some guy you met while hunting, a guy that took off and you don't know where he is. His name was Peanut, and you don't know any other name."

"Peanut. Me and Peanut stuck up the convenience store?"

"And he had the gun," Seth said.

"And he had the gun." Aaron repeated, his face knotted in concentration.

"Yeah, he had the gun."

Ten minutes later they were deep in the woods. Riding the rough trails, gnarled with tree roots and large limestone outcroppings, and shaded by the overarching limbs of hardwood trees, was much more difficult in the half-light of the moon than Seth had anticipated and he crept along.

For the next three hours, they picked their way along the trail, occasionally hitting low spots where water gathered, splashing onto their boots and jeans until their shoes were drenched.

Finally Seth, reaching an overlook, stopped for a break.

"What are we stopping for?" Aaron asked.

"Let's look at your head."

They dismounted and took seats on a downed oak that stretched alongside the trail. Aaron's forehead was still bloody. Seth stood and bent over his brother, using his lighter to illuminate the wound. A piece of glass was sticking out of his skin.

"Hold still a minute," he said. He pulled out his pocket knife and gently pried the glass out of the wound. The cut began to bleed again. "You got any of that bread left?"

"I ate it," Aaron said. "And I'm still hungry."

Seth cut a sleeve off of a sweatshirt he'd brought along in case it got really cold and wrapped it around his brother's head.

⏳

SETH AND AARON wrestled the machines down a long series of switchbacks, many washed out and full of mud the consistency of burnt motor oil. Seth's hand began to ache from squeezing his brakes. They were still miles from home around midnight when disaster struck.

Seth was turning his ATV through a steep, sharp right-hand curve when he saw, too late, that a section of the trail had collapsed. He hit the brakes hard, but his machine slid into the ditch and, out of control, headed straight for a twelve-foot drop-off. Seth bailed at the last second, landing hard on his back, his head whipping against a boulder.

He woke some time later to a sharp, grating pain in his ankle, already so swollen it pressed against the leather of his Red Wings. The moon was further west than it had been.

Aaron was seated next to him, scratching off instant lottery tickets with his pocket knife. The fog of his breath drifted across the moon.

"How about a little help?" Seth said.

Aaron reached out a hand, grasped Seth's, and pulled him to a seated position. Seth saw stars for a moment.

"Win anything?" he said.

Aaron held up a ticket. "A thousand dollars, if I could ever cash it in. You hurt bad?"

"Broken ankle, I'm guessing. How's my ATV?"

"Landed on its side down on the next switchback. I'd say it's totaled."

"Man, this is a mess if I ever saw one," Seth said. His teeth began to chatter.

"I counted the money," Aaron said, "while you were out. I didn't have nothing else to do."

"And?"

"Two hundred and twenty-three dollars and seventy-five cents."

"Damn."

"What do we do now, smart brother?" Aaron said.

"Let me think," Seth said, rubbing the knot where his head had collided with rock. "I got to get off this mountain. I might die out here in the cold with my injuries. Once a man gets a concussion, you never know what complications can set in."

"Well we can't two-up on my ATV, not on these trails."

"I'll tell you what we got to do," Seth said, keeping his voice calm and business-like. "I need to borrow your ATV. Otherwise we'll get caught up here. There's too many people use these trails during the day for us to go undiscovered."

"But what am I supposed to do?" Aaron said.

Seth patted him on the shoulder. "You can still walk. I can't. You hike out, catch the fire road at the bottom of the mountain and follow that on out to the highway. I'll come pick you up with Mom's truck. If you don't see me, thumb a ride into town."

"Won't that look bad if the cops see me?"

"I wouldn't worry about it," Seth said. "I'll have your ATV back at the house. I'm more worried about them finding mine wrecked up here."

"I don't like it."

"Well who does? And don't forget about Peanut."

"Peanut?"

"Your partner, if you get caught."

⏳

SETH LABORED DOWN THE MOUNTAIN, cursing with pain every time he used his bad foot to change gear. He ended up leaving it in second most of the way, sacrificing time for a lower pain level. He almost cried with relief when he finally hit the dirt road that led past their shack, around five a.m.

He glanced at Harmony's truck as he parking the ATV. The way his ankle hurt, he thought, he shouldn't be doing any more driving. He needed to ice it down, and probably go get an x-ray if it didn't feel better soon. And if Harmony caught him with her truck, how would he explain?

Besides, with Aaron's good looks, he assured himself, his brother would get a ride as soon as he stuck his thumb out.

⧗

SETH FELL asleep on the couch shortly thereafter, and when he woke around eleven his mother had already left for work. There was still no sign of Aaron.

By noon, Seth was deeply worried by his brother's absence. Had the cops caught him? Would they be coming for him next?

To his relief, the swelling of his ankle was down considerably. Maybe it was a sprain, not a break. He remained worried about his other problem, though—his ATV, lying abandoned on the mountainside. If the cops found it, it would lead them directly to him.

And he only had Aaron's word that it was trashed. Perhaps with a little work he could get it back in running order. If not, maybe he could drag it away from the trail and bury it under some rocks.

Around one o'clock he decided that he couldn't wait any longer; he had to find Aaron, and he had to check his crashed ATV. He wrapped his ankle in elastic bandages and covered it with duct tape so that it felt stable. He also stole a couple of the pills Harmony took for her back, which left him feeling lightheaded but pain free.

He slowly worked his way up the mountain on his brother's ATV, riding like a rookie, slow and stiff, all to keep from putting weight on his ankle.

He was only a few hundred yards from the crash site when he forded one of the larger creeks spilling off the mountain. As he bounced up the far bank, he caught a glimpse of something lying on the edge of the creek downstream a few yards. He stopped, rolled back. Even though the body was lying on its face, he could tell it was Aaron.

He sat stone still for several minutes, just listening to the water. He felt the cold now that he'd stopped moving, and there were ice crystals in his beard.

He got off the ATV and hobbled down the bank toward his brother. Aaron's legs were in the water. The back of his skull was thick with dried blood, and his clothes were soaking wet.

Seth grasped Aaron's jacket by the shoulders and dragged him up onto the bank, then rolled him over. His brother had never had a particularly bright expression, but it had never been as vacant as it was now.

He couldn't look at Aaron's face for long. Instead, he returned to the creek and studied the place where the trail forded it. There he saw the muddy boot prints where his brother had entered the creek, and on a large boulder in midstream he saw more dried blood. Aaron must have slipped on a wet rock in the dark and fallen, his head striking the boulder.

Still at a loss about what to do, he left his brother and continued up the trail on Aaron's ATV until he reached his own. It was on its left side and it took all the muscle he had to right it. He inventoried the damage. Fortunately it was mostly to the body panels, hunks of plastic that he could replace at his leisure. He unbolted what he couldn't wrench back into position, and straightened the handlebars as best he could. Crossing his fingers, he hit the starter. It ground for a minute and caught.

He rode his ATV down to where he'd left Aaron, then limped back up the mountain and returned with Aaron's.

He sat there for a few minutes, looking at the ford. His brother was dead and there was nothing he could do about that. He also contemplated jail.

Time, he thought, for more practical concerns. How was he to play this? It wasn't too long before he came up with a plan.

He rode his brother's ATV into the creek and stopped halfway across, front wheel in a hole. He managed to tip the machine on its side. He then retrieved his brother's body and placed it downstream of the ATV, his head near the boulder that was stained with his blood.

Lastly, he pulled out the lottery tickets they'd stolen and stuck them in Aaron's jacket pocket. He felt like a traitor setting up his brother to take the fall, but what else could he do?

⧗

Now WHAT HE needed was an alibi. As he rode home, he thought about his cousins Chris and Barry Couch, jailbirds that would as soon lie to cops as breathe. It would probably cost him all he'd cleared from the holdup, but at this point he was a desperate man.

He rode down to the Black Diamond Bar & Grill and found his cousins in their usual spot next to the jukebox, so they could impose their selections on anyone feeling generous enough to squander a quarter.

The two had no trouble remembering that they'd played poker with him in Chris's trailer the night before, in exchange for a hundred dollars each. If they hadn't been family, Seth would have worried that his money wouldn't go far, but he knew things about his cousins that the cops would be very interested in finding out, so there was a bit of a Mexican standoff to support his alibi.

Now, all he had to do was wait for Aaron to be found. He tried to avoid thinking about his brother's body out there in the cold.

To his dismay, it started to snow an hour later, big, wet flakes that fell in clumps like goose down. In two hours, three inches were on the ground and the blizzard was already pushing it into drifts. The weatherman estimated that they could get a foot or more before nightfall.

Harmony returned home late afternoon, released from work early because of the storm.

"Where's your brother?" she asked as she placed a bag of groceries on the countertop.

Seth had polished off the vodka, and took some time coordinating his response. "I don't know for sure."

She stopped putting groceries away and turned to him, hands on hips.

"I haven't seen him since yesterday afternoon," Seth said. "He was going to hang out with some tourist he met on the trail, a guy named Peanut."

"So where do you think he is now?"

"He and this Peanut guy were talking about riding into Elkins, so I figured he met some girl and got lucky. And now he's probably snowed in."

"Damn it, why'd you let him take off like that? That boy is too gullible to let run with strangers."

"Did it ever occur to you that I might not want to spend my life as a babysitter? You don't give him enough credit anyway. He can make his own decisions."

"Like he did yesterday?" she said. "I just hope he's safe in Elkins and not out on some godforsaken trail trying to ride home."

"What you want me to do?" Seth asked. "Go try to find him?"

"Don't be an idiot."

⌛

AFTER FRETTING through a couple of pilsners, Harmony called the Sheriff's Department. They had no reports of stranded riders in Elkins, and they didn't seem much interested in the possibility that someone would have been dumb enough to get caught out on the trails during the blizzard.

To Seth's surprise, a sheriff's deputy did make it out to their house later that afternoon; she had a plow attached to the front of her Chevy truck, doing double duty clearing the road as she responded to calls.

The deputy, a middle-aged woman packing extra pounds above and below a duty belt tight as a tourniquet, had obviously put two and two together and came up with the equation Aaron = Marlington. She questioned Harmony about Aaron's movements without mentioning the holdup, but his mother caught onto the tenor of her inquiries and asked the deputy why she was asking such questions.

"There was a holdup in Marlington last night," the deputy said, watching Seth out of the corner of her eye. "They got away on ATVs. We think this might be the same guys that have committed three other holdups in the county in the last month, although they never used ATVs before. One clerk on an earlier holdup was shot bad."

The deputy turned to him. "Where were you last night?"

Seth was still processing the frightening possibility that he could be charged with holdups he didn't commit, so it took him a moment to respond. He was glad he'd set up the alibi, although he knew it sounded thin. His mother, to his dismay, was shaking her head as he spoke.

The deputy also wasn't pleased with Seth's story about the stranger Peanut, especially when Seth said he'd never seen the guy. She asked Seth for a DNA swab, and, with his mother staring daggers at him, he couldn't help but comply.

"We'll do what we can when we can," the deputy told Harmony as she prepared to leave. "But we don't have the equipment for a backcountry rescue with all this snow, if it comes to that. If you hear from him, please tell him it's in his best interest to contact us."

"I understand," Harmony said, and continued to gnaw on her thumbnail.

When the deputy left, she turned to Seth. "You want to tell me about that?"

Seth remained composed. "I can't believe Aaron would steal, although the way he described that Peanut guy he sounded pretty wild. Maybe he's the guy that's been doing all these holdups."

"Bull," Harmony said, slumping onto the couch. She leaned forward, elbows on knees, and rested her forehead in her hands. "There's only one person that could convince Aaron to break the law."

"I was playing poker," Seth said. "Like I told the cops."

"You've never had any trouble lying to me, have you? I always did my best by both of you. How'd you grow up to be so goddamn evil?"

☒

THE THAW DIDN'T COME for almost two weeks, weeks during which Seth found himself staring out the window of the house for hours at a time. Even when the thaw came, the first couple of days the water running down the creeks was so heavy they were unfordable. It wasn't until the third day that Seth, his ankle feeling back to normal, was able to get on the mountain on his ATV. He couldn't stand the thought of his brother being up there any longer, even if finding Aaron himself would probably convince the cops he'd been in on the heist.

Given the conditions, he wasn't surprised that it took him the best part of two hours to reach the ford where he'd left his brother.

But the body and the ATV were gone. The stream was out of its banks, the once-bloody boulder submerged.

He could understand how Aaron's body might have been washed away, but what about his ATV? It was too heavy to be moved by the water. Someone must have stolen it. Did they drive off with it while Aaron was still lying freshly dead in the creek?

He stepped off his ride and followed the creek down the mountain. It wasn't far before it disappeared into a thicket of rhododendrons the size of a dump truck. Hung up in a snarl of fallen tree limbs on his side of the creek was a lonely boot, the same type that Seth was wearing. He reached out and grabbed it by the heel.

When he turned it over, a foot fell out and landed back in the stream, floated into the dense foliage. Before it disappeared, Seth could see bite marks in the flesh.

☒

SETH WAS SURPRISED by the depth with which he missed his brother.

He no longer found any joy in trail riding and took to spending his afternoons hanging out with his cousins at the bar.

Therefore, it was a coincidence that he was at home one afternoon three weeks after the holdup, playing a video game against himself, when the sheriff came to call.

The sheriff was a massive man, with arms that would rip the sleeves out of a tailored shirt. At Harmony's invitation, he took a seat at the kitchen table.

"We finally got the DNA test back on that holdup in Marlington," he said, speaking across the room to Seth. "It wasn't a match for you."

"No surprise here," he said. "I wasn't there."

"Well your brother was," the sheriff said.

Harmony shot Seth a murderous look.

"Your DNA is close enough to the blood we found on the store floor that it had to be from a sibling. You don't have any other brothers or sisters?"

Harmony shook her head. "The two of them are all I got."

The sheriff idly fingered the tips of the star he wore on his chest. "I'm not believing for a minute that you weren't with him," he said to Seth. "But I don't have any evidence tying you to those holdups. Yet. Next time, though, I'll be right in your face, and I guarantee you don't want that."

"You'll never catch me breaking the law," Seth said. "You can bank on it."

Harmony didn't say anything until the sheriff left. Then she unloaded.

"You little a-hole. I know he's dead. I can feel it in my heart. He'd never have run away by himself even if he was guilty, not unless you were leading him."

"You think you're the only one that misses him? We never had anybody except one another. I miss him like I'd miss my leg if they took it off."

"If you loved him so much, why'd you lead him to his death?"

He didn't have the heart to deny it yet again. Let his mother think what she wanted; she'd never loved him anyway.

"Yeah, that's what I thought," she said to his silence.

She stood and crossed the room into her bedroom returned with the shotgun and a couple of shells in her hand. Loaded it, then handed it by the stock to Seth.

He took the shotgun, mystified. "What's this?"

"It's our family heirloom. I figure now's the right time to pass it along to you."

He took the gun and laid it in his lap, trying to decipher the expression on his mother's face as she stared out the window at the mountain, a cup of cold coffee sitting at her elbow.

PEGGY ROTHSCHILD

Peggy Rothschild grew up in Los Angeles. Always a mystery-lover, she embraced the tales of Nancy Drew and the Hardy Boys before graduating to the adult section of the library. An English major in high school, she switched to art—her other passion—in college. Peggy has authored two adult mysteries, *Clementine's Shadow* and *Erasing Ramona*, and one young adult adventure, *Punishment Summer*. She is a member of Sisters in Crime National and Los Angeles. Find her at peggyrothschild.net.

THE COOKIE CRUMBLES

PEGGY ROTHSCHILD

THIS IS the God's honest truth: Momma never loved me. At least not the way she loved my big sister, Marnie. I once complained about it to my aunt and got the "mothers love all their children equally" speech. After that, I kept my mouth shut on the subject.

At least Dad and Gramps adored me. And I them. They made me feel special, like my thoughts mattered. The car accident that took them away turned me into a sad little lump two weeks after my ninth birthday. I didn't understand why they were gone and, through the fog of pain and loss, it didn't dawn on me for almost a week that no one loved me anymore.

Now, I've got to be fair—a concept Gramps drove into me—Momma had other things on her plate besides being interested in me.

Keeping the house looking just-so, losing that last five pounds, and, of course, Marnie. Golden-haired. Gorgeous. Graceful. Bigger than life, she took all the love and attention Momma had to give.

Momma wasn't crazy. From my earliest memories, Marnie was special. When she danced, her toes barely touched the earth. A feat I failed to replicate, no matter how hard—or how many times—I tried. And her voice. She had a five-octave range, never hit an off-note, played piano by ear, and could harmonize on the fly.

Most days—at least according to Momma—Marnie was perfect. But Momma refused to notice the scratches on my arms or bruises on my shins. Apparently appearing perfect makes a person cranky.

Momma had big plans for my sister. Enter her in a few local beauty pageants, then go regional, before moving up to the talent shows. Marnie would fix all of Momma's broken dreams.

Of course, I didn't see that when I was nine. All I saw was me alone, with no one caring whether I brushed the tangles from my mousy hair or scrubbed off the day's smudges in the bath. No one caring what I wore to school. And no one caring whether I succeeded there. Or failed. So of course I succeeded. Because the hell with them.

The hell with Momma and Marnie for making me an outcast in my own home.

When I was twelve, Momma pulled Marnie from school and took her to the beauty parlor where they both got their hair done. The next morning, Marnie put on the cornflower blue dress that matched her eyes. Momma scrutinized her appearance, then noticed me. "Better get going or you'll be late for school."

I took my time getting dressed. Finally the door to the garage snapped shut behind them. They were headed to Marnie's first big talent show—all the way up in Nashville, an eight-hour journey. Momma touted this fact many, many times before they departed, saying Marnie could use the drive to practice her song and her acceptance speech. I'd been deemed old enough to stay home alone.

After four days of skipping school, watching TV at all hours and eating nothing but microwaved wraps and burritos, I got the idea to make a "welcome home" surprise for them. Momma never liked to have anything fattening in the house, but after a contest win, she and Marnie sometimes allowed themselves a treat.

I poked around in Momma's white-on-white bathroom until I found the chocolate laxatives I knew she kept there. They were maximum strength. Perfect.

I scanned her cookbooks in search of cookie recipes, made a list, then dug into my small stash of cash in order to buy flour, brown sugar, butter, and a bag of chocolate chips.

On the six-block walk to the grocery store, I passed a man running a mower across the lawn of a large house, the smell of diesel mixed with the rich scent of pine. He didn't raise an eyebrow at a kid my age being out of school. No one at the store gave me the hairy eyeball either. I was starting to wonder if I might be invisible.

At the last minute before heading to checkout, I bought a bag of chopped walnuts. If the chocolate laxative gave the cookies a funny taste, adding nuts might explain it away.

By block three of the return trip, my arms ached from the weight of the flour and sugar. But tired muscles would be worth it. I smiled at the idea of Momma and Marnie taking turns rushing to the bathroom. A part of me knew I was being mean. Gramps certainly wouldn't have approved. But why'd they have to leave me behind?

Back at home, I threw out the frozen food wrappers and washed the dirty cups and plates I'd left in various rooms. After re-reading the recipe, I prepared a batch of doctored cookies, carefully inserting a quarter of a piece of laxative in each. I stayed within earshot of the oven timer's tick-tick-tick. If I burned the cookies, Momma and Marnie would never eat them.

The smell of baking chocolate was still hanging in the air when Momma and Marnie stormed through the front door. Momma dropped her suitcases onto the tile floor, nostrils flaring. "Do you know what your sister did?"

I'd never seen her look that way at Marnie. Me, sure, but never my perfect, golden-haired sister. I gulped and held my tongue. Marnie stood, shoulders back, red-eyed but defiant.

"She changed the song she was supposed to sing," Momma said. "Tossed out the patriotic medley we'd worked on. For weeks." She glared at Marnie. "You remember how many weeks we worked on it?"

Marnie stared past Momma like she was invisible.

"And for what? So she could sing a filthy song by some Top Forty Diva."

Giving a theatrical sigh, Marnie said, "Beyoncé's a legend."

"I don't care if she's Cher reincarnated."

"Cher's still alive."

Momma's face turned crimson. "The judges wanted a show of patriotism, not a song about sex."

Head held high, Marnie picked up her suitcase and left the room.

Momma sniffed the air. "What's that smell? Chocolate?"

"I made cookies. Thought they'd make a nice surprise for you."

"Winners get cookies. Not song-changing losers." She stomped out of the house, muttering something about getting dinner.

That night, Momma banged plates as she dished out servings of the Caesar salad she'd picked up earlier. Neither my sister nor mother spoke while we ate but, like members of some weird food cult, both speared every crouton they uncovered and placed it on the side of their plates. The fact that Momma failed to tell the deli to hold the dreaded caloric cubes was a testament to how mad she was. Like I needed additional clues. Normally an oversight like this would've had me smiling—croutons were my favorite part of any salad. But tonight, the first one I tried to swallow lodged in my throat. After forcing it down, I focused on pushing around the soggy lettuce.

The hum of the refrigerator briefly broke the silence, but not the tension in my gut. Marnie remained serene, seemingly unaffected by the sniffs and stormy stares Momma sent her way.

Unable to sit still any longer, I swung my legs back and forth.

Momma sighed. "Must you make that scraping sound with your shoes?"

I froze. I didn't know how to act. My whole life, Momma and Marnie had been a team. A sharp rap on the front door made me jump.

Momma rolled her eyes. "Settle down." She slapped her napkin down and left the table.

Curious, I leaned my chair back and watched Momma put an eye to the peephole. Then her face brightened, and she whipped the door open. "Why Mr. Trask. What brings you here?"

The low murmur of voices followed, then Momma fluttered into the dining room, an overweight, over-tanned man in a shiny suit and bolo tie at her side. "Marnie, you remember Mr. Trask? From today's competition? He's come all the way from Nashville to talk to you."

Her adoring gaze looked nothing like the eye-daggers she'd been throwing minutes earlier.

Marnie dabbed her lips with her napkin, then rose and shook his hand. "It's lovely to see you again, Mr. Trask."

"I'm sorry you didn't place in today's show." Still holding her hand, he stepped closer. "In my opinion, you were the best of the bunch."

The way Mr. Trask smiled at Marnie made my belly twist in a new way. He looked like he wanted to break off a piece of her and gobble it up.

Momma continued to flutter. "Yes. My Marnie is very talented."

Mr. Trask's wolfish grin widened. "I'd like to make sure more people know just how talented this little lady is." He wrapped his other hand around hers, sandwiching her slender fingers between his meaty paws.

Marnie shook back her golden hair. "I know my song choice didn't exactly fit the criteria…"

"No, but it beautifully demonstrated your vocal range." He turned to Momma. "I'd like to take Marnie under my wing, act as her representative. Get her into the national spotlight."

"Oh my." Momma patted her chest like her heart was a wild animal in need of calming.

"Of course, I'll have to arrange for professional photos—at my own expense, obviously." He stroked Marnie's hand. "Your head shots were adequate, but I think we can do better. Maybe even as soon as this week. And I'd like to bring her to New York to meet my contacts."

"New York?" Momma's smile faltered. "I don't know…"

"Of course, I'd want you to come along, too."

Momma's smile returned. "That sounds wonderful." She turned

to me and snapped her fingers. "Get those cookies. Now we've got something to celebrate."

Would they leave me behind when they flew to New York? And for how long this time? I retrieved the plate of neatly arranged cookies and offered them to Mr. Trask.

"They don't have nuts in them, do they?" His oily gaze slid from me back to Momma as if I couldn't possibly understand the question. "I'm allergic."

I opened my mouth, but Momma's fierce look shut me up.

"I never put nuts in my cookies." She practically simpered at the man.

He took two. "A multi-talented woman. Master baker as well as an experienced guide to her equally talented daughter." Mr. Trask leered at my sister again before popping an entire cookie in his mouth.

Though they'd both now been deemed "winners," Momma and Marnie passed on dessert. Bile mixing with the remnants of Caesar dressing at the back of my throat, I set the plate on the table and retreated to my room.

I didn't come out even when the sirens screamed to a halt in front of our house.

Whatever else happened, I doubted Momma and Marnie would desert me by rushing to New York anytime soon.

At least not with Mr. Trask.

EDITH MAXWELL

Edith Maxwell is the Agatha- and Macavity-nominated author of the Quaker Midwife Mysteries, the Local Foods Mysteries, and award-winning short crime fiction. As Maddie Day she authors the Country Store Mysteries and the Cozy Capers Book Group Mysteries. Edith lives north of Boston with her beau and two elderly cats, and gardens and cooks when she isn't killing people on the page. She is a member of Sisters in Crime National, New England, and Guppy Chapters, the Short Mystery Fiction Society, and Mystery Writers of America. Find her at edithmaxwell.com.

THE STONECUTTER

EDITH MAXWELL

I FIRST SAW the stonecutter working in a pool of illumination as I strolled near the cemetery on a summer evening. Sweat shone on his face as he chiseled a gravestone. Darkness surrounded him. Anyone walking nearby was lit up like on a movie set, but as soon as they passed, the black night swallowed them whole and they ceased to exist. I gazed at him for a few moments from the darkness and wondered who he was.

When I saw him enter the library a few days later, I noticed he did not look American. Portuguese maybe, or Italian. It was the style of his slacks, and leather shoes of a cut not made in this country. It was the set of his jaw, unused to English vowels. It was the open collar of his shirt, the texture of the cloth.

I was in my usual post behind the library's reference desk when he came in. He leaned forward and spoke to Jill at the main desk, and then headed into the stacks, toward where we keep books on town history. Watching him walk away, I saw an efficiency of movement, tough muscles under that European shirt, a firmness in the slacks.

Part of my job is, of course, helping people find information, so off to the history section I headed. I smoothed my hair as I went. I rounded the corner of the stacks and stopped. He sat at a table, its deep cherry hue gleaming like fine art in the morning light from the window. Several books were open in front of him, and he was copying something in a careful script on a pad of paper. His hair grew low on his forehead, and he had a full head of it combed straight back, dark and thick even though the lines on his face etched many years of living.

The air was quiet. The man stood and turned to the shelf on his left. His finger ran across the titles with the care of a connoisseur, as if he loved the sensation of the bindings more than the meanings of the words.

"May I help you?" My voice was loud in the stillness, and he turned quickly.

"Yes?" He bowed slightly and his eyebrows rose.

"I wondered if I could help you with anything." Oh. He didn't know who I was. "I'm the reference librarian."

"Ah." It was a soft, resonant voice. Our eyes linked together. He smiled at me, but his eyebrows, thick like his hair, drooped at their outside edges and his chocolate eyes did the same. "No, I have found what I need. But thank you." His accent sounded familiar, with its non-English stresses and softening of consonants.

I nodded.

"You have a fine library. A good collection."

"Thank you. May I ask what you're working on?"

He then showed me his interest: a book on genealogy, the old logs of fishing captains, a history of Gloucester. He explained that he was researching when some of his relatives had come to New England from Portugal—so I was right about that—and where they had lived in the area.

"I visited Portugal once," I said as I looked out the window. It had been my first trip alone after James left this world nine years earlier, my first excursion after the trouble with that had blown over. "Here's what I remember. I was inland in Belmonte, and the sun was intense. The hills were dry, covered with gray olive trees. Rocks pushed up out of the soil. But everyone was generous, they fed me, they wanted to practice their English."

He nodded in understanding.

"Then I went to Porto on the coast. I ate *mariscada* and drank real port wine, not the sweet stuff you find here."

"Yes, yes." He shook his head in amazement. "I am from Porto."

"You are?"

He nodded.

"I loved the market on the waterfront," I said.

"Yes. My grandmother sold fish there. There is nothing like it here."

"Then I went to the south. The blue and white tiles looked Arabic and the houses could have been Tunisian adobe. The beaches were empty, just beautiful. That's what I remember."

We stood there. We smiled at our separate memories, until a teenager slouched by. A tinny sound emitted from her earbuds and broke our bubble.

I cleared my throat. "How long have you been here?"

"We have been here for, let's see, ten years."

The "we" deposited a lead weight in my stomach.

"My son and his family, they are here too. But my wife is ill. She does not go out. So I work, and I do my studies here, and I play with my grandchildren."

"I see."

⌛

LATE THAT EVENING I sat on my porch with a glass of cognac. A breeze waved the scent of sweet peas past me like a letter from my childhood. Fernando Andrade was his name, he had told me, and then had asked me to join him in a coffee next door. When I told him mine was Eleanor, he called me Eleanora, in a musical five syllables, and I felt foreign and special. We talked over our coffees in the café for as long as I thought I could stretch my break. When he said he wanted to take me to eat *mariscada* in a Portuguese restaurant he knew in the next town, I didn't ask why he didn't have to be at home for dinner. We arranged to meet the following day.

After work the next afternoon, I changed my shoes and crossed over to the park, picking up the pace until I was at my power-walk speed. The air amid the greenery was mild. It smelled of summer: a strong, sweet flower, a distant sprinkler, the earth's scent rising. I thought more about Fernando. I suddenly wanted to escape this life I had enclosed myself in: comfortable and unspeakably routine.

At home, I showered and then did not dress in my usual tailored clothes. As a sea breeze danced with the curtains, I put on a long maroon skirt and matching silk blouse. My hand was steady as I applied cologne to the backs of my ears, my wrists, my temples, and I could hear Mother saying, "Always put scent where you have a pulse." I added a dab between my breasts for good measure, shaking my head at my foolishness. I pulled on tall leather boots from Lisbon, as old and comfortable as gloves and, parading in front of the mirror in my own private fashion show, I felt twenty-two, but my reflection showed a woman with silver hair on the path to old age.

"Well, you don't look half bad, really," I told my image, surprised at this feeling of anticipation. It had been a long time.

I was waiting on the porch when Fernando drove up in an older model Volvo, pristinely clean and maintained. He met me at the passenger door. When he turned to look at me, I saw raw red lines on one cheek.

"What happened?" I said, alarmed. They looked like scratches from something very sharp.

"Eleanora, it is my wife. She is schizophrenic, and became upset when I said I was leaving." The pain was in his eyes again. "It is hard for her to stay on her medications. They are hard on her. She paces and sees demons. Sometimes she calls me the devil."

"Oh. I didn't know." The delicious excitement I had felt about the outing agitated with fear of this new information.

He caught my eyes with his. "Don't worry, she is with my daughter-in-law."

I watched him and waited. I kept my hand at my side, and prevented it from stroking his other cheek.

He took a breath and let it out. "This has happened before, and it will happen again. Now, if you will come with me, it is time for dinner."

At Casa do Mar, we ate small, pungent olives the color of night. We drank Dão wine. We feasted on *mariscada*'s succulent seafood, the tender squid in *lulas guisadas,* and paper-thin potato slices fried to a crisp. We didn't only eat. He spoke to me of his years cutting stone, about his love for the permanence of gravestones. He said he would search for a pattern in the granite to match the deceased's personality.

I told him about not being able to have babies, how I couldn't bear to be around young children for many years. How, when I finally volunteered to help with the Girl Scouts in our town, I delighted in their energy and fresh approach to life.

We didn't talk about his wife or James, about the near future or the current war. We rode the wave of the present as if the walls of the restaurant were the edges of the world and our only cares were here in front of us.

We ate slowly. We sipped our wine and asked for more. Finally the waiter cleared our plates. Fernando had joked with him in Portuguese throughout the evening, and now asked the waiter to bring something, but I didn't understand what.

Two tiny cups of espresso appeared in front of us, and two small glasses of a clear liquid.

"*Bica e bagaço.*" He pronounced this with great satisfaction. "This is the finest coffee and our national liquor, *bagaceiro.* We finish all good meals this way." He took a sip of his coffee and lifted his glass to me.

"Here's to you, Eleanora."

"And to you."

A lilting Fado played in the background as the waiter set tables for the next day. We were the last diners to leave. Fernando pulled out my chair for me, and then offered me his arm. He smelled of smoke and wine and old-world cologne, and the cloth of his shirt was smooth against muscle. Then, halfway to the door, his arms took mine and we were dancing. Slowly we moved to the melancholy Lusian folk song. I stood almost as tall as he, and when my cheek touched the wounds on his, he pulled me closer, and I felt like I'd been there all along.

We began to see each other as often as we could. He cooked *mariscada* for me in my kitchen while I weeded my herb garden. He told me stories of his grandsons and I made him laugh with tales of my scouts. Once he told me that the only food his wife would eat now was Portuguese kale stew, which no one else in the family liked. We worked on his genealogy together and visited the former house of his great uncle down on the point. We drove north where we didn't know anyone and walked on a beach arm in arm. We spent long hours in my bedroom, enjoying each other's bodies and tracing the lines of our lives. We went dancing, although we drove into the city to do so.

"Are you happy, Eleanora?" he asked me one day as we sat in the garden at dusk. Iced tea cooled our hands. A gentle wind off the Atlantic swept the mosquitoes away.

I nodded. I didn't tell him that at night, alone, I dreamed of freedom with him, of a future without his wife.

I asked him the same question.

"I am happy with you, my friend," he said, clinking his glass with mine, but the pain never really left his eyes.

I saw them in late August near the medical building. She was gaunt and pale, with white streaks piercing her dark hair. A lit cigarette shook in her hand. Fernando looked grim. He held her elbow like he was trying to persuade her to go somewhere she didn't want to go.

When I asked once why he didn't place her in an institution where professionals could look after her, he told me, "It is my duty to care for her. I am her husband, after all."

I looked sharply at him. "What about your duty to love? To me?"

He just shook his head and kissed my hand.

⧗

ON THE LAST day of September, right before a fierce thunderstorm, he brought me an armful of red carnations. I watched him at my kitchen sink. In the darkening afternoon, he clipped the ends of the stems under running water and arranged each flower with care in a heavy glass vase. His stonecutter's hands were as gentle with the blooms as they were when they touched me.

"I didn't know men like you existed," I said, addressing the compact strength of Fernando's back.

He turned to me. "I am just me, not 'men like me.'" A tropical rain blew in and, as the gale beat the windows, we talked into the night. Our conversations sometimes now tasted bittersweet. We wove a cocoon of our passion and caring. We dared not look outside it.

⏳

ONE DAY in late October Fernando did not show up for a date to go bicycling in the state park. He was always prompt, and called from his cell when he was to be late. I waited for an hour, and then went alone. I rode slowly on the path through brilliant leaves and the detritus of summer: sagging vines, ferns chilled into brittle tan ghosts, the treacherous red beauty of poison ivy. The light was slanting low as I rode home.

I couldn't call him. I felt physically sick from worry and uncertainty. Had something happened to him? Had he fallen out of love with me? Was he just exhausted from leading a double life? I was as miserable as a teenager in my fretting, and as mad as one, too.

Walking home from work two days later I felt a hand on my shoulder as I passed the coffee shop.

"Eleanora."

"Fernando." I looked at him as if he had been missing for a year. I couldn't soak up enough of his skin, his thick hair, his sad eyes. "Where have you..."

He took my arm and said, "May I walk you home?"

I looked at him and nodded. As we walked, he was silent and gazed ahead of us, not at me. My heart began to feel a comradeship with the end of the season and the cold breath of winter.

We sat in the swing on my porch side by side until he finally spoke.

"I have decided to take your advice, Eleanora, and place my wife where she is safe."

I felt the warmth from his arm against mine. We could finally make a life together, this man and I.

"I'm so glad, Fernando," I said, reaching for his hand.

"Don't be." He shook his head. "I have found a residence for her. It is two days driving from here, and I will be living there with her." His voice was of a gentle steel, but the edges of his mouth quavered. "We leave on *Dia dos Mortos*. On Saturday."

"Why so far away?" I shivered. Sunlight, sparse in its autumn feebleness, lit up the blood-red blossoms of a chrysanthemum on the porch, but it didn't warm me. "Why now?"

"I am sorry, Eleanora." He put his arm around me and I leaned into his scent and his strength. I was sad to the bone and furious at once.

"Fernando," I said after a long silence, turning my face to his. My heart raced. "You can't leave me. I won't let you."

He stroked my cheek once, slowly, softly, then put his hand down. "I cannot help my life. I cannot abandon my obligations."

I thought frantically. "Come by tomorrow. Please? Just one last time? I have the day off. We could…"

He put up a hand to stop me. "I will come in the afternoon. But only for a moment."

I stared as he walked away.

⧖

THAT NIGHT I couldn't sleep. I tangled in my sheets, searching my crazed thoughts for some solution, some way to keep him with me. I wanted to cast my net over him and draw him toward me through the water of our lives, like an enchanted Azorean fisherwoman. Today was Wednesday. I couldn't bear the thought that I would never see him again after tomorrow. I climbed out of bed and paced my house. My skin burned as if I were ill. I opened a window, but the north air chilled me and I slammed it shut. A full moon lit my garden, shimmering on the purple monkshood flowers and the dark red asters.

My heart rate slowed as I gazed outside. Maybe I could sleep now.

⧗

GHOULS IN SPIDER webs leered at me as I walked into the Cape Ann Market when it opened at eight the next morning. I'd forgotten about Halloween. I tossed several bags of candy into my basket before picking up kale, onions, garlic, cilantro, and chicken stock. By ten o'clock my kitchen smelled like it was dinnertime, the air fragrant with sautéed alliums and greens. I went outside, pulled on gardening gloves, and filled a wheelbarrow with weeds and dead plants. I clipped a handful of leaves in the hardy section of my herb garden and added them to the stew.

The temperature dipped low with the sun as I sat on the porch swing in my parka that afternoon. The trick-or-treaters would need to wear PJs under their princess dresses and zombie costumes tonight. My eyes followed Fernando as he walked toward me, his head down.

We sat in silence. Fernando covered my hand with his. I looked into his sad eyes and squeezed.

"Here." I stood and extended the handles of a small bag to him. "I made her some kale stew."

Fernando grasped the bag. He rose, then embraced me. He made his way slowly down the steps.

"*Até logo*," I called after him. I'll see you soon.

He glanced back, shaking his head.

⧗

I WALKED SLOWLY through the cemetery late Saturday morning. Families sat in the cold on picnic cloths. A slender woman in black laid a mass of flowers on a grave then raised a glass of red wine to the headstone. Children played hide and seek. The sad All Soul's Day festivities seemed to include almost the entire Portuguese community.

When I arrived home, I turned on the local news. Fernando's picture flashed. My hand covered my mouth of its own accord. My ears throbbed. My feet felt numb. I leaned toward the screen.

"Local authorities are investigating the suspicious death of area man, Fernando Andrade." The young newscaster looked into the camera and shook his head, eyebrows knit in TV sincerity. "We talked to his son, George." The image switched to a tall man with Fernando's hair and sad eyes. "We can't think who would want to hurt him. My father was a good man, a husband, a father, a grandfather. He was about to move with my mother, who's mentally ill, to a residence where she could receive the care she needs." The camera switched back to the newsman. "Police are looking into the origins of a soup that was apparently a gift to the family, and say they have identified a person of interest."

The thin wail of a siren grew louder. I left the television and walked out back to sit by the stone Buddha that watched over my garden. I felt my cell phone in my pocket. The phone Fernando had called me on. My heart was an icy stone that chilled me from the inside out. He said he didn't eat kale stew. As sirens grew near, I wondered what kind of granite would suit the personality of Fernando Andrade.

PETER DICHELLIS

Peter DiChellis concocts sinister and sometimes comedic tales for anthologies, e-zines, and magazines. He is a member of Friends of Mystery and the Short Mystery Fiction Society, and an Active (published author) member of the Mystery Writers of America, Private Eye Writers of America, and International Thriller Writers. Find him on his blog about short mystery and crime fiction: shortwalkdarkstreet.wordpress.com.

CALLINGDON MOUNTAIN

PETER DICHELLIS

THE ODD CALLINGDON Mountain story began for me with a phone call last winter. But I still remember every detail, every twist, because what happened in the end has forever changed, in a small though vital way, how people look at me and how I look at myself.

The man who called me wailed into the phone. "This murder is killing the resort's reputation, it's just killing us."

I imagine so, I recall thinking. I bet it was a tough break for the victim, too.

"Nobody but you can help us," the man pleaded. "You solved a bewildering murder case before, almost exactly like this one. Do you have any idea of the chaos we're experiencing here?"

Yes, I did. The media was buzzing with news of the perplexing murder at the legendary Callingdon Mountain Ski Resort. Fanciful headlines trumpeted IMPOSSIBLE CALLINGDON MOUNTAIN KILLING! and INVISIBLE CALLINGDON MOUNTAIN KILLER? But whether reported by newspapers, TV, radio, online news, or the true crime blogs I followed, the strange story was always the same.

A new promotional event at Callingdon Mountain featured a celebrity skier named Donegal Cain. As part of the event, and in view of a dozen witnesses, Cain climbed into one of the resort's enclosed gondola trams for the mile-and-a-quarter airborne ride to the top of Callingdon Mountain Peak. Though the gondola would hold up to eight people, witnesses confirmed that Cain departed alone, and very much alive, cheerfully waving to an admiring crowd through the gondola's window. The gondola then sailed skyward, hanging from its mechanical cable, without incident and without stopping. It remained in full view the entire ten minutes it glided through the air on its ascent to the mountaintop. So nobody could have entered or exited the gondola's enclosed compartment along its route. But when the gondola arrived at Callingdon Mountain Peak, Donegal Cain's dead body was discovered inside, alone, stabbed in the back with a knife from one of the resort's dining rooms.

The man who'd called me, a top administrator at the resort, wailed into the phone again. "Just think about it, Donegal Cain was alive when that gondola left for the mountain. And he was alone. And after that, nobody could have gotten in there with him. Nobody. Yet someone got inside, killed him, and then disappeared, all while the gondola was in mid-air. And the killer had the nerve to use one of our own steak knives."

"Sir," I said, "this is a matter for the police, not a private investigator."

"Police. We've got more police here than you can count, and they're all baffled. The State Police, the County Sheriff's deputies, even a Callingdon City Police part-timer who thinks he's a detective because he writes mystery stories."

"Sir, the investigating officers will not welcome a private eye meddling in their case."

"Wrong. The resort has a lot of political influence, both with the state legislature and the Governor's office. We'll put in the word. After all, back when you were a cop you solved a murder just like this one, a murder nobody else could solve. We'll tell our politician friends all about how you found a dead victim in the snow with two sets of footprints leading to the body. One set of footprints for the victim, a different set for the killer. But there were no footprints going away from the victim's body. So how did the killer leave? You solved that one and you can solve this one—and before our snow melts, if you don't mind. This is bad for business. *Very* bad for business."

"I was a patrol officer then, not any sort of detective," I said, though long ago I admitted to myself that I'd solved the case of the missing footprints by pure luck. I eventually failed my police department's detective exam three times, left the force, and hung out a private eye shingle. I now make a wearisome living snapping photos of wandering spouses for suspicious wives and jealous husbands. Taking a crack at solving a real mystery was a tonic I craved at my core. Yet how could someone like me expect anything but frustration from the Callingdon Mountain case?

"If you come to Callingdon Mountain right away, I will pay double your usual fee," the administrator said. "And I guarantee full cooperation from the local authorities. Full cooperation."

As much as I tried, I couldn't resist such a peculiar and challenging mystery, not to mention the money. "I'll do it."

⧗

THAT EVENING, at my invitation, two Detective-Sergeants from the Major Crimes Unit of the State Police joined me in the posh restaurant at The Callingdon Mountain Grand Resort Hotel. They sat across from me at the table, listening while they devoured the expensive dinners I'd bought them as a peace offering.

"Full cooperation?" Detective-Sergeant Harlan Trut bellowed. He stopped attacking his steak long enough to poke his fork at my face. "Do I look like the kind of person who'd give a low-rent gumshoe like you full cooperation?"

No, he sure didn't. A scowling giant with a long snout nose and a mane of black hair greased back on his enormous head, Trut looked like a mutant descendant of Godzilla and the Bride of Frankenstein.

Detective-Sergeant Jennette Zoya, a tall woman who moved like a fit athlete, glanced up from her grilled salmon and joined the cooperation festivities. "Here's the one thing we can tell you," she confided to me with a smile. "The Chief Medical Examiner is ruling it a suicide."

"Suicide?"

Detective-Sergeant Trut ogled his steak but set down his knife and fork, pointed his thumbs in the air, and raised his bulging eyes toward the ceiling. "That's what the higher-ups want. Suicide. Makes things easier for everyone. Even for us."

"Much easier for us," Zoya emphasized.

"C'mon," I said. "Donegal Cain committed suicide by stabbing himself in the back with a steak knife while riding a gondola to the top of a ski mountain?"

"The Chief M.E. thinks it was a lucky strike," Zoya said.

"Or maybe unlucky," Trut said.

"The knife entered Cain's lower back in the one spot that would do the job," Detective-Sergeant Zoya continued. "Exactly the right angle to rupture almost every internal organ down there. That gets him dead, pronto, sitting on his butt, slumped in the corner of the gondola. If the knife entered an inch in any other direction, he'd be home sleeping on his stomach. Lucky strike."

"Still don't see how it's ruled a suicide," I said.

Trut pointed his thumbs in the air again. "The higher ups," he repeated. "Maybe someone got *their* full cooperation."

⧗

THE NEXT MORNING I phoned the resort administrator's office from my room at a budget motel, located on an access road a few miles from the pricey resort lodgings. I had plenty of unanswered questions, but mostly wanted to know whether I should continue investigating the case.

"I'm so sorry, he's out of the office," the administrator's executive assistant said. "He's meeting with his contacts in the state legislature to ask for their help in ending the terrible publicity from this horrible incident. But he instructed me to give you my full cooperation. What may I do for you?"

Help in ending the terrible publicity? Like obtaining a phony suicide ruling?

My instincts screamed that Donegal Cain's death was a well-planned murder. But how was it committed, by whom, and for what purpose? I decided I'd persist in my detective investigation.

"I'd like to talk to anyone who interacted with Donegal Cain at the resort and everyone who saw the gondola depart for the mountain peak or arrive there," I told the executive assistant. "Do you know whether any of those people are still here?"

"I imagine most of them are. Would a complete list of all the witnesses help you?"

I was astonished. Maybe my luck had finally turned. "That would be wonderful."

"One moment, please. I think I have exactly what you're looking for."

She put me on hold but returned within a few seconds.

"I found it," she said. "I have an email here that says if you need any information at all, just contact Detective-Sergeants Harlan Trut and Jennette Zoya of the State Police. The email says they'll give you their full cooperation."

"Of course. Thank you."

⌛

OKAY, it was time for some old-school detective work. Exactly the kind of work I always wanted to do. As part of my preparation, I'd loaded my phone with news photos of faces in the crowds at Donegal Cain's promotional event. All I needed now was to match the photos to people at the resort. I steered my decade-old jalopy from my motel's parking lot to Callingdon Mountain's base lodge, near where Cain's gondola ride began. I checked the photos and eyed the room.

Right away, I matched photos to two people. But they couldn't tell me much. A young woman divulged Donegal Cain was a "total horn dog" and a jilted girlfriend probably killed him "with like, voodoo or something." An even younger guy would only say "I bet that dude can ski better dead than I can alive" before hitting the slopes to prove his point.

Undaunted, I scanned the room again. Another match. Angular nose, high cheekbones. Dark eyes, olive complexion. Long black hair flecked with strands of silver. An intense woman, thickset, perhaps forty years old.

"Excuse me, ma'am?"

"Yes?" She spoke with a conspicuous accent. Eastern European?

I explained what I was doing.

"Oh, yes," she said. "I first saw that poor young man the night before he died. He told me he doubted he would live through the morning."

"He said that?"

"Oh, yes. It was shortly after I fell asleep. Perhaps midnight. That is when he came to me at the resort hotel."

"Came to you?"

She handed me a business card. "I am Madame Fortunata, the most learned psychic in all of the Callingdon Mountain region. You shall have my full cooperation. How may I help?"

"Wait. It was dream? You saw Donegal Cain in a dream?"

"No, no. Not a dream. A vision in my sleep. And I learned more as well. I heard a woman with a shrill voice arguing with a different man, not that poor young man Donegal Cain. But from the arguing, it is certain the poor young man was at the center of a lover's quarrel. He ended a passionate affair, very passionate, with this shrill-voiced woman. The other man did not approve of Donegal Cain."

"And the voices were part of your vision?"

"No, no. The voices kept me awake until thirteen minutes before midnight. The vision came later, while I slept."

I recalled the news photo that led me to her. "You said the vision was when you 'first saw' Donegal Cain. The night before he died. What about the next day, the day he died?"

"Oh, yes. I was there when he left for the mountaintop. I saw everything. After the poor young man Donegal Cain went into the gondola car, another man followed him inside. Then two more men. I heard shouting and then laughter. Then the three men left and the gondola departed with the poor young man Donegal Cain alone inside it, smiling and waving through the window."

"What did the three men look like?"

"Large men, very large. The first one wore a blue parka. The same shade of blue as the gondola. The same shade of blue as the sky that day. The other two men ran into the gondola after him. After the man in the blue parka."

"Anything else?"

"Oh, yes. Tell me please, do you suspect me of this killing?"

"Why would I suspect you?"

"It is a simple matter, very simple, for me to place a curse on someone, anyone really," she stared directly at me. "And cause their death in a most unusual way."

"Is there something you're trying to tell me?"

She studied me for a moment. "I predict the solution to this mystery will be utterly unexpected. To discover it, you must first uncover a diabolical plan crafted by a conspiracy of evil forces, some of them shrewdly disguised as friends or allies."

As soon as Madame Fortunata left, a trim older couple, who must have overheard our conversation, approached me. I didn't recognize them from my news photos, but I didn't assume the photos captured everyone who'd attended the event.

"Are you trying to find out what happened?" the woman asked. "We were there when they found his body." Her teeth made a slight clicking sound as she spoke.

"Barney and Betsy Blankenstoop," the man said. "Happy to help."

"You were on Callingdon Mountain Peak when Donegal Cain's gondola arrived?" I asked.

"We saw everything," Barney said.

"Everything," Betsy agreed. Click, click. Her teeth again.

"Tell me about it."

"When the gondola arrived, a young lady opened the door, looked inside, and screamed 'My God, he's dead,'" Betsy said. Click, click. "Then an older man yelled to the crowd 'I'm a doctor,' and pushed past the young lady to go inside." Click, click. "When he came outside again he shouted 'Call 911, maybe it's not too late.'" Click, click, click. "But the young lady screamed 'No, no. He's dead, I saw him. I saw him! He's dead and it's all my fault. All my fault.'" Click, click.

"And people were calling 911 on their cellphones," Barney said. "They were screaming 'Send paramedics, he's been stabbed.'"

"How could they know he'd been stabbed?" I asked.

"The young lady said so. She yelled it," Betsy said. Click, click.

"No, dear. It was the older man," Barney said. "By then, the young lady was just standing there, staring at the ground and moaning, as if in shock."

"I'm sure the young lady yelled about the stabbing," Betsy insisted. "Her voice reminded me of our great-niece, Loretta. Quite a deep voice." Click, click.

"Lorna is the one with the deep voice, dear. Loretta has a shrill voice."

"No," Betsy said. "Loretta has the deep voice, almost like a man's." Click, click.

I interrupted the couple to show them the news photos on my phone and see whether they recognized either of the people they'd seen at the gondola. They picked out two photos of the young lady and one of the older man. I thanked them and, as was my habit, handed each one a business card, requesting their contact information in return.

The instant they walked away, still debating the timbre of their great-nieces' voices and Betsy's teeth still clicking, a husky man, probably in his early sixties but built like a barrel of muscle, positioned himself in front of me. He leaned into my face. "You should have checked in with me first. Roy Lutano. Head of resort security. Let's talk in my office. Now."

He placed his hand, about the size and texture of a baseball mitt, atop my shoulder and guided me toward the exit.

⏳

LUTANO'S OFFICE was a windowless cubbyhole at the far end of a dank underground hallway. He shut the door behind us and snapped the deadbolt.

"Privacy," he said.

"I'm sorry about any confusion," I told him, "I'm working for—"

"I know exactly what you're doing." He eased into his office chair and signaled for me to sit. "Wish you'd checked in with me about this gondola business. Maybe we can help each other."

I stole a glance at his tiny office. A dozen framed photographs stood on his desk. A lovely woman who I supposed was his wife and a slew of pictures I guessed portrayed their adult children and young grandchildren. Lutano's only other office decorations were paperback book covers torn from Michael Connelly mystery novels, affixed to the walls with cellophane tape.

As it turned out, Roy Lutano had been hired on at Callingdon Mountain after losing his job as a town constable after a local election swept out the mayor and the rest of the council. I gathered the resort administrator and police shunted him aside during the Donegal Cain investigation. Lutano's curiosity and pride, along with his love of a good mystery, compelled him to learn what really happened in the gondola. I reflected on my own so-called detective career and decided I both liked him and empathized with him.

"Mind if I ask what you found out so far?" he asked.

"Wish I could tell you. But anything I find goes to my client first."

"Fair enough. But could you mention me in your report? I'm the new guy here, stuck in a basement office, and I could use some publicity. Like I said, maybe we can help each other."

"Delighted to," I said. "What can you tell me?"

"Well, whatever happened up there, the snowboarder probably wasn't part of it."

I nodded as if I knew what he was talking about. "The snowboarder never even entered my mind. What convinced you?"

He looked at me as though I were a befuddled toddler. "For one thing, after we pulled him out of Cain's gondola he rode to the top in another one. So he was mid-air in another gondola, behind Cain's gondola, the whole time. Unless he turned into some kind of invisible flying ninja acrobat." Lutano shook his head. "Not likely, even for a hot-dogging freestyler used to all that screwball jumping and spinning and flipping upside down on the slopes."

"And of course Donegal Cain was alive when you pulled the snowboarder away from him."

Lutano leaned forward. "We didn't really have to pull him away, not really. Soon as we told him what was going on, he apologized, took a quick selfie with Cain, and went looking for another gondola. Nice enough guy. Just wanted to get to the Peak and freestyle back down. Hard to tell which one of them was more stoned, though."

"You mean…"

"Donegal Cain. Eyes so bloodshot they matched his parka."

"Red parka?"

"Blood red. One of those oversized, overstuffed ones. Paramedics had to cut it off him with shears to get at the knife underneath."

I nodded again as I recalled what Madame Fortunata had told me. "You said 'we' pulled him out of the gondola?"

"Myself and a temporary security guy I hired for the event. College kid. But forget about him. Art student. All he seemed to notice was the snowboarder's parka was the same shade of blue as the gondola. Same shade of blue as the sky. That's the only thing the damn art kid talked about. How all that blue blended together."

Lutano shook his head again. "Some think it was murder, others say suicide, others say some kind of freakish accident. And some say we'll never know."

My detective radar pinged. "Haven't heard the accident theory. What kind of accident?"

"Freakish, like I said. Maybe Cain filched the knife from the resort restaurant, Lord knows why, and hid it in his waistband. He was too stoned to stand up, fell down the wrong way, and took an unlucky poke."

Another attempt to shield the resort's reputation from a shocking murder, I wondered? "Accident seems unlikely."

"Everything about this crazy mystery is unlikely," Lutano said. "Why would the solution be any different?"

I showed him the photos of the young lady and older man the Blankenstoop couple had picked out. "Ever see either of these folks?"

"Sure. That's Marlee Wilson. She's an assistant in the resort's marketing department. Set up the Donegal Cain promotion. And the man's a top sports doctor, Dr. Armand Wilson. Never met him."

"Both named Wilson?" I asked. "Married? Related?"

"Who knows? Common enough last name."

"But Marlee Wilson knew Donegal Cain?"

"Sure. Maybe the doc did too."

"Why do you think so?"

"Cain took a spill and broke a couple of bones last winter. Still in a lot of pain from the surgery, at least that's what everyone says. A big sports doc like Wilson might get involved in something like that."

⧗

NEXT STOP, the resort's marketing department to interview Marlee Wilson. She wasn't there. She'd taken an "unexpected absence" according to the department manager, who invited me to sit in the lone visitors' chair in his cramped work cubicle.

"I guess it makes sense, after what happened," the manager said from behind his desk. "But it's not like her to just leave a voicemail and take off."

"What did her voicemail say?" I asked.

"Listen for yourself." He punched a couple of buttons on his phone and another to put the phone on speaker. A woman's shrill, quivering voice filled the cubicle.

"Hi. It's Marlee. I'm so sorry for what happened. It's my fault. I'm responsible for everything. I never should have…done it. I'm taking some time off to decide how to handle what I did. I hope you understand. I'm so, so sorry. I know I shouldn't have done it."

I didn't think Marlee's voicemail rose to the level of a confession and I didn't know for certain who I could trust, so I decided I'd notify Detectives Trut and Zoya after I spoke with Dr. Wilson and learned more. I figured the successful doctor would stay at The Callingdon Mountain Grand Resort Hotel, the best accommodations the resort had to offer. I confirmed his room number and found him there. Easy enough for someone with my cheating-spouse peeper experience.

"I've already spoken with the police," Wilson told me as he stood blocking the half-opened door to his generous suite. "I'm sure you can get whatever you need from them. Besides, a friend in the state legislature informed me Donegal Cain's death was ruled a suicide. Everyone knows Cain's injuries and botched surgery ended his career as a competitive skier. He must have been despondent over it. I understand he became an unstable drug abuser as well."

"I doubt the suicide ruling will stand," I said from the hallway. "And after what I learned a few minutes ago, the police will be too busy looking for a young lady named Marlee Wilson to talk with to me. Maybe you could spare just a minute?"

"My daughter had nothing to do with this," he said.

"Your daughter."

"Marlee, of course."

"You know where she is?"

"Why shouldn't I just slam the door in your face?"

"I haven't told the police what I learned about Marlee yet."

He glared at me and his face flushed. But he stepped aside and let me in. Barely. We sat across from each other in a seating area immediately inside the suite's entrance. He'd grudgingly moved his parka from one of the chairs so I could sit. An overstuffed dark maroon parka.

"Just tell me what you saw and heard," I said. "That's all I'm asking."

"I'll tell you what I told the police. Nothing more. When the gondola arrived, Marlee opened the door, looked inside, and screamed 'Oh God, he's dead.' I looked inside and saw what I assumed she saw, Donegal Cain sitting in the corner, slumped over, both of his eyes closed and his face deathly pale. I went in to try to help him but realized there was nothing I could do. He was still breathing but barely had a pulse. He needed emergency hospital care, immediately. So I came back out of the gondola and shouted for someone to call 911. Then somebody in the crowd began screaming that Donegal Cain had been stabbed."

"Was your daughter the one who screamed he'd been stabbed?"

"Leave her out of this. She's been through enough heartache with Donegal Cain."

"Meaning?"

"You need to leave. I told you exactly what I told the police. Now get out. And leave my daughter alone. She already spoke with the police. There's nothing more to say."

"Your daughter knew Donegal Cain. Did you know him too?"

"I'm not the one who botched his surgery, if that's what you're asking."

It wasn't. "Where is Marlee? The police will need to see both of you again, right away."

"I've told you everything I know. Now, do I need to call Security or will you get out of my room?"

⏳

As soon as I left Dr. Wilson my cellphone buzzed. It was the marketing department manager who supervised Marlee Wilson.

"Marlee just called," he said. "She's coming to the office. She said she wants to explain. I wasn't sure who to tell."

"When do you think she'll be there?"

"Twenty minutes. She said she knows what she did was wrong and she won't run away from it. Do you think Donegal Cain committed suicide because of her? Everyone is saying he killed himself. Or maybe it was an awful accident, nothing anyone did on purpose." The manager's voice dropped to a hoarse whisper. "I know Cain was definitely alive when he left for the peak because I went to the departure ceremony at the base lodge and I saw him go into the gondola. Then he waved through the window as the gondola left. Should I have told you that when we spoke earlier?"

I didn't answer his question, just thanked him and ended the call. Grateful for my habit of always exchanging contact information, I phoned resort security head Roy Lutano. Because the solution to the impossible Callingdon Mountain mystery finally hit me. I told Lutano everything. He agreed with my analysis.

"Do you have the authority to make an arrest?" I asked.

"No, but with reasonable cause I can detain anyone on the property until the police arrive."

TWO DAYS LATER, with the Callingdon Mountain killer in police custody, I finished my report to my client. I covered every detail, connected every dot, laid out where every piece of the puzzle fit.

The telltale clue that finally registered with me: the red parka. With Donegal Cain "sitting on his butt, slumped in the corner of the gondola," as Detective-Sergeant Zoya described, and the lethal knife beneath his oversized and overstuffed blood-red parka, Marlee Wilson couldn't have seen Cain had been stabbed in the back, as a confused Betsy Blankenstoop stated Marlee had screamed. Nor could anyone in the crowd know he'd been stabbed, as an uncooperative Dr. Wilson had intimated.

Which meant, only the killer could have known.

Perhaps more obvious to someone with sharper detective skills than mine, just one person was in the gondola with Donegal Cain when it was remotely possible to commit murder: Dr. Armand Wilson.

But what exactly happened?

The prominent sports doctor, enraged at "total horn dog" Donegal Cain for mistreating his daughter, implemented a simple, but effective, plan. He introduced himself to Cain before the promotional event in order to provide the pain-stricken skier with feigned sympathy and two high-dosage prescription opioid pills.

Before the gondola departed for Callingdon Mountain Peak, Cain was, as Roy Lutano described, merely "stoned," but by the time he reached the mountaintop he was unconscious, slumped in the corner of the gondola, apparently dead but actually still alive.

A waiting Dr. Wilson entered the gondola and lifted Cain's thick parka to insert the knife into his lower back at the precise angle the skilled surgeon knew would prove fatal.

Only the killer could have known then that Donegal Cain was stabbed, so it was a nervous Dr. Wilson who inadvertently divulged the stabbing to the crowd, in the deep voice— "almost like a man's"—that Betsy Blankenstoop heard.

But it was Marlee Wilson's shrill voice that Madame Fortunata had heard arguing the night before. The hurtful end of the "passionate affair" between Marlee and Donegal Cain, prompting the argument between Marlee and her father. Then the furious Dr. Wilson crept downstairs from his suite to the hotel restaurant and pilfered a steak knife, which he easily concealed in his own parka, setting in motion his plan for the mysterious Callingdon Mountain murder.

And Marlee Wilson's seemingly damning voicemail? She was not involved in the killing and knew nothing about her father's involvement. She'd violated resort policy by booking Donegal Cain's promotion for "personal, not professional" reasons, she confessed. And therefore she felt responsible for whatever had happened to him.

What of her department manager spreading the rumor Cain's death was perhaps an accidental stabbing in the back or Madam Fortunata's "vision" of Cain in her sleep and her "conspiracy of evil forces" prediction?

Simply the manager's noble but absurd attempt to protect Marlee if she was involved and the ramblings of a self-proclaimed psychic.

Luckily, spotting unreliable evidence is not my weakest detective skill.

Finally, I never could verify who might have influenced or requested a suicide ruling. I didn't want to press my client about it and couldn't determine whether Dr. Wilson played a role.

In the end, I guessed it didn't matter much. I also guessed the

Medical Examiner ran a standard toxicology screen on Cain, but concluded opioid pain-pills were part of the skier's post-surgery prescription regimen.

⧗

MY REPORT GAVE former town constable Roy Lutano well-deserved praise for aiding the investigation and detaining the deadly doctor until police arrived. But as it turned out, Lutano didn't need my help. He retired as head of resort security to collect a small municipal pension and write a debut mystery novel based on the strange Callingdon Mountain murder.

So I applied for his vacated security job and got it. Working at the resort for a steady paycheck provided a refreshing life-change from sporadic gigs skulking outside no-tell motels with a cheap camera.

As a bonus, even now, whenever I stroll the grounds of the gorgeous Callingdon Mountain resort, people smile, nod at me, and whisper conspiratorially to their companions. And why wouldn't they? After all, I'm the famous detective who solved the impossible Callingdon Mountain murder mystery.

MARY DUTTA

Mary Dutta traded New England and a career as an English professor for a new life as a college admissions reader in the South. A member of Sisters In Crime National, Central Virginia, and Guppy Chapters, "Festival Finale" is her first fiction publication credit. Follow her on Twitter @Mary_Dutta.

FESTIVAL FINALE

MARY DUTTA

FROM A DISTANCE, Charles Attlee looked a lot like his author photo. Up close, he presented a faded, fortyish version of the twenty-something literary boy wonder of his press kit photo. Like a Dorian Gray in reverse. Hailey Fields had paused, momentarily uncertain, before approaching him at the airport and introducing herself as his chaperone for the book festival. Attlee resembled his younger self about as much as she resembled the acclaimed author she'd naively planned to become.

The book festival director had encouraged the local university's MFA students to volunteer, stressing the unprecedented access to eminent authors that chaperoning would provide. An opportunity to receive advice, guidance, maybe even an introduction to a literary agent. Hailey had planned to network her way into the charmed circle of literary luminaries. Attlee, however, seemed to consider her more of a personal assistant than a colleague. He had handed her his messenger bag and sent her to fetch him a cup of coffee before they had even left the terminal.

He soon revealed her other role: captive audience for a ceaseless monologue on his breakout novel and subsequent accolades. When Attlee invited her to accompany him to his hotel room after checking in, Hailey had worried that she was in for a #MeToo moment, but she realized he just needed to continue the incessant stream of self-centered conversation. He had talked non-stop while he hung his clothes in the closet, laid out his toiletries on the sink counter, and put his laptop in the room's safe.

"You know," he said. "I always use the year I was a National Book Award finalist to set the code on the safe. I figure, what are the odds a hotel maid will know that? But then, one time, when I was delivering a keynote in Savannah," he paused and touched a finger to his lip. "No, I lie, it was when I went to Denver to receive that prize. Anyway, I stopped for a haircut and it turned out the hairdresser was a big fan. So really, you never know."

Hailey wondered why he couldn't direct all his verbiage to the page and finally publish the second novel that he had never managed to produce. Once hotly anticipated, popular expectations for the book had long since cooled to when-hell-freezes-over. Had Charles Attlee shown any interest in her or her own writing problems Hailey could have shared her struggles completing her debut novel, two years in the writing and still not considered a viable MFA thesis by her alleged advisor. She had planned on benefitting from a lot more academic mentoring when she had taken out the massive student loan to fund her degree.

But Attlee ignored her and directed his attention out the hotel window, where he had spied a new audience in the throngs of book festival attendees in the plaza below. "Let's go," he said, handing Hailey his bag again and heading out without casting a backward glance to see if she was following.

Once outside, Hailey trailed him through the crowd and down the adjacent street. Despite his persistent efforts to make eye contact with every passerby toting a festival book bag, no one seemed to recognize him. When they reached a bookstore with a window display of book festival authors, Attlee flung open the door, forcing Hailey to grab it before it smacked her in the face. The author plunged inside. With a flourish, he plucked his book from the display, signed it, and returned it to the owner. Hailey didn't tell him that the bookstore owner had confessed, in an interview in the local paper, that without a significant bump in sales from the festival she would be forced to shutter the store. Attlee didn't know it, but his signed first edition was most likely headed for a going-out-of-business sale.

The author's ego apparently satisfied at last, they returned to the hotel and the first of the panels on which he was to speak. Hailey spent the next two days accompanying him from panel to panel, listening to the same stories every time, the same stories he had told her, the same stories he told in every interview. The only time things got interesting was when an audience member refused to relinquish the microphone until he finished bashing the literary star system that kept a has-been like Attlee making the rounds at the expense of, in his telling, lesser known but superior writers like himself.

Hailey sympathized with the outraged questioner as a festival staffer wrestled the microphone away. Her MFA program had its own star, Jason, in whose shadow they all labored and who was living the life Hailey had planned for herself. Jason had a fellowship while Hailey was burdened by debt. Jason had an apartment with mountain views while Hailey had a decrepit space overlooking a yard choked with overgrown azaleas and cherry laurel. Jason had literary agents handing him their cards at the festival, while Hailey wandered from table to table in the bookseller area, wondering if she would languish unpublished forever.

Jason, of course, was chaperoning the festival headliner. As she sat clutching Attlee's bag the morning of his final festival appearance, Hailey saw them sitting together, looking quite chummy. She wondered what her fellow student had been expected to do for his charge. Probably not place his lozenges and a bottle of water at the precise center of the podium and then run back to the hotel room to fetch a different tie ten minutes before he took the stage.

Hailey doubted that the headliner had planned to attend Attlee's reading until the night before. How many years had the once-hot author been reading the same excerpts from that long-ago bestseller? But the previous evening, Attlee had stunned the crowd at a meet-the-authors event by announcing that he planned to read the first chapter of his newly completed, much anticipated second novel. The festival director had proposed a toast, and for one brief shining moment Jason, raising his water bottle, had looked at Hailey with genuine envy.

Catapulted back into relevance, Attlee had held court for the rest of the evening, basking in the spotlight he had wrenched from the headliner and sending Hailey back to the bar for repeated refills. The new book, he promised, was a complete departure from his earlier work. And no one had seen it—not his agent, not his editor. "In the words of a fellow Bard," he declared, "'we few, we happy few' will share in a critical moment of modern literary history here at the book festival."

In light of Attlee's announcement and the festival's immediate, ferocious social media marketing, the next morning's reading was moved from a meeting room to the hotel's main ballroom. An anticipatory buzz greeted the festival director's hastily rewritten author introduction, swelling into enthusiastic applause when Attlee stood to speak.

The author approached the podium and placed a manila folder on it, smiling out over the capacity crowd. As he opened the folder, a frisson of excitement ran through the ballroom. Attlee picked up his bottle of water, twisted it open, tilted his head back, and drank. Seconds later, he staggered back from the podium and collapsed. The festival director charged back onto the stage and knelt beside the author, who had gone into convulsions. "Is there a doctor here?" she shouted.

The room rapidly descended into pandemonium. Three people, presumably medical personnel, rushed forward. Hailey fought her way through the crowd to join them, passing Jason on the way. He was headed for the nearest exit with a protective arm around the headliner, as if author collapse might be contagious. Hailey made it to the stage and stood next to the podium, still clutching Attlee's bag, as though her responsibilities involved chaperoning him all the way into the next world if need be. People all around pulled out cell phones, some calling 911, some filming. By now, Attlee was shielded from view by the three people hovering over him, desperately attempting to keep him alive.

Within minutes, the crowd parted to allow stretcher-bearing EMTs to reach the stage, and moments later to transport Charles Attlee to a waiting ambulance and down the street to the medical center. The author was dead on arrival.

The festival director and Hailey waited in the hotel manager's office for the police. An officer entered and took a seat opposite them. He walked them through the morning's events and Attlee's entire time at the festival. The director described the author party the night before and the incident with the angry audience member at the panel. Beyond those two events she had not actually spent much time with the dead man. She deflected most questions to Hailey, who had been with the author almost constantly and, it appeared, had been the last person to speak to him before his death.

"I don't think I can be much help," Hailey said. "The last thing he said to me was, 'Please go get my blue tie.'" Although he had not actually said "please." Ever.

The director asked if the police had found a manila folder anywhere on the podium or the stage, explaining about Attlee's revelation of his new novel. The officer shook his head.

"It was such a zoo," said Hailey. "Anyone could have taken it."

"I need to find those pages," the director said. "And I need to get out there and do some damage control." The police officer agreed to let her go for the time being, leaving Hailey alone to answer questions.

"Mr. Attlee seems to have collapsed due to whatever he drank from that water bottle," said the police officer. "The bottle you apparently put on the podium."

Hailey stared at him. "I...I mean, I don't..."

"Where did you get that water, Ms. Fields?"

"The shelf under the podium," she said. "The festival staff stocked all the podiums with water bottles. I just reached under and grabbed one."

"We'll confirm that," said the officer. "Now, would you be able to describe the man who caused the scene at the panel yesterday?" he asked.

"Definitely," said Hailey, "he accosted Charles Attlee again later that day."

"Accosted how?"

"We were in the plaza outside the hotel," Hailey said, "and the man came up and confronted Mr. Attlee about having him kicked out of the panel. He actually shoved him and said he'd pay for trying to silence other writers."

The officer made a note. "Did you witness anyone else confronting Mr. Attlee?"

"No, that was the only problem," said Hailey. "He had a nice interaction with the woman who owns that failing bookstore down the street. He signed a book for her. She's probably planning to sell it for a lot of money now, since it was the last thing he signed before he died. Maybe she can even save her store."

The officer made another note.

"Other than that, he didn't interact with a lot of people," Hailey said. "People didn't really seem to recognize him. He said…" She trailed off. "I feel bad telling you things he told me in confidence."

"Anything you tell us could help us find out what caused his death."

Hailey nodded. "Well, he said he felt like a failure, like his moment was over a long time ago and he was kidding himself that he was ever going to write that second book he had planned to publish."

"But the festival director said that he was planning to read from his new novel this morning."

"I wondered about that," said Hailey. "He really did seem depressed. And he hadn't said anything about a new book before last night. Maybe he was saving the news for his big announcement at the party, or maybe…" she trailed off again.

"Maybe what?"

"Maybe there was no new book," she said. "Maybe he just wanted to enjoy one last moment in the literary limelight. He knew he couldn't deliver the book, so he pretended he was about to produce it and then staged his death."

"You think he committed suicide?"

"I don't know," said Hailey. "But now that he's dead people will always wonder what happened to the manuscript he claimed he had. The great novel that was never published will forever be the great novel that was never found. Maybe it was his way of writing a happy ending to the sad story of his failed career."

"Interesting theory," the officer said, scribbling more notes.

"Well, I have his bag," said Hailey, handing it over, "and there's no manuscript in it."

Not anymore, anyway. Hailey had pocketed the flash drive containing the manuscript and had already changed the author's name on it to her own. She planned to show it to her advisor Monday morning. And she had removed Charles Attlee's laptop from the hotel safe when she had gone back to retrieve his tie. She would dispose of it as soon as she left the hotel, along with the folder she had snatched from the podium in the chaos following Attlee's collapse. She was sorry no one would ever know her own greatest work of fiction, the convincing tale she had told the police of a desperate bookseller, an envious author, and a despondent writer who still took the time to confide in a young MFA student. Just as no one would ever know that an English major had managed to extract cyanide from a cherry laurel bush in her yard, and that she had shown the forethought to retrieve a water bottle with the ambitious Jason's fingerprints to refill with poisoned water and plant on the speaker's podium.

Charles Attlee's best-laid plans for his literary rebirth had come to naught. But he had told the truth. The book festival would see its critical moment of modern literary history. Only Hailey Fields would be the one telling the story, complete with her own happy ending.

Just like she had always planned.

LESLEY A. DIEHL

Lesley A. Diehl retired from her life as a professor of psychology and reclaimed her country roots by moving to a small cottage in the Butternut River Valley in Upstate New York. In the winter she migrates to old Florida—cowboys, scrub palmetto, and open fields of grazing cattle. The author of several mystery series, mystery novels, and short stories, Lesley is a member of Mystery Writers of America, Sisters in Crime National, and Guppy Chapter. Find her at lesleyadiehl.com.

LUNCH BREAK

LESLEY A. DIEHL

"IF MY OLD lady sent that crap in my lunch box, she'd be wearing my fist in her eye." Ralph watched Ben fold back a corner of his sandwich, look at the contents and grimace.

"Peanut butter and jelly. Not so bad. Anyway, Myra didn't make it. I did." Ben took a large bite out of the white bread and washed it down with a slug of coffee from his thermos. He coughed as the dry bread and peanut butter stuck in his throat and gulped more coffee to dislodge the lump.

The two men sat in the only shade available on the site, their legs stretched out in front of them, backs against the trunk of a gnarled and bedraggled live oak, accidentally left standing when the ground was leveled by the bulldozer. The roar of an earth mover several lots over obliterated their words for a moment. Ralph reached into his jeans pocket and extracted a wrinkled handkerchief. He wiped his forehead. "God, I hate August in Florida, especially here. At least on the coast you get a breeze off the ocean. Here you get the smells from the swamp."

The coast. Ben remembered the coast well. His three-bedroom house in Vero Beach, his job with Data Com as an electrical engineer. And his wife. Back then she fancied herself somewhat of a gourmet cook. Now she spent her time watching television in their rented singlewide, sucking up as much junk food as he would bring home to her.

"Myra's got some heart problems. She can't get around too well, so I do most of the shopping and make my own lunch," Ben said. Why was he defending her to Ralph? Because Ralph expressed out loud what Ben felt in his heart. Times were tough. Why couldn't Myra buck up and help him out?

"Sorry, old boy." Ralph munched on his roast beef. The horseradish sauce oozed out of the bread and ran down his hand. "Want some?"

"Naw." Ben shook his head, although if he were to be honest, he'd like to grab the sandwich away from his co-worker, shove it into his mouth and slug down the icy cold lemonade in Ralph's thermos.

Ben thought back to life before he lost his job. He never saved a penny of his more than adequate salary. Why should he? Who would predict he'd lose his job and find himself living in a trailer in the middle of a scrub palmetto field forty miles from the coast? He was lucky to find this job, part-time roofer. No benefits, no health insurance, and Myra's medical bills were crippling them. Last week the doctor said she might need heart surgery. Where the hell were they going to get the money for that?

"She's taking her health issues really hard. She just sits in front of the television all day and half the night. Doesn't move."

"What's the doc say? Wouldn't she be better if she dieted and got some exercise?"

"She's too depressed. He put her on antidepressants. We're waiting for them to work." Ben crumpled up his sandwich wrap and stuffed it into his lunch box.

"You know, buddy, this isn't just about her. What about your needs? Give any thought to asking Helen out for a little fun? She likes you."

Helen was the waitress at the bar Ralph and Ben stopped at for a beer some days after work. One beer for Ben. More for Ralph.

"I'm married, man, and I take my vows seriously. C'mon. Back to work." That should shut up Ralph. Yet Ben couldn't get the thought of Helen out of his mind the rest of the afternoon.

⧖

"I'M HOME, honey, and I've got your bananas." Ben set his lunch pail on the kitchen table where he found his wife, her face shiny with sweat. "It's hot in here. Why don't you have the air conditioner on?"

She looked up at him, spoon in midair, something brown and syrupy running off the side of it. "Because you obviously forgot to pay the electric bill. You need to get a better job. And why are you so late getting here? I was forced to eat all this ice cream and chocolate syrup without the bananas. How can you have a banana split without bananas?" Her voice rose in pitch and volume, then broke, and she dropped her spoon onto to the table. Myra's chins quivered as tears joined the sweat running down her cheeks. Her cries stopped abruptly as she reached for the bananas in Ben's hands. "Grab that other half gallon of ice cream out of the freezer, would ya?"

Ben could see nothing of the tiny, blue-eyed, perky, full-of-life woman he'd married ten years ago. Right now, he hated the mound of flesh that sat in front of him. And yet, he felt sorry for her. Myra wasn't able to adjust to the changes in their financial circumstances. Were it not for her cousin, Renny, who lived in Okeechobee, Ben knew Myra would be even more impossible to live with. Renny took her out to a movie now and then, and the two of them had lunch together once each week. But what stood in the way of his reaching out and hugging Myra to comfort her was the image of Helen's face when she served him his beer last weekend in the bar.

"I'll call the electric company tomorrow." He turned away from his wife, the image of Helen's flirty smile still filling his mind.

"So I've got to spend the entire night in this hot box? I'd think you'd be a little more considerate of a woman in my condition."

"Pack a bag, and I'll drive you to Renny's. You can stay there until we get the juice back on."

He stopped at the bar on the way back home, but Helen had already left for the night.

X

EARLY THE NEXT MORNING, he went by the bank and emptied his savings account, then took the cash and contacted Florida Electric and Gas. They informed him they'd turn the electric on in forty-eight hours. He drove to Renny's house to let Myra know she'd have to stay there for another day or so.

"Last week it was your phone. This week the electric. Don't you make any money at that roofing job? Can't you find anything better?" Renny stood with her hands on her hips, her face wrinkled up in disgust.

Ben wondered if nagging ran in the family. "I'll see about a pay-as-you-go cell phone," he said.

"You should, you know. What if Myra needs emergency medical help?"

Oh yeah, thought Ben, like another load of chocolate syrup, a tub of ice cream, and a bushel of peanuts. The tires spit gravel as he spun out of the drive.

X

"YOU'RE FIFTEEN MINUTES LATE," Ben's foreman notified him when he got out of his car at the job site. "Better not be late again or you'll find yourself out of here. There's no end to the people who'd kill for this job."

Ben began to wonder what he'd kill for, and it certainly wasn't this job. Maybe a little distance from Myra and her cousin. Maybe more than that.

"You here or somewhere else?" asked Ralph. Ben climbed onto the roof and began to shift the shingles into position.

"I'd sure like to be someplace else." Ben slapped shingles into place and applied the nail gun to them, beginning the dreary, repetitive, sweaty, mind-numbing work for the day.

Instead of joining Ralph at the bar that night, Ben begged off, telling him he had groceries to buy.

"The ball and chain need more bologna or are you feeding her lobster by now?" asked Ralph.

"Shut your trap. You don't know what you're talking about." Ben threw his empty lunch pail into the back of his truck and drove off without another word to Ralph.

He knew Ralph found his attitude toward his wife irritating, but worse yet, he also figured Ralph felt sorry for him and thought he should grow a new pair.

He nosed the car into an empty space near the building and walked into the library. Ben located the computer terminals at the rear of the main room.

"We close in less than a half hour," said the woman behind the checkout desk.

"I won't be long," he promised.

His internet search brought unexpected results. He thought Florida would have more poisonous scorpions like ones found in the southwestern states, but the most common one here was the brown scorpion. It could deliver a painful sting, but not a deadly one. He wondered what would happen if a person with medical problems experienced many stings. Could an individual die under those circumstances? How could he find out?

The woman who had warned him of the impending closure of the library stopped at the monitor he was using. "We're closing, sir, as I told you."

Ben looked up into brown eyes. They weren't Myra's icy blue ones, so he decided to take a chance.

"I just moved my wife here from the coast and we're living out of town. She's deathly afraid of scorpions. She has a heart condition, and she's worried she might get stung and die. I told her I'd look into it. You live here long?"

"I was born here. I only heard of one person dying from

scorpion stings. A little girl. She was diabetic, I think. Got hit about ten times. She died. It can happen, although it's rare, but I guess if enough of them got you, well, I'd be worried, especially if I had something wrong with my heart."

"I wish I could move her someplace safer, but we're kind of down on our luck right now. I lost my job."

"You're a good man to be so worried about her." The woman gave him a warm and somewhat inviting smile. He returned the look. She backed away from him. "I've got to close up now."

He walked out of the library considering what he had learned. Myra might be vulnerable. Those disgusting-looking creatures were all over the place, probably because he didn't mow the lawn and the trailer was so old and rusted, it had holes in the floor where they could come in, find food, and build their nests. It was a death trap for Myra, he decided, an opinion he shared with Ralph the next day.

"Don't they sell spray at Home Depot for those buggers?" asked Ralph.

"That stuff's poison. In that little space, Myra'd breathe it in, and the poison would kill her."

"Might not be such a bad idea. Get a guy out of a bad situation, you know?" Ralph gave him a knowing smirk.

Ben stopped his work and turned on Ralph. "What are you suggesting?" He no longer pointed the nail gun at the shingles, but at Ralph.

"Whoa, buddy. Just kidding." Ralph held up his hands as if to ward off his friend. "Although there's nothing so attractive to a woman as a widower, and I'm talking here about Helen."

"I'm not interested in Helen." It was a lie, of course, but one he wanted Ralph to buy, and one he wished he believed in himself.

⌛

BEFORE HE STOPPED by Renny's after work to pick up Myra, he drove to the trailer to make certain the electric worked and to turn on the air conditioner. Myra wouldn't be happy if she had to wait for the hot tin can to cool down. Then he paid a visit to the old shed behind the trailer, a large, empty coffee can in his hand.

Myra didn't comment on the coolness of her house once she returned. Instead she headed for the refrigerator and stuck her head into the frosty cold of the freezer. "There's less than a half gallon of ice cream here. Be sure to pick up some when you go to the store."

"Have a good visit with Renny?" Ben asked, determined to keep his cool.

Myra ignored him, reached into the cupboard, and extracted a box of cookies from the shelf. "Renny's husband, Hank, was out of work for a while, but he didn't settle for some crappy job roofing. He's a real go-getter. Beat the pavement until he found something with good pay. Kept their house. Got direct TV, internet and everything. She's off shopping at the outlet malls tomorrow. If I were able to walk better, I'd go with her. Not that I could afford to buy a thing. Not even at an outlet mall. I used her phone to order me some of that fancy rum cake I saw advertised on television. I hope that won't be too much for you to handle. Maybe you'll have to cut out your beers with the boys, huh?" Winded from her speech, she dropped her overstuffed frame into the recliner rocker and explored the inside of the cookie box.

"One beer every now and then with Ralph, that's all."

She stopped chewing her cookies. He thought she was about to ask him a question, a question he knew he wouldn't want to answer. But she shrugged her shoulders and grabbed two more cookies out of the box.

"I guess one beer can't hurt. If that's all it is." She let out a cackle, spewing crumbs down the front of her blouse. "Any lemonade left?"

Ben sighed and turned away from the sight of his wife. He didn't remember her always being so self-centered. He'd given her everything she'd asked for before he lost his job. Now he was a failure in her eyes.

On the other hand, Helen liked him well enough, and the librarian thought he was a kind man. He thought of himself as kind, and Myra was suffering.

He ought to do something about that.

HE LEFT for work early the next morning, tiptoeing out of their bedroom, not wanting to awaken his wife. He'd left her a present on the pillow next to her head. He wondered if she'd be surprised.

By the time Ralph arrived at the job, Ben was whistling a tuneless song and nailing shingles in place.

"This is supposed to be the hottest day this month, and you're acting like there's a breeze blowing down from the arctic. What's up?"

Ben refused to meet Ralph's eyes. "Nothing much."

At lunch the men sat leaning against a Sabal palm, trying to catch the bit of shade provided by what was left of it after the bulldozer had attacked it. The tree leaned at an unnatural forty-five degree angle, most of its fronds lying dead on the ground, foreshadowing the fate of all the vegetation which once grew abundantly on the development site.

"Not eating today?" Ralph noticed Ben hadn't brought his metal pail and thermos.

"Too hot." Ben sipped water from a plastic bottle.

Ralph sneaked a sideways glance at his co-worker. "Myra still on strike?"

Before Ben could answer, the foreman drove up in a four-wheel drive truck, the company's logo on the door panel obliterated by mud baked by the sun into a thick layer of dirt.

"Your wife and her cousin dropped this off for you." The foreman handed Ben his lunch pail. "She said you left in such a hurry this morning, you forgot to take it." He sped off in a cloud of rocks and dirt.

"Well, now, no wonder you're so pleased this morning. Looks like you had a little come-to-meeting talk with Myra last night, and she's back on track. Good for you, ole buddy." Ralph clapped him on his back.

Ben opened the lunch box rivulets of sweat rolling off his forehead and down his cheeks.

"So whatcha got there?" Ralph leaned over toward Ben to get a better look.

At the bottom of the lunch pail was a plastic container, one of those double-lined ones, Ben noted, the kind that could keep contents warm or cold. He slowly lifted the lid.

Ben peered in without hope. "Ceviche." He spoke in a monotone.

"Ceviche? Never heard of it. What is it?"

"It's seafood marinated in lime juice, but not cooked."

"Raw? Ugh! But you said Myra was a great cook. I could give it a try."

"You won't like it." Ben dropped his head to get a closer look at what Myra had made. He identified fish, octopus, shrimp, and a darker ingredient. Myra was a culinary innovator, but something about this made him wonder. He pushed at it with his fork, and he thought it moved its tail higher over its back. Probably just his imagination. Several hours in the citrus marinade and the fridge, even if it was what he thought it was, it had to be dead. He leaned closer to the container. Nope. It was what he thought. He sighed, held the morsel aloft on his fork, shoveled it into his mouth and chewed. Crunchy.

He'd have to let Myra know he ate the entire container.

VICKI WEISFELD

Vicki Weisfeld's short stories have appeared in *Ellery Queen Mystery Magazine* and *Sherlock Holmes Mystery Magazine*; her story "Breadcrumbs," which appeared in *Betty Fedora*, Issue 3, won a 2017 Derringer Award. Her stories are included in the anthologies *Busted: Arresting Stories from the Beat, Murder Among Friends,* Bouchercon 2017's *Passport to Murder,* and *Quoth the Raven,* contemporary stories inspired by the works of Edgar Allan Poe. A member of Sisters in Crime National, Mystery Writers of America, the Short Mystery Fiction Society, and the Public Safety Writer's Association, Vicki is a reviewer for crimefictionlover.com and TheFrontRowCenter.com. Find her at vweisfeld.com.

WHO THEY ARE NOW

VICKI WEISFELD

THE DAY after deadly Hurricane Alex hit, our duty sergeant gave my partner and me the kind of assignment I dread—the kind that reminds you that no matter how brave or smart or rich or good-looking you are, no matter how good a planner or how much "in control" you are, the indignities of old age lie in wait.

A Department of Children and Families investigator had called the Delray Beach Police Department about a possible homicide at an assisted living community called Sunshine Rest. She'd been called in because they had three storm-related deaths, and one of them looked suspicious. Bill Buxton and I were following up. The patrol officers were busy directing traffic at intersections where signals were out, checking alarms, and a million other things, so her request came straight to us detectives.

Bill and I breezed past Sunshine Rest's empty guardhouse through wide-open gates. If one of the reasons people moved there was to feel safe, the storm had shattered that illusion. The left side of the main building's front portico had collapsed, and the wind had uprooted shrubbery, flung the memorial benches into the koi pond, and strewn the grounds with trash. Sunshine Rest's gates and high walls couldn't keep a hurricane out.

I'd been called to Sunshine Rest a time or two when I was a patrol officer and remembered its layout. A main building housed the dining room, activity rooms, and administrators' offices. Healthy seniors lived in five three-story apartment buildings on the grounds. Those that couldn't manage on their own were relocated to the nursing facility—sometimes temporarily, more often…well.

Dr. Marta Acevedo and one of the forensic investigators were hauling equipment out of the county medical examiner's van.

Marta waved. "Hey, Yolanda, this must be the big time if you and Bill are here."

"Just checking up on you," I said.

"What's up?" Bill asked her. He and I had been partners for two years. I'm hotheaded in certain situations, but Bill keeps his cool. Saves me from myself.

"The problem's in the nursing unit," Marta said. "Lost a big piece of its roof and its electricity. Three patients died up on the second floor. No physician on duty, so I have to take a look." Shadows under her dark eyes proved she'd had a long day already.

"What about the apartment residents?" I asked, scanning the battered landscape. From missing roof tiles to a fallen parking canopy that turned a couple of Cadillacs into convertibles, damage was visible everywhere.

"All okay. Security staff did a check."

"Apparently one of the deaths is"—Bill waggled his hand back and forth—"so we're checking it out. Not the first time a natural disaster provided cover for murder."

We passed through the main building and out the back. The nursing facility was down a short walkway, its doors propped open with cement blocks. Given the ninety-five degree temperatures and no air conditioning, they hoped to catch a breeze. Ironic, considering.

Inside, the bitter-sour smell of saturated drywall overlaid a sloppy mess. Maintenance staff tackled the puddles in the dim hallway. As fast as they mopped, the seeping water returned.

"*¿Luces de emergencia?*" I asked.

The maintenance man apologized. The building had lost its

back-up generators. "*Rayos*," he said. Electricity from the sky—lightning—had left them without electricity on the ground.

"*Ay, mi madre*," Marta said. "*¿Escaleras?*"

He pointed us to the stairwell, and we climbed, avoiding the hazardous farrago of broken ceiling tiles, twisted metal, and other debris mostly pushed to one side. Plasterboard dust covered the treads. Marta fanned herself with her sheaf of paperwork. "This says a lot already. Imagine residents negotiating these stairs."

I could picture it: fragile residents—terrified, confused—the roaring storm, total darkness.

We found the nursing home administrator, Greg Thornberry, pacing the upstairs hallway, sunlight pouring through the open roof. We introduced ourselves. "What happened here?" I asked.

In a voice ragged with exhaustion he said, "When that goddamn roof went, my staff and I worked like dogs to get these people out of harm's way." He wiped his hand across his forehead, leaving it covered in white powder, like he'd been dredged in flour. "Most of them are downstairs now, packed in two and three to a room." He didn't actually say, "like sardines," but I bet he was thinking it. His hands and forearms were bruised.

Was that from hauling patients and beds?

"We just couldn't get to them all soon enough. And they couldn't make it on their own. Slow as Christmas."

A woman wearing a flimsy nightgown tottered across the hall, a dented walker the only thing holding her up.

"I can't run an efficient operation in this chaos," he said.

"Much less a compassionate one," I sympathized.

His head snapped toward me. "Compassion is the social workers' job. And the nurses'." He tapped his chest. "I'm an MBA. I run this place like a business. The only way."

Bill shifted foot-to-foot, frowning at a pile of sodden mattresses.

"But—" I started, an edge in my voice.

Bill must have heard it and headed me off. He asked about the number of residents in the facility—forty-five. Twenty had needed to be moved.

"Some of them aren't with us permanently," Thornberry said.

"They've had a procedure or a fall or whatnot, and we monitor them here until they can return to their apartments."

"I see." I hoped I'd never be old, afflicted with whatnot, and under the supervision of someone like him.

"Listen, I have to check on the residents downstairs. Can we talk later? Give me half an hour?"

"Sure," Bill said, being congenial. Thornberry had made a bad impression on me, and both men knew it.

⧖

MARTA and her assistant moved two bodies to the end of the hallway, where the roof remained intact, and covered them with sheets. Their beds were too wet to bother with. Bill and I joined her in the room where the third resident had died.

"Nothing suspicious about those two." Marta gestured toward the bodies in the hall. "Flying debris hit one of them. Part of a window frame was still on top of her. I think the other one had heart failure. I'll verify that. This gentleman, however," she indicated the body in the bed, "he's interesting. Major trauma to the back of the head, which is probably what killed him. We'll know for sure once we get him on the table. Here's why it's suspicious. Someone knocked on the head like that usually falls forward and lands with their arms and legs every which way. But here he lies, flat on his back, limbs neatly arranged, as if he were laid out. Crazy stuff happens in a hurricane, but his room? Hardly disturbed."

The forensic investigator took photos and measurements, and he and Marta made notes. More techs would be arriving to dust for fingerprints, look for hairs and fibers, the usual meticulous aftermath.

"Possible weapon there." The investigator pointed to a walking cane with a decorative brass knob on the floor next to the bed.

Marta examined the back of the dead man's skull. "That knob might explain why his head looks like this."

A staff member delivered a residents' roster, courtesy of Thornberry. Reading from the list, I said, "The victim's name is

Tim Wood." Glass crunched underfoot, and I bent over a broken picture frame. "This him?" In the black and white photo, two men grinned into the camera, a ballpark in the background.

Marta squinted at the photo. "That's him."

Bill pointed to the other man. "That's Branch Rickey." His jaw dropped. "Is he *that* Tim Wood?"

"Who?"

"Don't they teach anything in school these days? For decades, Timber Wood was the country's greatest sportswriter. Baseball was his specialty."

"Timber Wood and Branch Rickey?" I asked. Marta rolled her eyes.

"Tim was really great at predictions." Bill was on a roll. "He'd study a baseball team's roster, monitor the off-season trades, watch a few early games, and predict who'd be league champion."

"That's useful," I said, thinking about my brothers' fantasy sports obsession. I glanced through the other names on the list. "Oh my god. And across the hall is Gloria Major. I love her movies...*if* that's her."

"Never heard of her," Bill said.

"1950s Hollywood epics? Men in togas? Racing chariots? Don't tell me you never watched them."

"Nah."

"I'll go talk to her. Who knows? Maybe she saw something."

The moment I stepped into the room I knew the woman in the bed was Gloria Major, former Hollywood star. Nightstand cluttered with cosmetics, filmy peignoir draped over a side chair. She was sitting up in bed, reading *Variety*. I introduced myself.

"Is he dead?" Her voice was rough and cigarette-worn.

"Who?"

"Tim, of course." She side-eyed me. "You're too late."

"Mr. Wood *is* dead. How do you mean, 'too late'?"

"Isn't it obvious?" Clearly, she'd pegged me for an idiot. She turned a page.

"I'd like to ask you some questions."

"And I'd adore giving you some answers, but I'm fresh out." She turned another page.

I leaned against the wall. "*Hero of Sparta* is my favorite film of yours. I love the scene where you bid farewell to Leonidas before he leaves to fight the Persians."

She glanced at me before returning to her magazine.

"Afraid I lost track of you after that."

She put *Variety* down. "After the big epic wave died, I did twenty years of training videos, all with the theme of 'if the little lady can do it, so can you.'"

I laughed. "Really?"

"Really. Boring as hell, but I still get the occasional royalty check. I learned to change a tire, use a hand truck, run a forklift, weld. Once I was supposed to move a shipping container from a dock to a ship, but the crane was too high. Freaked me out."

"Wow," I said, meaning it.

"Sit down."

I sat. "Last night must have been rough."

"Pandemonium. The staff yelling at those poor old folks. The storm howling. The residents howling even louder. They wanted us to move downstairs. I refused. If I'm gonna go, I'm gonna go right here with my few bits. Precious little that it is."

"How long have you lived here?"

"Years. My apartment's in Building C, but I've been in here since I fell a couple days ago. Never planned on being here, but I'm going home soon. I'll miss Tim. His apartment was right across the hall."

"Why was he here?"

"Cardiac flare-up. They were keeping an eye on him. We were both due to be discharged."

"Why are you living here in Delray Beach?"

"My son's idea. He moved me out here to be close to him, then promptly took a job in Boston. I stayed put. Didn't relish the cold. Weather. Hunh."

"You got a big dose of it last night."

"That's not the worst." She craned her neck to look past me, as if for a lurking eavesdropper. I recognized the move from *Moon over Pompeii.*

"Please tell me."

"Who could sleep? So about four a.m., I decided to check on Tim, and I saw someone sneak out of his room."

"Wasn't it dark?"

"Too dark to see who it was, but there was a lot of lightning while the hurricane's eye passed over, and I saw a silhouette in Tim's doorway, then a dark shadow slip down the hall. That scared me, so I came back into my room and climbed into bed."

"Why did that scare you?"

"Because Tim has a priceless collection of baseball memorabilia. He was sure someone would try to steal it. It's supposed to go to Cooperstown, when the time comes." She chewed her bottom lip. "I guess it's come."

I gave her a minute. "Can you describe this intruder? Man or woman?"

She shrugged. "He or she wore a hoodie under a rather voluminous long, dark raincoat."

"Interesting. Here's my card." I handed it over. "If you remember anything else?"

⏳

WHILE MARTA WAITED for help in removing the bodies, Bill and I went in search of Thornberry. We found him in his office.

"Well?" he said, pronounced "Weh-yull."

"The medical examiner thinks Mr. Wood's death was foul play," Bill said. "Preliminary, but likely."

"Foul play? With the roof gone, furniture blown to bits, debris flying a hundred and fifty miles an hour?"

"Not in his room." I sounded testy.

Stop arguing with the man.

"Are you in charge of this whole place?" Bill asked.

"All of Sunshine Rest? No, sir. I run the nursing facility, or nursing home, folks used to call it. Don't confuse it with 'home.'

Home is the apartments. There's a whole separate admin team for them."

Our conversation with Thornberry was interrupted numerous times. Staff had can't-wait questions. Anxious family members phoned for updates. As our investigation proceeded, a few of those people proved interesting.

One was Tony Radke. He wore a blue nursing uniform, dark rings of sweat looped under his arms. "Mr. Thornberry," he interrupted, too exhausted to notice the conversation in progress. "It's not cooling off down here a damn bit. We've got wet sheets on them and Janine got ice from somewhere, but it's not enough."

"Tony, y'all need to handle it, even if you have to load them into the van and your private automobiles and drive them around with the AC cranked up. I can't have any more bodies on my watch. You hear?"

"Yessir." He shuffled away.

"He's upset about Tim, like a lot of folks," Thornberry said in a low voice. "He helped with Tim's rehab. Spent a lot of damn time with him."

"Maybe having some good conversation was part of the rehab," I said.

"You a clinician?" Thornberry asked.

"My sisters are nurses. They believe in care of the whole patient."

"Maybe so, but here, we've got performance standards to meet. Handholding's not in the job description."

My irritation with Thornberry was on full simmer.

The administrator worked his jaw, assessing me. "You have no i-dee how many government rules we put up with. Plus, most residents' families live up north. They visit once or twice a year, *if that*, and let dad and mom dwindle and die alone. But they'll haul ass down here faster than that"—he snapped his fingers—"if they think *we* neglected any little thing. They'd make my life hell. Them and their lawyers. No ma'am. We check all the boxes, and don't have time to do more."

"Is it possible you had an intruder upstairs last night?" I asked.

"Nope."

"Gloria Major says—"

"Crazy as a bedbug," Thornberry snorted. "Some of our residents'…faculties are diminished, and they don't think too clearly in the best of times. Which last night was *not*."

"What about Tim?" Bill asked. "He was a legendary sportswriter."

"And never stopped talking about it. His mind was ok, and his memory was *too* good, if you ask me. People like that, questioning everything, make my job harder."

That left Bill and me momentarily speechless. Thornberry saw our raised eyebrows and added, "He had a long list of complaints. Nothing for you to worry about."

Statements like that never stop me from worrying. In fact, they fire up the worry machine.

A maintenance man banging on the open door brought good news at last. He wore a dark uniform, steel-tipped shoes, and a Yankees cap. "Roof men coming. I yell a lot, now we in morning first thing."

"It *is* an emergency," Thornberry said, unimpressed.

"Not to roof men it ain't." The maintenance man—"Stan" his embroidered name tag read—squinted at us, something more to say. "I not knowing those dead women, but Tim, I feel bad. Could shoot the breeze like business of nobody."

"Yes, well, leave us," Thornberry said. "We're in the middle of something."

Stan spun around like a person with useful work to do.

"Shame I have to let him go," Thornberry muttered.

"Really?"

"Likes the track too much. Pompano Park, Hialeah. Can't have that here. Vulnerable residents and whatnot. Did a great job last night, though. Carried residents downstairs like they were his own kids."

"He has quite an accent for someone named 'Stan,'" I said, interested by the gambling.

"He's Hungarian or Slovakian or something. Full name's Konstantine Suslak."

"Funny about Tim Wood," Bill said, back on our earlier topic. "They said if he was as interested in the weather as he was in sports, he could have put the National Weather Service out of business."

"Heard that one too," Thornberry said. He might as well have said, "So what?"

The man's lack of respect had my Cuban blood bubbling. "So you have this famous sportswriter and right across the hall an *estupenda* actress like Gloria Major—"

"Yeah, well, this may not be the life they planned when they were in their prime, but that's not who they are now, is it?"

Bill laid a placating hand on my arm. "We'll have more questions, but that's it for now," he said.

As we neared Thornberry's door, a chubby man with a bright blond hairpiece nearly knocked us down. "Where's Mother?" he panted, while I studied how his fake hair sat at a strange angle, as if blown off-kilter by the storm. "Her room's—"

"Mr. Vance, she's in the commons room." Thornberry's tone became unctuous. "We had to move most of the second-floor residents. The roof." He gestured vaguely heavenward.

"Is she okay?"

"She's fine. We gave them lunch and started our cleanup—"

Vance eyed Bill's badge, clipped to his belt. "I heard about Tim. He's really dead?"

"Afraid so," Thornberry said.

"That awful storm. Poor Tim. Mother liked him. I took her to his room for a chat every day."

None of us mentioned that Tim Wood's departure from Sunshine Rest was murder.

"Go find your mother, Mr. Vance, and I'll join you momentarily." When the man left, Thornberry muttered, "Chats with Tim? Give me a break. His mother hasn't said an intelligible word since her stroke two years ago. Now this place is the son's social life. Pitiful."

We followed Thornberry into the hall. Gloria was ambling along, munching popcorn. Thornberry brushed past her.

"Be not so hasty in your departure that you neglect your duty to those who serve you," she said with a little bow in his direction, which he ignored.

I put my fist to my mouth to keep from laughing. It was a line from *Hero of Sparta*. Gloria caught my eye and gave a one-shoulder shrug. I said, "Tell Bill about Tim Wood's collection of baseball stuff."

"There's a fortune in that," Bill said.

"Especially since his collection goes way back," Gloria said. "He'd whittled it down, but he said what's left is priceless."

"Definitely worth stealing?" Bill asked.

"Worth killing for too, maybe," she said.

"Tell Bill what you saw last night."

She repeated her sketchy story about Tim's hooded visitor.

"So was the collection with him, in his room upstairs?" Bill asked.

"No way. It's locked up in a safe back at the apartment."

Gloria started to say more but was interrupted. A member of the medical examiner's team came to tell us they were ready to remove the bodies. We needed to leave too. The smell of the place was getting to me, and we wanted to check Tim's apartment.

⧗

BY THE TIME we got over there, it was nearly dark. Building C, where Tim had lived, was considerably less damaged than the nursing unit. Its emergency generator hummed, and the hallways and apartments were dimly lit. Residents had been asked not to overtax the system by running their air conditioners, and many doors were propped open for airflow, more out of hope than expectation.

Bill unlocked Tim's apartment door, his bulk blocking my view when he flipped on the lights. He stopped short. "Holy…"

I peered around him and "*Ay-yi-yi*" burst out of me. The

apartment had suffered extensive damage, and it wasn't from wind and water. Plants were overturned, their pots shattered. Glass and mirrors smashed. Cabinet doors and drawers hung open, their contents spilling out. In the bedroom, the mattress was slit open, clothing pulled from hangers, shoeboxes emptied.

"Serious aggression," I said.

"No kidding. Looking for the collection? D'you think they found it? Or maybe they couldn't find it and went to the nursing unit to make Tim tell where it is."

"And he wouldn't…?"

"Or did," Bill said.

"Either way, they had to kill him."

"Okay, we get the crime scene folks back here." Bill pulled out his phone.

I tried to imagine the level of anger or wantonness that could produce this much chaos. "And nobody would have heard it over the noise of the storm."

"Most of them probably don't hear so well anyway."

THE NEXT MORNING we met with the head of security for the entire Sunshine Rest complex. He printed off a list of the keycards that had accessed Tim's apartment since he was admitted to the nursing facility.

"Who do they belong to?" Bill asked, frowning at the ten-digit numbers.

"The first two, housekeeping. Staff doing their regular Wednesday cleaning, judging by the dates," he said. "If the apartment had been ransacked before they got there, they obviously would have reported it. The night of the storm, someone used a master key registered to the nursing facility. That'll be the one of interest. The one last night—"

"Was us," I said.

"Right."

"Who has access to the nursing facility's keys?"

"Between us, security over there is crap. They keep good track of the narcotics—the nurses are on top of that—and most of the time they're pretty sure where the patients are, but as far as building security? It never occurs to them anyone would want to break *in*. Securing master keys is not a priority."

"So if someone knew where they're kept, they could just take one?" Bill asked.

"Night of the storm? Anything might have happened. Total chaos."

"What about cameras?"

"The nursing unit cameras went black when the generator was knocked out, but there's one on the front door of Building C. Let's take a look."

The recording showed nothing but storm until nearly four a.m., when we saw someone matching Gloria's description of a hooded figure. Unfortunately, with the blowing rain and with him—or her—hunched over in the wind, all we saw was a smeary blob. About thirty minutes later, the blob left, possibly empty-handed.

The rest of the day we interviewed residents and staff, trying to find out more about the intruder and whether anyone was especially interested in Tim's collection. What we learned was that lots of baseball fans retire to Delray Beach. I paid another visit to Gloria to finish our conversation from the day before.

⏳

BY THE TIME Bill and I returned to the station, my head pounded in the thumping rhythm set by the roofers. Our colleague Javier Batista had been working the phones and the internet, checking staff backgrounds.

"Present for you." Javier handed me some papers. "Cooperstown faxed a rundown of the collection Tim promised them. Now that I know what to look for, I can see if anything turns up on eBay and contact baseball memorabilia websites."

"Great. We can check local pawn shops and stores that carry this kind of thing," I said. "Anything else?"

"Sunshine Rest's staff seems pretty clean. But Thornberry himself has a checkered job history. No one will say why. The corporate office implied he either makes it good here, or his career with them is finished."

"He did say Tim Wood was a complainer," Bill remembered. "He might have thought Tim would take his complaints up the ladder."

"In general he had an attitude about Wood. I wonder."

Javier interrupted my musing. "There's one bad apple. The maintenance worker with the gambling problem, Stan Suslak. Behind on his mortgage. Car repossessed. That kind of thing."

"I'll talk to Beanie, see if Suslak's out in the deep water," I said. Juan García—Beanie—was a confidential informant who knew the local moneylenders, the ones who didn't advertise on bus stop benches.

Javier continued, "Crime scene report's on your desk. I can tell you what's in it. *Nada.*"

Javier was right. Our investigators had thoroughly examined the room in the nursing facility and the apartment. No prints, no hairs, nothing.

☒

BILL and I spotted Thornberry and various staff members we'd interviewed moving through the cafeteria line. Lunch was a cold buffet until the kitchen could be fully operational. We joined Gloria Major at a big table where she sat alone, spooning yogurt over a bowl of fruit salad.

"Hope you like sandwiches," she said.

"We already ate," I said. "Place looks to be getting back in shape." At least it was swept, and new glass filled the windows.

She licked the spoon. "I'm moving back to my apartment tomorrow. Can't say I'll be sorry to say goodbye."

We'd invited several people to join us, and, one by one, they did. First Nurse Radke and the maintenance man, Stan Suslak.

"Again, who did you say knew about Tim's collection?" Bill asked.

Before any of them could answer, Thornberry walked up, carrying his tray. "Everyone. It's all he talked about."

"Afternoon." My smile was probably about as welcoming as an alligator's.

He plunked into a chair and set his paper plate and cup of soda on the table.

"Well, was anyone especially interested in it?" Bill asked.

"Not me," said Thornberry.

Mr. Vance arrived, slow-rolling his mother's wheelchair, her lunch tray semi-balanced in one hand. "Mind if we join you?"

Since we invited you, no, we don't mind.

"Have a seat." Bill leaned out of the way in case Mother's lunch took a dive.

"Thank you." Vance said. "Mother, you remember Detective Yolanda and Detective Bill?"

Not in a million years.

I said, "I think around the table here are the people most interested in Tim's collection, except for Mr. Thornberry, who frequently protested he wasn't."

"What would I do with it? Look at it?" Thornberry asked.

"Doth he protest too much?" Gloria asked and received a glare from the administrator.

"Sell it," Suslak said.

He needs cash. No surprise that's the first thing he thought of.

Vance tried to smooth things over. "Me, I'm trying to get rid of stuff. Mother lived in our house forty-seven years. You wouldn't believe——" He chuckled. "But, irregardless, Tim wasn't selling." He took the plastic wrap off a tuna sandwich, gave half to his mother, and started eating the other half.

"You all found those old stories of Tim's so interesting." Gloria batted her eyelashes at the men across the table.

"Lots of interesting people here, Gloria." Vance smiled and patted Mother's hand.

"Tim did know a lot of people," Gloria said.

"Most of them dead," Thornberry said. "I always wondered how many of his stories were actually true."

"All of them," Nurse Radke said with confidence.

Ah. A true believer.

"Some, maybe." Gloria shrugged. "But I wonder. Just like I wonder about 'the collection.' Did he try to make it seem like more than it was?" She speared a grape, looking thoughtful.

"Absolutely not," Vance said, spraying the table with bits of tuna fish. "It was full of one-of-a-kind treasures."

"Did you ever see it?" Bill asked casually.

"No, of course not," Vance said. "It's locked up somewhere,"

"In safe," Suslak said. "He show it me when I fix AC in apartment."

"When was that?" I asked.

"I dunno. May? When weather get warm."

He would have known where Tim kept it. And have easy access to a master key.

"I saw it more recently," Radke said. "I went with him to the apartment to pick up clothes and personal items. We spent about an hour going through it. Amazing." Radke gave Thornberry a guilty glance. "He had some paperwork to finish, so I carried his suitcase back, and Gloria brought him over here a while later."

Ditto Radke. Knowledge and access.

"I remember." Gloria studied her perfect manicure. "I wheeled him all around the complex for a mini-excursion. Two weeks later I had my fall and we were neighbors again. In here."

Bill leaned back in his chair. I stirred my coffee.

"What you don't know," Bill said, "is that the collection is gone."

"Stolen?" Suslak sounded outraged.

"Can't be." Distress filled Radke's voice.

"Gone," I said.

"But where?" Vance whined.

"On its way to Cooperstown," Bill said. "Tim's will was crystal clear about that. We opened the safe in front of his lawyer and a probate judge, and they authorized it."

"We retrieved the safe from the apartment, and that was that." I brushed my hands together.

"But it wasn't *in* the apartment," Vance said.

"Tim's apartment? No, it wasn't there. It was in Gloria's apartment. Remember, he was worried about theft? He had her move it to her place. Only someone who'd been in Tim's apartment very recently would know it was missing. Mr. Vance, apparently that's you."

Vance jumped up from the table, protesting, and glanced at his mother as if seeking a defense she could no longer provide. Another bite of sandwich occupied all her attention. Thornberry and Radke looked shocked. "Mr. Vance."

Suslak was surprised too. "She not move sixty-pound safe."

"Listen, Suslak," Gloria said, "I know my way around a hand truck. You should see my videos."

I was glad Nurse Radke wasn't the culprit. He seemed dedicated, unlike his boss. It would have been a pleasure to snap the handcuffs on Thornberry's wrists, but it was Vance who had given himself away and soon burbled the truth.

As Bill and I drove back to the station, following the squad car with Vance slumped in the back seat, I watched workmen hauling tree branches and armloads of shredded palm fronds to the curb. Over the whine of chain saws, I said, "You know, Thornberry was wrong."

"About what, specifically?"

"He said the residents aren't who they were. Tim with his predictions and Gloria with her acting—that's exactly who they were."

JOHANNA BEATE STUMPF

Johanna Beate Stumpf is a German millennial, living and working in Norway. She is fairly new to fiction writing, but she did enough academic writing to earn a Ph.D. in Computer Science from the University of Oslo. Johanna is a member of the Oslo Writers' League. Find her at johannawritesstuff.wordpress.com.

THANK YOU FOR YOUR COOPERATION

JOHANNA BEATE STUMPF

MARSHA GLANCED at the timestamp in the corner of the screen. It was exactly eight twenty-two and forty seconds. The surveillance program switched the camera angle on the big screen. She let her eyes slide over the small screens to her right. Everything was quiet. There were very few people in the subway stations she was monitoring; the morning rush of regular commuters was over and the tourists hadn't yet woken up. The program automatically showed a new camera angle on the big screen. Eight twenty-two and fifty seconds.

Marsha pressed a few buttons on her keyboard and the big screen switched to manual control. A few more buttons and the camera angle changed again. The screen was now filled with a wide view of the main entrance of Greenbrook Station. The time stamp read eight twenty-two and fifty-six seconds. Four seconds later a handsome middle-aged man carrying a red umbrella stepped into the frame.

Punctual like clockwork. Marsha loved that about him. She blushed as she realized what she had been thinking. Love. Did she really love this man? She had never even spoken to him.

The man with the red umbrella walked to his usual spot on the platform, turned, and waved directly at the camera. Marsha giggled like a schoolgirl.

Six weeks ago the same man had walked onto her platform, the big red umbrella opened above his head. Marsha had pressed the button on her microphone and recited her usual lines. "The opening of umbrellas inside the station is not permitted. Please close your umbrella. Thank you for your cooperation."

The man had awkwardly closed his umbrella and waved apologetically to the camera. This was a bit unusual but at that point she had not paid special attention to the situation. The program had automatically switched to the camera of the next subway station.

The man with the red umbrella had been reading a book when Greenbrook came up again on the big screen. The camera angle allowed her to see the cover. This time Marsha did a double take. The man with the red umbrella was reading the same book she'd been reading on her morning commute.

The next train arrived and the man with the red umbrella closed the book. Once again he looked directly at the camera, as if he knew she was watching him in that very moment. He smiled a big smile, winked, and stepped on the train.

Marsha had sat in front of her screens as if struck by lightning. Sometimes people waved at the cameras. Mostly children and teenagers. But no customer of the subway train services had ever winked at her. What was that supposed to mean?

Since that day she had watched the man with the red umbrella every morning. He came onto the platform at exactly eight twenty-three and took the train at eight thirty-one. Marsha had come to look forward to those eight minutes every day. The man always carried his red umbrella and a book, walked up to the same spot, waved at the camera, and started reading. Each week he had a new book. Marsha began to order the same books online, reading in the evenings and on the weekends to keep up. It felt as if she was slowly getting to know him.

Marsha was forced to admit that she had a crush on the man

with the red umbrella. Still, she tried to convince herself that it wasn't real. Unfortunately, that didn't help much. Two weeks after their first encounter, Marsha was watching him intensely when a couple of teenagers began pushing each other around on the platform, coming dangerously close to the tracks. Marsha pressed her microphone button and recited the usual directive: "No fighting on the platform. Please stay behind the yellow line. Thank you for your cooperation." When the teenagers started laughing, she realized that she had been moaning the last line, her mind and body still consumed with thoughts of the man with the red umbrella.

The man with the red umbrella looked directly into the camera, smiled, and winked again. Marsha blushed and giggled in front of her screens, relieved that no one could see her. One day she would talk to him, she thought. One day. She just didn't know how. Or when. But one day.

The man with the red umbrella closed his book. It was eight thirty and forty-six seconds. The train was about to arrive at the platform. He turned to the camera, smiled and waved.

And then he did something he had never done before. He touched his mouth with his left hand, pursed his lips, and blew over his palm in the direction of the camera.

He blew her a kiss. Marsha hiccupped. A kiss. This had never happened before. Her stomach exploded in sparkles and butterflies. She couldn't sit any longer and jumped up from her chair. This was a sign. The man with the red umbrella wanted to meet her, too. She was sure of it.

The next morning, Marsha hung over the side of her bed, phone in hand. She'd read somewhere on the internet that if you were upside down, you sounded like you had a stuffy nose. She chose her supervisor's number from her list of contacts. The phone rang, answered almost immediately.

"Amanda?" she asked. "It's Marsha. I'm sick, I can't come in today."

Amanda's answer was sympathetic. Marsha instantly felt guilty, but she couldn't go back now.

"Yes, I think it is better if I just stay in bed today," she said, and coughed meekly.

Marsha arrived at Greenbrook Station at five minutes past eight. She waited outside for fifteen minutes, afraid that if she loitered on the platform for too long she might draw the attention of her replacement.

Inside, the platform looked different. It felt strange to be there in person, instead of having a bird's eye view through the lenses of the cameras. Nevertheless, she soon found the man with the red umbrella's usual spot.

She waited. The eight twenty-one train came and people went on and off. The hands on the big clock on the wall moved slowly. Eight twenty-two and thirty seconds. Marsha suddenly felt an urge to use the bathroom. She ignored it. Forty seconds. She started fidgeting with her hair. Fifty seconds. Her eyes raced back and forth between the clock on the wall and the entrance. Eight twenty-three. Marsha held her breath.

Nothing happened. No one entered. Then, after an eternity, someone stepped on the platform. Marsha made a step in the direction of the person before she realized that it was just a young mother carrying a toddler. Marsha looked at the clock again. Eight twenty-three and twenty seconds.

The man with the red umbrella was late. Except the man with the red umbrella had never been late before. Had something happened to him? Was he sick? Marsha paced back and forth on the platform, waiting, scanning every person that entered. But the man with the red umbrella didn't come. After an hour Marsha left the platform and went home, wondering, worrying. What had happened to the man with the red umbrella? Would he come back? Or had the kiss actually been a kiss-off?

When Marsha entered her office the next day she found a note on her desk. "See Amanda ASAP," it read. A black hole opened in Marsha's stomach. Had Amanda found out that she hadn't been sick yesterday? Had one of her colleagues seen her standing around at Greenbrook Station and reported her? Marsha shivered involuntarily. She threw a glance at the clock on the wall and another thought struck her. She had to be back in her office in twenty minutes or she would miss the man with the red umbrella. She dropped her bag and hurried to her supervisor's office.

"Marsha," Amanda said. She sounded tired. "Sit down."

Marsha sat down on the chair opposite her supervisor's desk.

"Two days ago there was a break-in at Fourth Street Bank. It happened during the day, although they only discovered it after closing up." Amanda looked at her expectantly. Marsha looked back blankly. Why had Amanda called her in to tell her about a bank break-in?

"Do you know where Fourth Street Bank is?" Amanda asked.

"No," Marsha said, still unsure about where this conversation was headed.

"Fourth Street Bank is directly next to Eastwick Station."

"Okay," Marsha said. Eastwick Station was one of the subway stations she monitored. But she still didn't understand what this had to do with her.

"Your Eastwick Station," Amanda stressed.

"Yes, but…" Marsha trailed off. She didn't know what to say. All she wanted to do was go back to her office to watch the man with the red umbrella.

"Look at this," Amanda continued, turning her screen to Marsha. "Our data analysts compiled these files yesterday."

Amanda clicked a button and a video started playing. It was a view of Eastwick Station, the same view Marsha watched everyday. The platform was almost empty. Three men in hard hats entered, carrying big plastic boxes. The camera angle changed while the men moved quickly to the wall at one end of the platform. The camera was on the opposite end of the station, the men small figures in the distance. Two of them started doing something on the wall, while the third one set up barrier tape. The camera angle changed again. Now the men were in the corner of the screen, recorded by the camera directly above them. They took heavy machinery out of the plastic boxes and started using it on the wall.

"What are they doing?" Marsha asked.

"They are drilling a hole," Amanda said, with a sigh.

Marsha looked at her puzzled.

"Why?"

"Marsha," Amanda said, jumping up. "They are drilling a hole to the safe of Fourth Street Bank, that's what they are doing. They are preparing a bank robbery. "

Marsha shrank back as Amanda settled down in her seat.

"They have been doing this every day for weeks," Amanda said. "Have you never seen them before?"

Marsha shook her head. Amanda sighed again.

"Marsha, all of these files were recorded during your shift. How could you not see them?"

Marsha stared at the screen as if seeing the platform for the first time. This had been recorded during her shift? How could that be? How could she have missed such an obvious misdemeanor? All the activities were in plain sight of the cameras. She should have seen this. How was it possible that she was seeing this for the first time today?

The men in the hard hats had finished working and were packing the machines away. From another box they pulled a large plastic sheet. As they attached the sheet to the wall, the camera angle changed again. From the opposite side of the station, it became clear that the sheet had a life-sized picture of the wall printed on it. Onscreen it looked completely untouched.

"Marsha," Amanda leaned in and spoke softly now. "The police will be here in a moment to speak to you."

Marsha nodded numbly. Her eyes wandered over the screen trying to find something to hold on to. In the corner she found the timestamp. It showed eight thirty and forty-seven seconds. Marsha held her breath. The men on the screen jumped on the next train and disappeared. Eight thirty-one.

The next file loaded and started playing. The timestamp jumped back to eight twenty-three. The men entered the platform. The video was eight minutes long. Each of these videos was eight minutes long. Marsha slowly led out her breath. She thought of the man with the red umbrella. The kiss he had blown to the camera two days ago. She understood now what it meant. She had hoped it meant he liked her. She had been afraid it meant goodbye. But it meant something else. Something completely different.

It meant thank you.

Thank you for your cooperation.

WILLIAM KAMOWSKI

William Kamowski is Professor of English at Montana State University in Billings, where he has taught writing, literature, and mythology. His recent publications include a novel, *Buckeye's Ballet*. "Last Thoughts" is his first venture into crime fiction. Find him at williamkamowski.com.

LAST THOUGHTS

WILLIAM KAMOWSKI

THE RESEMBLANCE WAS ALMOST TOO FITTING. MUCH alike in many ways, the three girls were likewise subtle, silent in their agreement to shape their deaths as he had suggested. None had said, "I'll do it now." They simply followed his scripts into their last thoughts.

So each story—Spark's drowning on the first page of the local section in the *Seattle Times*, Cobbie's "fall" reported a month later on the same page, and today, Ivy's two-paragraph obituary announcing her "unexpected death in the garden she so loved"—came as a light, warm surprise with his midmorning coffee.

For all his time on the screen with them, Timothy preferred to read the final news in the paper. On the screen, even at the most intimate turns of conversation in their many email exchanges—about butterfly strokes and point shoes and growing rue—there was that distance, safe though a little frustrating, comfortable though cool. Somehow, too, that distance was necessary, like the detachment of therapists from their confiding patients. Yet now, with all three gone, he wanted to be near them again, and the newspaper seemed to close up the space, especially Ivy's obituary, apparently written by the family she had never mentioned.

The idea of talking them out of their sad lives had come in

fragments over a month of half-tipsy musings at Rottweiler's Tavern and Tugboat Andy's. These were cheap bars where he would not have been a regular drinking three-dollar happy hour drafts if he had not been driven, finally, to underpaid freelance consulting on small business PC systems. He had lasted just a month, despite the good salary, processing the endless data at Digital Warehouse; before that, just two weeks selling laptops to cyber illiterates at Better Deal.

If he had had the cash to retain a lawyer to begin with, he would never have quit LoveOverFortyOnline. He would have bought it. The owners had snatched the copyright on his program LoveFortyMatchPoint, and it was now driving their website for older hopefuls in internet mating—stolen from him by a couple of second-tier leeches who couldn't write a program and didn't know the first word to say to an older woman.

For that matter, what did they know about older men? Only twenty-two himself, he had fleshed out the program's romantic details from his mother's and aunt's open discussions about recharging their love lives in their forties. Mom and Aunt Lennie had run the range of "hard-copy" strategies in the aging singles world. He just translated their strategies and quests into online adventure.

At times, family could be a real resource.

Yes, he could congratulate himself on a few other successes in design as well, and confidentially with friends if he'd had any. He was particularly pleased about cracking into Trader Troy's organic health foods site where he had inserted sensuous pictures of puffed cheese worms, beer-battered bacon logs, and the all-in-one deep-fried dinner (his own creations). To the Toyota dealer who had gouged him for transmission repairs on his aging Celica, he meted out a harsher treatment with the same bit of pride: a jamming field that blocked the keyless starter systems on an entire lot of new cars. And hacking into Jefferson Behavioral Health Clinic's receivables to "adjust" his therapy bill to "paid" was really quite the coup—less entertaining perhaps, but the level of the challenge …Well…

It was a little painful being unable to claim the achievements publicly.

The same with the girls, though he was a bit worried about that brief slip in Rottweiler's to the belligerent gamer who played *Offed* and *Dead Maidens* online and kept droning on and on about his picking up girls as easily as the animated belles in *Snatchem*.

It wasn't actually a slip, then, because there was no truth or motive behind it at the time. Without forethought about his reply to one-up the boastful gamer, but with that straight, honest face that always worried his mother, he'd told the game-junkie-ladies-man, "I do better than that in chat. I drop some suggestions tuned to whatever the girl is feeling at the moment—excited, happy, insecure, sad—sensitive sounding things like how she might dress for a wedding, or how she might let down a hopeful fellow gently, or how she might land the next guy with a bit of talk about a little tattoo in just the right place. That girl went out and got inked with a set of cherubs circling her navel. They come round." And then the idea came round, though it seemed a bit of a surprise at the moment: "Hey, I could sketch out the scripts for the sad ones' deaths and they'd follow my directions."

"You couldn't sketch the circuit for a vibrating dildo, or land a girl who's horny enough to use one," the gamer had said.

Timothy had been a bit drunk too, but, unlike the gamer, he let offenses slide by when he glowed. So in response he simply muttered "gamer" a little under his breath, just loud enough to be heard, and dismissed him with a half swivel of his stool. Why belittle a guy who was just a slopwork janitor in a research lab? Just a *gamer*, not a *programmer*. He'd stifled a silly urge to return to the subject of LoveFortyMatchPoint where the doomed boasting exchange had begun. Instead, he'd pocketed his Visa card, signed the standing credit tab for his drafts, and slapped the ballpoint on the tab to punctuate his exit before Gamer Boy grated his ear again about picking up chicks.

But next evening, in Tug Boat Andy's, where the essence of the air was beer, and the exception cheap cocktails, he picked up—well, was picked up—by Shala, twice his age and half her former charms. The pub was full and she asked to share his booth until a stool came free at the bar, but she never took that stool.

It was awkward. He slipped up badly on the first go-round, but she didn't seem to mind, kept him all night in her high-rise studio, until he'd gotten most of it right—or, to her liking anyhow. "Don't worry…don't get discouraged…we've got the whole night. Unless you *want* to go home early."

He knew she was using him, but he didn't mind much. Wasn't he using her, too? It was only his fourth time since high school. But he didn't know how much of a use until he returned to Tugboat Andy's two nights later and sat himself in the booth where they'd met, hoping she'd return. As he sat there, alone in his musings, he heard the voices of two women, out of sight in the booth behind the stained oak partition to his left. Shala was talking to a friend.

"So if you see him here, just befriend him. He'll come home with you. He won't get it right on his own, but he does anything you ask, and he follows directions like a dream."

Katie was the same as Shala—his mother's age, but never married, a lonely, needy lady in a vintage one-bedroom on First Hill. Speaking of needy, he told himself, the old cliché "Beggars can't be choosers" might be revised to "Beggars choose beggars." And he smiled in realizing that he'd begun a bit angry during his night of compliance with Katie, though he had not asked to go home early.

But he was half their age and he would do better. They had not done better and were not going to. And then it all came together: he'd seen Katie and Shala many times before, only twenty years younger and vulnerable, on all the My Faces and My Places and the gush-blogging and bleed-out sharing sites that offered so many ways of saving face or, really, losing face, without knowing it in the deceptive comforts of self-revelation.

With that thought, whatever anger he had felt over Shala, Katie —over his own incompetence, his fawning performances with them in bed—warmed into a confidence he was more accustomed to. What Shala and Katie really needed was his help twenty years ago. They didn't have to become what they had become.

They didn't have to become…anything.

He knew he could do this, better than anyone, and without the blatant violence of those lowlife predators who occasionally made the news, but more often the TV crime shows. It was simple enough on any of the social media platforms to locate the needy ones who lived around Seattle, especially the girls who used their real first names. But even the careful ones eventually dropped a clue about location.

The swimmer was too easy—went for long workouts in Lake Washington—and the shoe girl shopped in the upscale Chaucette's downtown. The gardener girl (actually, she was twenty-eight but looked younger) finally mentioned a specialty nursery she ordered from in West Seattle.

As easy as it was to locate subjects nearby, he had lost quite a few cautious ones at first. He should have chatted a little more before suggesting the email. He had planned a fatally drugged wine in one of her mock masses for "Just Mary," who, at twenty-one and on her mission to become America's first female Catholic priest, had been newly denied admission to the seminary.

He had envisioned a tragic vertical cartwheel from the scaffolding to spoil the season's opening home game with "Plain Pam"—imagine calling herself that—who rediscovered daily on social media that she hadn't the looks to make the basketball cheer squad at UW.

Then there was "Cheddar," who ate thirty pounds of extra sharp cheese a week for breast enhancement. He had lost her before he had quite worked out how the cheese might be pleasantly tainted.

Sure, he had expected some losses—not hard to see why they might mistake his hasty intentions for harmful. Relax, *listen*, then chat.

That lesson learned, he recalled another lesson from his favorite psychology teacher. Professor Grissley had emphasized that the "longings" in those who fail socially are sometimes disguised as odd ways to gather attention, recognition, or even companionship. Spark, Cobbie, and Ivy were all guarded in that way, masking their needs in their quirky, self-involved postings.

A little legwork in the concrete world complemented the internet searches, learning a few things about them that they hadn't posted: a favorite latte drink at Starbucks, the best cozy mysteries at Barnes & Noble, the choicest seafood at Pike Place Market. Without letting on that he knew their favorites, theirs became his and supplemented the rest of his own fiction: he was Wayne Pastern, a forty-year-old Portland fitness trainer with greying sideburns, who turned up in a dozen planted references when googled. That, too, was fitting for gaining the confidence of a swimmer, a girl who grew up with ballet, and a botanist who raised herbs and naturopathic medicinals. To each, he barely mentioned his Portland job and dropped his "name," figuring they'd look him up and find he was "legitimate."

Playing to their caution and indirection, he patiently, gradually fashioned softer suggestions to "talk" by email, which eventually secured Spark, then Cobbie, then Ivy. Mail was better than chat because it could unfold slowly, gradually, carefully. It gave them the time they needed to think.

Besides, the mail could actually "sound" more like caring conversation than chat, which too often slid into self-promoting cleverness and repartee. And he'd absorbed enough of such caring conversation—from the mutual supporters, the ego-savers at the cosmetic counters, and outside the fitting rooms at Penney's and Nordstrom's, where friends flattered friends, and where he pretended to shop for gifts. Such unbelievable crap it seemed at first. But almost always that talk seemed to bolster the needy.

"I'm not just friending you, I'm *befriending* you." It was a terrible line, painful, and he knew it. Credible only to the credulous. But they didn't seem to think so, or care.

Yes, pretty poor stuff, but not traceable back to him behind his spoof email address, behind the unregistered desktop—self-assigned compensation from Better Deal—in the basement storage unit, and behind the Trojan Horse in the teacher's upstairs apartment on Queen Anne Avenue. (Yes, he admitted reluctantly, the scam-spam fellows had something to teach him after all.)

WITH THE FIRST ONE, Spark, the swimmer, he came to realize that if he asked just so—just a little meekly, or even a little sheepishly—to meet her, she'd turn him down easy without cutting him off. She'd feel more comfortable, more secure having said no to him, still more comfortable thinking of him as mail from two hundred miles away in Portland, and she would never, then, ask to meet *him*. The learning process was a delicate challenge.

"I understand," he replied to her kind refusal. "You're right. That's the beauty of what we do: we keep our own space. To meet would be an ending." Another dreadful line, but…

"Yes, and my swimming is my space, a place to be alone."

Despite his careful, acquired patience, he broke his own new rule with Spark by going to watch her swim out into Lake Washington the next day at Madison Park Beach. Yet it was for the best that he went there. He hadn't noticed on her posts, and couldn't in her email, but at the beach he could see immediately what was wrong: the swimsuit and the cap, so unattractive, so neutering, like those on the Olympic swimmers, sleek and fast, yes, but inelegant, off-putting. She wore only what was expected of her by her team, by her coach, by her mother, by training, training, training. So he nudged the conversation toward her suits as if he'd only seen them on her posts.

He convinced her to visit a Victoria's Secret where, too quickly, nervously, she picked out a beach robe, charged it in an awkward moment with a shaky screen signature, and left in a flustered hurry, as she admitted to him later. Good enough for now. A week later he doctored an address label on a Victoria's Secret swimsuit flyer and left it in her mailbox on top of *Swimmer's Monthly* (she'd think she made the mailing list with her credit card purchase).

"…You can't swim off like this. Let them know you were pretty all along. Let them know how pretty you are now. Let the suit be slow, slight, elegant, for your last swim. There's no hurry. Let your hair drape and trail…"

She never mentioned the mailer, but told him she was planning to go back to the mall for a suit.

"…let your hair trail slowly with a ribbon waving through it.

There shouldn't be any hurry. There's only the water that's been your comfort, your home all along."

⧗

THE SHOE GIRL, Cobbie, was a bit odd in a different way: all that money, and she bought her only happiness in shoes, mostly at Chaucette's, and only when the young man with the soft hands was on shift. She lived alone in a sixth-floor apartment on Mercer Island, drove through the tunnel and downtown to Pioneer Square to buy shoes, then uptown for a walk about Seattle Center or Lake Union, on the pavements or the docks, whichever best set off her shoes of the day—and all of them posted on her wall like a Macy's website.

With Cobbie, he thought he had miscalculated from the way she signed off so quickly in her last message to him. But the quickness must have been to keep the resolve that they had worked on together: just "Bye." And two evenings later she had "fallen" as he had imagined it to her.

It did seem especially right, since she had done most of the talking, dropping ideas to him in her typing flurries:

"...and I saw this stupid ad: 'Clothes make the man, but shoes make the woman.' Then I realized that it wasn't so stupid in another way. I mean, we always talk about being in other people's shoes, don't we, and why not? So I buy shoes that are not me and I slip into them and they're like me and not like me and I like that ..."

"I've noticed when you talk about all the different shoes on your page you have a little different style for each pair, like a writer shifting voices, just small subtle changes that seem so right, so genuine..."

"...but the high heels *really* change me. They're really, really *not* me. I'm flats and sandals, but I've learned to walk in all these heels better than anyone I know. The downstairs neighbor complained a few times about my practicing, but not anymore. I glide. I do, as gently as I used to in a *pas de bourrée*."

"You should post a video, show how it's done. So many women

make heels an awkward exhibition—walking peg-legged on stilts and clomping like horses."

"…and my foot's that perfect size 8B, not too large or clunky, not too small to notice."

And so he replied, when she let up and let him, that flats, especially sandals, showed a person's most natural side.

"Thanks, you *are* a friend, not just some blab-blog post-it-all person that friended me. You befriended me." She said it as if she had discovered that turn of phrase herself, as if he had never written it to her.

Coming upon the silver sandals in Banana Republic was a bit of luck. He sent them to her, size 8B. Just a symbol of her own true nature, he said in the gift note and repeated in the email, the last to her. Yes, he was afraid he overdid it there—not to mention his talk about Mercury, the airborne messenger of the gods with the winged silver sandals, and her own mercurial nature that could slip into the style of others—but apparently not. From her, just "Bye," and two days later she let herself go.

⌛

THE BOTANIST'S posts were a case study in pathos on her best mornings, bathos on an average afternoon, and agonizing embarrassment, even for the readers, on her worst evenings. She called herself Ivy, pretty corny for a gardener, except that the name was short for *Ivory*. Her wall was an endless scroll of plants with human names: Mario for marigold, Daphne for daffodil, Mindy for mint, Sandra for pachysandra, Drake for mandrake, Camille for chamomile.

She grew from pathetic to sympathetic after she agreed to email: "…the plants—they respond to my care. They don't run away. They grow in a way that I would grow if the men…if I … No, that's too egotistical, too egocentric."

And so he grew into his poised empathy: "But there's nothing wrong with trying to find someone like yourself to respond to. It's not your fault that so very few men are as caring as yourself, as nurturing. How is it wrong to wish men more like yourself?"

And then, "*Ironic*, isn't it, that I've got the whole world on my roof—240 species from literally everywhere, 241 if the mandrake survives—its root goes deeper than any planter—and not a visitor to see them. Well, only this Cassie—a shy one herself. I think she mistook my orientation at Caffe Ladro. She came home with me that day. She came by a few times after and couldn't quite say what she had in mind, pretending some interest in the mandrake, the maca, the horny goat weed—the aphrodisiacs, I mean. I could have smiled at her or cried for her."

For Ivy, the whole world was ironic, and she was a shy soul in its bitter shell, but he could not acquiesce to her veiled, perhaps unconscious, plea to visit her.

"Your garden, your plants—they can help *you* now…"

It all sounded so absurd, even with the other two successfully rescued from themselves. Still, with this third girl, he had these wavering moments when he recalled again his surprise, his regret perhaps, that anyone would be taken in by suggestions that a healthy psyche would reject in an instant. But these three could not see through to an alternative, and so those moments, his wavering instants, passed into hours of shaping kind ways out for them.

With Ivy, he had learned yet more of patience, and it paid. He told her he would give her a little time to sort through her thoughts, to search through her rooftop garden for that special plant which might bring her final comfort. No need for her to write back until then. And he'd write the end of the week in any case. Friday, he'd said.

But Ivy was gone by Tuesday, according to the obit, and now a nagging point returned to him: It was a bit disconcerting that the police had not bothered to read Spark's or Cobbie's email, as far as he could tell, because their deaths had been declared accidental. Likely they wouldn't check Ivy's email either. Shoddy detective work really. Was it only the television cops who checked the deceased's correspondence? Disconcerting, yes, and disappointing that all his hard work would go unnoted, unappreciated, even. Still, he could console himself, knowing contentedly that the girls had been thankful to him at the end.

☒

KINCADE HAVRE, Seattle Medical Examiner, sensed that Detective Doorframe from Bellevue was halfway between impatient and bored, but she had done her work carefully and wasn't going to waste it in a rushed explanation.

"It was just a precaution I took in one of those 'what if?' moments—keeping the blood, I mean. I thought she just plain overextended herself, went out too far even for a competitive swimmer. Could have been a suicide though, and I couldn't completely dismiss the mother's opinion that it was. She claimed her daughter always wore those racing suits and a cap, never a string bikini like that one or a bow in her hair.

"Team or no team, she was a loner and just a freshman, according to her mother, and this skimpy suit was 'over the edge.' But, hey, not even mothers know everything their daughters wear when they're out on their own. Anyhow, I found nothing in the usual drug and toxin screens but, as a precaution, I kept a tube of her blood in the cooler."

Half a nod from Doorframe.

"There was another 'what if' moment with the faller—or the leaper—that the Mercer Island Force sent over. Now, she'd had maybe a couple servings of wine. Plus, the two witnesses—junior high sweethearts—said it looked like she was balancing herself on that railing, but the more they got to talking about what they saw way up on that balcony, the more they thought she might have been daring death to come get her. I don't know what happened on that balcony, especially since she had trained in ballet and could probably do quite a balancing act. Still, the silver sandals seemed wrong for a toe step on a railing."

Havre turned to open a drawer of a stainless steel refrigerator.

"I kept a blood sample from her, too, even though she wasn't drunk. I figured if anything turned up in the personals on her computer or phone, or from her family about her state of mind, I might have to reconsider a suicide and run additional tests. But no word from the family or the detectives who'd been too busy with the SAM sculpture heist and the Mercer boat launch shootings to think that these girls' phones or laptops needed their attention."

Doorframe's eyebrows pinched into a little more interest.

"I found the 'what if' in the third girl—actually she was older, in her late twenties, but she looked so young and girlish. She was obviously poisoned, and she had to know her last tea was lethal because she grew her own teas and she was something of an expert on plants, judging from the two hundred and some species on that apartment rooftop in Belltown."

Doorframe was *definitely* interested. Kincade continued.

"When I heard about her garden, I went there yesterday to have a look for myself: teas, spices, too many herbs I didn't recognize, flesh-eating flowers, aphrodisiacs alleged and actual, lots of poisonous stuff from mild to scary—oleander, nightshade, monkshood, and, of all things, poison hemlock, the Socrates brand. That was the tea root that finished her...funny though, the little patio table in the roof garden was set for two, but there wasn't any tea in the second cup, just water...anyhow, hemlock can be a relatively easy way to go if the muscle paralysis comes on early, and it could have."

"Socrates? Hemlock?" Doorframe puffed a breath through his lips. "Death with dignity? And courage?"

"Good guess, given her knowledge of flora and the library in her apartment. This time I ran drug and toxin screens for everything I could think of. That's when I found the 'what if' in her blood. It's some distant relative of the benzodiazepines, but I couldn't find a name for this particular variety. Turned out it's not on any market, legal or illegal. So I called my ex at Med Labs 21 over your way in Bellevue. Sure enough, this stuff is brand new, and it happens to be theirs. But it was shelved by Research and Development after the first 'off-the-record' human testing. It was supposed to be a breakthrough in anti-anxiety meds, among other things, to counter irrational inhibitions that lead patients to failure."

"Some kind of success drug?" A mutual smile from Doorframe and Havre.

"Nothing's ever going to be that easy. This drug works too well as designed and otherwise—virtually erases inhibitions and makes the subjects pliant, extremely vulnerable to suggestion. The labcoats at Med 21 were joking about selling this stuff to the carnival hypnotists. It's as bad as—no maybe worse than—the date rape drugs.

"So, as you've already guessed," Havre concluded, finally satisfied that she had one hundred percent of the detective's attention, "I screened the other two girls' blood samples for this Fearless Fog as the lab techs are calling it, and there it was in both of them."

"You've done half my homework for me." The detective smiled his first show of thanks.

DETECTIVE DOORFRAME SPENT the latter half of his Thursday afternoon drinking coffee with Chief Lintel because it had cost him less than two hours after lunch to figure out who had taken the Fearless Fog off the shelf at Med 21 and slipped it to the three women: Wendell Swiver, the young custodian with full access to the labs and a penchant for boring his co-workers about his triumphs in computer gaming and landing dates with the hotties.

Some of the coffee talk with the chief concerned the difficult and intriguing part: how to prove Swiver intended to *murder* the first two young women, since the drug itself was not toxic at the dosage levels in their blood. But that was a job for the busy suits in Seattle or Mercer where the women had died. They could pick up Swiver and plan their own strategy.

"IMPOSSIBLE." Used to talking to himself over the newspaper or at the screen, Timothy was suddenly wordless, except for "Impossible."

He dropped the local section of the Friday *Times* and checked the *Post-Intelligencer* on his screen. Same story:

A Seattle man, Wendell Swiver, was arrested Thursday in Bellevue for the suspected homicide of a twenty-eight-year-old Belltown woman. The police described the deceased only as a botanist found dead Tuesday in her garden.

Swiver is also being investigated in connection with the deaths of a female university athlete and a twenty-year-old Mercer Island woman. Their deaths in July and August, previously declared accidental, are now being re-examined as possible homicides.

Swiver was described only as a custodian who worked in Bellevue.

⏳

Timothy had not gone to the rented storage bin in Queen Anne to check his cloaked email since Sunday night, when he'd told Ivy he'd give her time on her own, and after reading her obit yesterday morning, he felt no need to check. But now…Yes, she might have left him something that would explain.

But there was no message from Ivy, and just one message dated Thursday at 10:31 a.m.:

Hey Programmer,

Nice chicks, really, they were, Spark, Cobbie, and Ivy. But they were just GIRLS in a GAME, and I told you: I know how to talk to girls and how to play the GAME, SET, and MATCH. As you know, that comes right after "LoveFortyMatchPoint." But I have to give you credit: a good modus operandi on your part. Set up things nicely for me. One thing though, Mercury's sandals were not silver. Thinking of quicksilver maybe? Better luck "BEfriending" your next set of girls.

Gamer

Oh yeah, P.S., I wiped all their mail between you and them. Kind of incriminating, don't you think? Even with all those precautions against tracing it to you, you never know what might get back to you—me, for instance. I'd close up that little basement office over in Queen Anne. And you should definitely check your credit card bill this month. It's been a little tight for me, and I had to put a few downloads on your tab.

Timothy grimaced. Hacked by a mere gamer—and none of the girls thankful to him in their last thoughts.

C.C. GUTHRIE

C.C. Guthrie's short stories appear in several anthologies, including *Fish Out of Water, Busted! Arresting Stories From The Beat, Landfall: The Best New England Crime Stories: 2018, Fishy Business* and *Me Too Short Stories: An Anthology.* A member of Sisters in Crime International and Guppy Chapter, she lives near Fort Worth, Texas. Find her on Goodreads.

A SURE THING

C.C. GUTHRIE

THE JOB OFFER came as another late season storm took aim at winter-weary Buffalo. Faced with the prospect of more snow, Rocco Sakarian only had one question for the caller: "Where's the hit?"

He'd heard of Oklahoma, thought there was a song about it, but had never been there. Wasn't even sure if it was in the south or the west. He ignored the voice squawking from his cellphone and pulled up the Oklahoma weather report. The state's forecast high temperature sealed the deal.

With thoughts of clear sixty-degree days clouding his judgment, Rocco didn't question why someone wanted him to kill an eighty-year-old cattle rancher. A job was a job. No worries about confronting a marathon runner, a weightlifter, or a tech-savvy millennial. It was a sure thing.

The prospective client went into justification mode, as they all did, so Rocco switched his phone to speaker, lowered the volume, and settled in to watch the live-action pinball game outside his front window. While a snowplow worked its way up the street, moving a mixture of dirty and newly fallen snow onto parked cars and sidewalks, the rival rancher spewed out complaints about Abigail Hawkins.

"…don't underestimate her," the voice said. "It has to be done before her kids get back in town on Sunday. You got that?"

Rocco pumped a fist when the plow slammed into a car.

The voice bellowed from the phone. "Hey, you still there?"

"Still here," Rocco said. "Heard every word. No worries. Gotta plan."

When the caller's litany of grievances slowed, Rocco seized back control and presented his fee and payment demands. Eager to rid himself of a troublesome competitor, the client accepted the terms.

TULSA WAS flat as Rocco expected, but the scenery changed as he drove southeast, and small mountains appeared on the horizon. In the town nearest the Hawkins ranch, he checked into an anonymous chain motel, and went in search of lunch.

He waited for his food, and checked out the location of the Hawkins place, something he'd meant to do before he left Buffalo. The map app showed the ranch on a minor county road several miles off a state highway. But the app didn't have a street view, so he couldn't see the surrounding area. Then he remembered, it didn't matter. Hawkins was an eighty-year-old woman. While he ate, he planned a side trip to Dallas to celebrate the successful kill.

Rocco left the restaurant and drove to Hawkins' property, where he had his first inkling this kill wouldn't be like all the others. Her house, perched high on a bluff, overlooked a river valley. One glance and he knew surveillance tactics that worked for hits in Trenton, Hartford, and Providence wouldn't work in rural Sugarloaf County, Oklahoma.

The roads around the ranch were also a problem. The paved ones had potholes that looked large enough to swallow his rental, but the dirt roads were the real threat. An encounter with a tricked-out black pickup drove home the danger when the big F150 blew past, the percussive blast echoing like a drive-by gunfire barrage.

Instinctively, he slammed his car into park and drew. Heart pounding, he swiveled, ready for a firefight, only to see gravel ricochet off the truck's wheel rims and rear fender as the truck disappeared into a blooming cloud of dust. He waited for his heart rate to return to normal and stared up at the bluff. The house at the top mocked him. There wasn't enough traffic on the road for him to blend in, and he couldn't sneak up undetected. From her high perch, Abigail Hawkins would either see him approach or hear the clatter of rocks bounce off the car on his drive up. He had to adjust the plan.

Blind without a street view on his map app, he was forced to explore the surrounding roads for a way to access Hawkins' land. Finally he chanced on a rutted track along the river near her land, hid his car behind a cluster of junipers, and set off on foot. Two bloodied hands and a torn sleeve later, he mastered the art of climbing through barbed-wire fence. He paused above a fast flowing creek to savor the triumph. Seconds later, the ground crumbled beneath him. An explosion of dirt, dead leaves, and old tree limbs engulfed him in an eight-foot drop that ended on a muddy spot beside the water. Debris rained down and he gasped for breath. But when he saw a large brown and tan snake four feet away, air exploded from his lungs. The snake's tail was raised and vibrating.

Rocco locked eyes with it and stared in trance-like fascination. Then he heard the sound. Faint at first, but it grew louder, more persistent, and closer. His eyes bulged at the strain to remain still. A snake bite might kill him, but an insect buzzing in his ear would drive him crazy. Without warning, the snake moved. It zigged left, zagged right, and slithered between a knot of twisted tree roots beside the creek. The moment the tail disappeared, he raced up the embankment and into the sunlight, his only thought to get away from the creek.

By the time he realized he was running in the wrong direction, away from the Hawkins land and back to the river, he didn't care. Primitive roads and wild kingdom adventures were not part of his plan. Fed up, ready to call it a day, he hurried across open pasture, on alert for other animal encounters, but all he saw were birds. They ran beside him and skittered ahead. High above, a dark shadow hovered, darted, and emitted a repetitive thrum. In the distance, a long-legged gray bird took flight and made a slow, lazy turn over the river.

Motivated by images of cold beer and rare steak, he picked up the pace when he saw the scrubby junipers that camouflaged his rental. Intent on returning to civilization, he didn't notice the car's pronounced tilt toward the river until he opened the door. After a series of savage kicks at the fender, he maneuvered the rental away from the river's edge so he could access the flat. While he changed the tire, the sun retreated behind gray clouds and a cool breeze chased off the afternoon humidity.

In the time it took Rocco to put away the flat tire and jack and return to the highway, the weather changed again. A pronounced green hue replaced the pewter-colored sky, and in the distance a bank of clouds formed a towering wall that darkened like a fresh bruise. Wind howled, rain sluiced down his windshield and oncoming drivers switched on headlights. Rising water prompted others to pull off the road, but he plowed through, never noticing that the time between lightening flashes and thunder crashes grew shorter.

After parking at the motel, he grabbed the door handle, ready for a sprint through the rain, when his car shuddered violently. Thunder rumbled, the sky lit up and an electrical transformer exploded in front of him. A glowing fireball shot sparks across the parking lot. Rocco peered through the top of his windshield, up at the storm that showed no sign of moving. He waited out the weather in his car and used the time to revise his plan to kill Abigail Hawkins.

The next morning, evidence of the storm's ferocity littered the motel property. A deflated soccer ball, part of a kayak, and a tricycle missing wheels were smashed against the fence that surrounded the swimming pool. A splintered tree branch with burn marks lay across the shattered windshield of the pickup next to Rocco's rental. But he saw the cloudless blue sky as a sign his luck was about to change. His optimism lasted until he spotted a flat on his car.

He gave the tire a therapeutic kick and started for the trunk, only to remember the spare was already in use. His only option was a call for roadside assistance and the hope that a cash payment, a tip, not big enough to be memorable, and his false ID would keep the transaction anonymous. While he waited for help to arrive, he paced the parking lot, muttered about poorly maintained roads, and vowed never to return to Sugarloaf County, Oklahoma.

By the time he had two new tires, the county courthouse was open for business and a line had formed in the Tax Assessor's Office. He eavesdropped on the conversations around him about topics he didn't understand. A portly man and a scrawny hawk-nosed woman in front of him debated a recent Sunday sermon. Behind him, a petite woman with chic gray hair, and a weathered woman who looked like she wrestled steers, discussed the merits of critter cams.

Ten minutes and thirty dollars later, Rocco left the courthouse with a spiral-bound book of maps that showed the ownership of every parcel of land in the county. On his way back to his car, he whistled a jaunty tune to celebrate his new plan to kill Abigail Hawkins. But the closer he got to his car, the more he questioned two flats in two days. When he noticed the Sooner State Farmer's Co-op across from the parking lot, he detoured to test his theory. He wandered through the store, looking at items he never knew existed and couldn't imagine needing, until he found his way to the sales counter. He flashed a grin at the young clerk. "My brother-in-law's birthday is coming up. I'd like to get him a critter cam."

She returned his smile with a mouthful of metal. "We don't stock the cameras, but lots of places sell them online."

He leaned in for long chat. "Do they really work?"

She gushed HD, LCD, SD, motion-activated, trigger interval, no glow, infrared flash, wireless-compatible techno-babble. The more she talked and shared what she knew, the calmer Rocco grew. With a logical explanation for the events of the last twenty-four hours, he left the store whistling another lively tune.

Back at his car, he found all four tires in working order and gave a silent cheer that he could return to his plan to take out Hawkins. But his outlook wavered when he found his car door unlocked. On the driver's seat was a burlap sack tied shut with a rope. Rocco surveyed the parking lot and relaxed. Most of the cars looked like his anonymous sedan. He forgot that he didn't believe in coincidences and reached for the bag. His fingers brushed against the rough fabric and the sack moved. He took a step back. It moved again.

"You okay there?"

Rocco's scalp tingled. He turned, forced a smile at the barrel-chested sheriff's deputy in front of him, and gestured at his front seat. "Hi, officer. Someone made a mistake. That's my car, but that sack isn't mine."

"You know what's in it, sir?" The deputy rested his hand on his holster and studied the bag.

"No, it was here when I came back from the courthouse."

"Sir, take a step back." After the deputy keyed his shoulder radio and asked George to respond to the courthouse parking lot, he gave Rocco a long look. "You aren't from around here, are you?"

Before Rocco could reply, the two women who stood behind him in the tax office line walked up. The deputy doffed his hat. "Miz Gail, Miz Rita."

They returned the greeting and eyed Rocco with frank curiosity but the arrival of a service truck emblazoned with the county logo stopped them from asking awkward questions and they continued on their way. The deputy greeted George and the two men stood a healthy distance from Rocco's car while they discussed the sack.

The longer the men talked, the uneasier Rocco grew. He was about to demand an explanation when a large black pickup drove up. A tinted window slid down to reveal the driver was the small gray-haired woman the deputy addressed as Miz Gail. She smiled at Rocco and waved the deputy over.

"Dub, I clean forgot to ask about your Aunt Lily. I heard she's in the hospital in Tulsa. Please tell your momma I'm thinking about y'all." She turned to Rocco. "I hope Dub gets you all fixed up. This is a nice town, and we don't like it when people have problems." She gave Rocco a wink and drove off at a speed that sent a spray of gravel shooting behind her.

"That Miz Gail, always thinking about others," Deputy Dub

said. "You'd never know she's the richest woman in the county and tough as nails. She once walked right up to a rabid coyote and shot it between the eyes before it could attack one of her calves. She's got the best aim in the county, man or woman, and nerves of steel." The deputy returned to George's side and the two men continued their discussion.

Finally, George ambled back to his truck and retrieved a pole with a hook. With a determined look, he transferred the sack from the car to a tall plastic container, maneuvered the rope off, and tipped out the contents. The deputy and George peered into the bucket.

George looked up at Rocco and narrowed his eyes. "So, Mister, who's out to get you?"

Rocco eased up to the container and looked in. At the bottom was a large brown and tan snake, its tail raised and vibrating.

"Been a long time since I've seen one that big," Deputy Dub said.

"Well-fed," George agreed. He shifted his toothpick to the other side of his mouth. "That is one big copperhead."

The deputy shook his head and gave Rocco a sad look. "It's a good thing Miz Gail isn't here. She'd be sorely disappointed that you've got all this trouble."

"Yessirree Bob," George said. "That snake would surely upset Miz Abigail Hawkins."

Memory of the woman's wink flooded back and Rocco felt his blood pressure spike. "The woman who just left was Abigail Hawkins?"

Deputy Dub cocked his head. "You know about her, do you?"

Rocco tamped down the rage he felt over her taunt. "My brother-in-law told me about the Hawkins Ranch. He and my sister plan to retire around here." He held up the book of maps and land descriptions. "They asked me to buy this on my way through town so they can match up online real estate listings with the location in the county."

He'd barely finished the explanation when the deputy and George began to pelt him with questions about why someone would put a venomous snake in his car. But he stuck to his story about being a stranger in town. Finally George clamped a lid on the container, put it in the back of his truck and left, followed shortly by the deputy.

Rocco gave his car one last check and drove to Hawkins' ranch. The whole time he plotted his revenge with new enthusiasm and didn't notice the bright blue sky dissolve into a muddy gray. The first thing he saw when he arrived was a black F150 pickup in the driveway. That was all the motivation he needed to implement his carefully calibrated new plan, Operation Double Down. On the county road in front of her house, he gunned his car engine three times and crawled past her property at a pace that demanded attention.

At the quarter mile mark, he executed a three-point turn and returned to his starting point. He repeated the maneuver two more times. On each pass, he eyed a string of outbuildings of various ages, styles, and sizes that fronted the road. The most interesting, a modern hanger-shaped metal structure, looked large enough to house an airplane. His curiosity piqued, he parked and went to inspect it.

Intrigued by the elaborate lock that secured the tall sliding doors, he leaned in for a closer look when the left front tire on his car exploded. He drew, turned, and dropped to a knee. The back tire blew. In disbelief, he watched a third shot shatter his windshield. Now he knew why someone wanted the Hawkins woman dead.

Sure that she was positioned high in the building behind him, he waited for her next shot to take out his gas tank, but the explosion never came. In the unexpected silence, he heard a persistent low-pitched hum. Above, just out of reach, was a bouncing shadow.

Thanks to his new friend at the Co-op, Rocco knew the drone was likely recording his every move. Before he could blast it out of the sky, it lurched around the corner. He followed and watched it hover briefly along the edge of the metal roof before it darted behind the building.

Before he could follow, a sharp clap of thunder broke his concentration and stopped him in his tracks. The gray sky shifted and turned an ominous shade of green. In the distance, a black wall of roiling clouds soared up. With the image of exploding electrical lines still fresh in his mind, he assessed the wisdom of standing next to a metal structure during a storm and returned to the front of the building where he found the big sliding doors open. Thunder crashed and his hair crackled seconds before multiple flashes of lightning lit up the sky. An extended blast of thunder masked the sound of a massive tractor roll out of the building. The large bucket on the front of the twelve-foot tall machine loomed above and blocked his view of the driver.

Confidant he was more nimble than the machine and could outwit the driver, Rocco stepped to one side. The tractor followed. At each turn, he responded more tightly until he was backed against the building, the tractor advancing. With the machine a scant three feet away, he ducked, shot past at an angle, and ran flat-out.

To his left was the edge of the bluff, steep enough the tractor might tip over if it followed him down. He could circle back to the hanger-like building and use it for shelter, but it could also trap him. The Hawkins house was in front of him. He ran for it, past a brick patio bordered by a curved pergola to the far corner. Through still-bare tree branches he watched the tractor roll up the drive and park behind the black pickup. He drew and braced for a shot. The machine stopped, the engine went off, but the cab door in front of him remained closed.

When light flashed in the cab's interior, Rocco knew he'd made a mistake. Hawkins exited through a second door, one on the far side of the cab, and was on the move. He kicked the side of the house next to a row of narrow foundation-level windows and almost missed hearing a hinge squeak and a door slam. He edged around the house for a better look, but a wide front porch blocked his view. Sure that she would burst out the back door shooting, Rocco looked for a better place to regroup.

The sky lit up and illuminated his choices. If he went down the bluff he would be forced to cross open pasture and risk a lightning hit or sniper shot from above. He could go halfway down and run the length. Lightning would still be a risk, but he was confident that Hawkins wouldn't follow and risk her eighty-year-old hips.

The wind shifted as he began his descent. Rain blew directly into his face, slicing at his skin like shards of glass and obscuring his visibility in the muddy slosh down. He felt rather than saw the ground level out. To his left was a notch in the bluff. A wide rock projected out to offer protection from the rain and lightning. He backed into the hollowed-out area and felt a wood doorframe built into the dirt wall behind him. From a crouch, he pulled open the door and counted to ten. When nothing happened, he stood up and stepped into darkness.

In front of him, lightning backlit a row of high narrow windows. Thunder crashed and the space went dark. Rocco balanced on the balls of his feet, ready to bolt when white light exploded in his face. It went out and was replaced by a pinpoint red beam. The dot moved from right to left and he imagined it crawl across his forehead before it paused in what he thought was a spot between his eyes. Then the red light dropped and stopped over his heart.

"You've got a choice," a woman's voice said. "You stay in my storm cellar, and we both know how this will end. You take your chances outside with the tornado, and you might survive so you can go back where you came from."

Rocco changed the plan again. He decided uncertainty was better than a sure thing.

ROSEMARY MCCRACKEN

Rosemary McCracken writes the Pat Tierney mystery series: *Safe Harbor*, which was a finalist for Britain's Debut Dagger, *Black Water*, and *Raven Lake*. Her short fiction has appeared in various collections and magazines. "The Sweetheart Scamster" was shortlisted for a Derringer award in 2014. Rosemary is a member of Sisters in Crime National and Toronto, the Short Mystery Fiction Society, Crime Writers of Canada, and the Mesdames of Mayhem. She lives in Toronto and teaches novel writing at George Brown College. Find her at rosemarymccracken.com.

THE SWEETHEART SCAMSTER

ROSEMARY MCCRACKEN

"MRS. SULLIVAN IS HERE for her appointment," Rose Sisto, my administrative assistant, announced at my office door.

I looked up from the papers I was studying as Trudy Sullivan slipped into the chair across from my desk.

"Good morning, Pat," she said.

I smiled at my client. Trudy's silver hair had been cut in an attractive new style. She was wearing more makeup than usual, and it accentuated her high cheekbones and deep blue eyes. She was also sporting a smart fall suit. New hairdo, new makeup, new clothes. She looked fabulous—and far younger than her seventy-four years.

"A new man in your life, Trudy?" But as soon as the words were out of my mouth, I wanted to bite them back. Trudy had been mourning her husband's death for the past three years. I wasn't sure how she'd take my flip question.

"As a matter of fact, there is. I'm seeing a nice gentleman."

I realized then how lonely Trudy had been. She was Ernie's second wife, and from what he'd told me, they'd had a happy marriage. She became my client after his accident, and I'd been meeting with her every four months. She was a reserved woman, not given to joining clubs and social groups, and I had the impression that she had few friends. Her two daughters lived in other cities, and Ernie's sons seemed to have dropped her after their father's death. Yes, she had been lonely, but now she had someone in her life.

And that made me sit up straight in my chair. As a financial advisor, I'm well aware there are complexities to grey romance that are seldom present in youthful relationships. Ernie had been a heavy gambler, so Trudy had to be careful with her money. But she had his big home in Toronto's Beaches neighbourhood and enough investment income to stay there as long as her good health continued. I wanted to know more about this friend of hers. A lonely woman can be an easy mark for fortune hunters.

"What's your gentleman's name?" I asked.

"Jim." She didn't give his surname.

"I take it Jim's retired."

"Oh, yes."

"You see him on weekends? Saturday night dates?"

"Not just on weekends." She lowered her eyes again. "You might say we've become very close."

This romance had got off to a galloping start.

"We're not living together," she said, "but who knows...?"

I needed to ask some hard questions about Jim. What he did during his working years, where he lived, if he had a family. But I wasn't sure how to begin.

"Let's go over your investment portfolio." I hoped an opening would present itself there.

My mind was clicking away as I showed her the changes I'd made to her investments and explained why.

"Does Jim work with a financial advisor?" I asked when I'd finished.

"I don't know. He's never brought it up and I've never asked him."

Of course not. Trudy's generation of women considers it crass to talk about money.

Then she surprised me by asking for some.

"I need a bit extra this month, Pat. Ten thousand dollars."

Ten thousand dollars. I was about to launch into my spiel about living within her budget, but she beat me to it.

"You're going to say I mustn't run through my money if I want to stay in the house. Well, I may sell it."

I nearly fell out of my chair. Trudy had been adamant about remaining in her home even though she would have had more money to live on if she'd downsized. Was Jim pressuring her to sell the house?

"It's something I'm considering," she continued, "but for now I need ten thousand dollars. Cash me out of some bonds."

It was her money, of course, but I wanted to know why she needed it. "You're planning something nice?" I asked.

She looked me in the eye. "A surprise for Jim."

I swallowed hard, and thought of contacting her daughters. But I quickly dismissed that idea. It would be a breach of client confidentiality.

I looked at the woman seated across from me. Trudy was a competent adult with every right to form a new relationship and do whatever she wanted with her money.

I told her the ten grand would be in her bank account in a few days. But I had grave misgivings as I watched her leave my office.

"You look worried," my business partner Stéphane Pratt said when he sat down in the client's chair five minutes later.

I told him about Trudy's new beau, and that she planned to surprise him with a lavish gift.

"You think he's one of those sweetheart scamsters?" Stéphane asked.

"Is that what they're called?"

"I watched a television program on sweetheart fraud," he said. "The scamster tries to win the affection of a lonely person, then takes over his or her financial affairs. When the money is gone, the sweetheart leaves the victim."

"Trudy was very astute when we went over Ernie's financial statements, and now she wants updates on all her holdings. I can't see her falling prey to one of those crooks." But I couldn't shake the idea that she'd been taken in by a con man who would leave her destitute and heartbroken.

Stéphane gave me a tight smile. "When people fall in love, common sense flies out the window."

A WEEK LATER, Trudy reached me on my cell phone. As soon as I heard her voice, I braced myself for a request for more money.

"I thought I'd let you know that Jim and I are getting married," she said. "I'm changing my will. My lawyer will send you a copy."

"Married!" Then I remembered my manners. "I wish you every happiness, Trudy. When's the big day?"

"Friday."

"This Friday?"

"We're not getting any younger, so there's no point in waiting. We'll go down to city hall with Jim's friend, Kenneth, and his wife. Then we'll all go out for lunch."

"The girls won't be at your wedding?"

"We thought we'd surprise Beth and Mary Lou afterwards."

Red flags went up in my mind. It sounded like Jim was pressuring her into a hasty marriage. Not giving her time for second thoughts. And by not telling her daughters until after the wedding, they couldn't talk her out of it.

I was about to ask whether she and Jim had drawn up a marriage contract, but she told me she was off to visit her hairdresser and hung up.

Once again, I thought of contacting her daughters, but my professional ethics prevented me. And there was a possibility I was mistaken. I'd never met Jim. He might be just the man to brighten Trudy's golden years. Then I thought of the will she was changing. Had that been her idea—or Jim's? And what were the changes?

After work that day, I dropped by Trudy's home with a bottle of champagne. The FOR SALE sign on the front lawn put me into full alert.

If Trudy was surprised to see me, she didn't show it. She was perfectly turned out in a plum-colored dress and a pearl necklace. As I handed her the champagne, a white-haired man hobbled into the hall with the help of a cane.

"My fiancé, Jim," Trudy said. "Honey, this is Pat Tierney, my financial advisor."

She took my coat, and Jim led me into the living room, where he poured glasses of sherry. He handed me a glass, and clinked his against Trudy's.

I raised my glass to them. "To the happy couple. May you have years of health and happiness together, although I see it won't be here. You're selling the house."

"Yes," Trudy said. "We're looking at condos downtown."

I wondered if Jim had a home of his own to sell, but I decided that this was a social call. I'd arrange a meeting with Trudy after the wedding to go over the financial implications of her new situation. I'd suggest that Jim attend as well. But there was one question I couldn't resist asking.

"Do you have a family, Mr.—"

"Call me Jim," he said with a twinkle in his eyes. "No family, unfortunately. My late wife Rita and I weren't blessed with children."

I settled into an armchair with my sherry. They took seats on the sofa across from me.

"How did you two meet?" I asked.

"On an Alaskan cruise in June." Trudy held up a hand. "Don't worry, Pat. It didn't cost me a penny. Beth and her husband, Steve, wanted me to see my new grandson. They paid for my flight to Vancouver, and I stayed with them a week. Then they put me on the cruise."

Jim took her hand and looked at me. "We were seated at the same table at the captain's dinner. We chatted, found we had common interests. I don't think either of us realized until then how lonely we were, Trudy without Ernie and me without Rita. We began seeing each other when we got back to Toronto, and...well, here we are." He gave Trudy a peck on the cheek.

I pasted a smile on my face, and they told me more about their wedding plans. Trudy said she'd made a reservation for a late lunch at La Madeleine, an upscale restaurant in trendy Yorkville, that they planned to spend the weekend at the Four Seasons Hotel down the street. They seemed to be looking forward to their life together.

I tried to find out more about their living arrangements. "When will you move downtown?"

"We'll stay here until the house sells," Trudy said.

Jim tapped his left hip with his cane. "I avoid stairs whenever I can, so a home without them makes sense. Fortunately, this house has a main-floor bedroom with an ensuite."

"Then why not stay here?" I asked.

"We thought we should make a fresh start," Trudy said. "In a home of our own."

It sounded like the sale of her house would finance the condo. With money left over for two to live on.

Trudy gave Jim a sunny smile. "Honey, I have a surprise for you." She glanced at me. "I've booked us on a cruise for our honeymoon. A ten-day Mediterranean vacation."

So that was what she wanted the money for. The cruise seemed to be her idea, but I wondered if Jim had planted it in her mind.

"Sweetheart." He took both her hands in his and chuckled. "And I thought you had your heart set on Niagara Falls."

I could see the lovebirds wanted to be alone, so I finished my sherry and wished them happiness again.

"I'll see you to your car," Trudy said.

Outside the house, she turned to look at me. "Well?" Her blue eyes were shining.

"I think he's landed quite a catch." I paused. "There are financial implications to marriage, Trudy. Jim will own half your home."

She put a hand on my arm. "Don't worry. I know what I'm doing." She gave me a little wave as I drove off.

Jim was charming, I mused on the way home. But was he too charming? And did he really need that cane? I still knew nothing about the man my client would marry in a few days.

The next week, I received a copy of Trudy's will. She had made Jim her sole beneficiary; her daughters weren't even mentioned. I learned Jim's full name, however. James Reynolds. Why did that sound familiar?

I needed to talk to Trudy about her will. Her daughters would be hurt when they learned she hadn't even left them her jewelry. I wrote a note on my calendar to call her in two weeks. I figured she'd be back from her honeymoon by then.

⧗

THE FOLLOWING MONDAY, Stéphane blew into the office suite just before ten. "Bonjour, *ma chère*." He placed a Starbucks latte on my desk and copy of *The Toronto World*. He pointed to the front page of the newspaper. "Take a look."

He had circled an article in blue ink. "Wealthy industrialist James Reynolds dead at 78," the headline read.

JAMES REYNOLDS, FOUNDER AND FORMER CHIEF EXECUTIVE OF THE REYNOLDS GROUP, WHICH DOMINATED CANADA'S AUTOMOTIVE SECTOR IN THE 1970S AND 1980S, DIED THIS WEEKEND ON A HONEYMOON CRUISE OFF THE COAST OF SPAIN.

EARLY SUNDAY MORNING MR. REYNOLDS WAS FOUND CRUMPLED AT THE FOOT OF A STAIRCASE ON THE DECK OF ROBERTSON CRUISES' PRINCESS MARIA. HIS WIFE, THE FORMER GERTRUDE SULLIVAN, SAID HE HAD STUMBLED COMING DOWN THE STAIRS. ACCORDING TO HER STATEMENT TO SPANISH POLICE, SHE CALLED FOR HELP WHEN SHE WAS UNABLE TO REVIVE HIM.

AN AUTOPSY REVEALED A SMALL AMOUNT OF THE TRANQUILIZER BENZODIAZEPINE IN MR. REYNOLDS' BLOOD.

THE COUPLE MARRIED IN TORONTO NINE DAYS BEFORE THE ACCIDENT.

I THOUGHT of Ernie's accident three years before. He and Trudy had been on holiday in Greece when he'd stumbled on a footpath along the top of a cliff and fell to his death below.

I looked up at Stéphane. "My God. It was Trudy who wanted to tie the knot quickly so Jim wouldn't have time for second thoughts. She must have slipped him some of Ernie's medication."

Stéphane looked puzzled.

"She gave him just enough to disorient him and cause him to fall —or be pushed—down that staircase. Jim told me he avoided stairs.

"I thought she was lonely after Ernie died," I went on. "But being alone doesn't necessarily mean being lonely."

A FEW DAYS LATER, I received a letter from Trudy's lawyer saying that she was transferring her account to another investment firm. I thought of going to the police, but what could I tell them? That she'd married a wealthy man who had died soon after the wedding? That he was her second husband to die in a fall?

I thought of her last words to me. *I know what I'm doing.*

She certainly did.

LISA LIEBERMAN

Lisa Lieberman, a historian of postwar Europe, abandoned a perfectly respectable academic career for the life of a vicarious adventurer through dangerous times and places. She writes a historical noir mystery series based on old movies featuring blacklisted Hollywood people on the lam in exotic international locales. Lisa is a member of Mystery Writers of America, the Short Mystery Fiction Society, Sisters in Crime National, and the New England chapter of Sisters in Crime, where she serves as Vice President. She has published essays, translations, and short stories in *Noir City, Mystery Scene, Gettysburg Review, Raritan, Michigan Quarterly*, and elsewhere. Find her at DeathlessProse.com.

BETTER DEAD THAN REDHEAD

LISA LIEBERMAN

I LEANED OVER THE BODY. "Nobody kills herself over a bad hairstyle."

"You didn't know Mimi Courvoisier."

I glanced down at her and quickly turned away. The esthetician lay sprawled across the black leather sofa in the Hospitality Lounge of the Rhode Island Convention Center, her face contorted in agony. The room was dimly lit, but I'd seen enough. Mimi had swallowed the contents of a bottle of hair dye. The empty bottle stood on the coffee table in front of the sofa. Beneath it was a note: I CAN'T LIVE WITH THIS COLOR.

"Couldn't she have just worn a wig until it grew out?"

"She hated wigs. Said you could always tell and believe me, appearances matter. In this business you've got to look authentic."

I gave my sister Alex a slow once-over, starting at her vermillion polished toenails peeking through the cut-out sandals with four-inch heels, working my way up the spray-tanned legs, past the tight skirt with strategic side slit, the shimmery V-neck top that showed off her cleavage. My eyes took in the gold necklace with a diamond pendant that nearly disappeared into said cleavage, moving past her flawlessly made-up face, the lips outlined in a darker shade, then filled in with a creamy gloss that complemented her nail polish, the expertly lined eyes, taupe-shadowed lids, mascaraed lashes, and shaped brows, coming to rest, at last, on the cascading blonde curls —a far cry from my own lank brown hair. You'd never have guessed we were twins.

"Authentic," I said, deadpan. I spoke out loud, but of course Alex had taken my point eons before I opened my mouth. Different as we were, we still knew each other's minds inside out, communing in a kind of nonverbal shorthand we'd perfected well before we entered kindergarten. Now, for example, I was aware of her annoyance with me in the way that you might pick out the top note in a complex perfume. It was noticeable, but it wasn't the essence of Alex's vibe at that moment. Nor did the sight of Mimi Courvoisier's dead body upset her, per se, although she felt badly about the dye job.

"Poor Mimi." Alex dabbed at her eyes with a tissue, careful not to blot away too much concealer. "Red was not her color, I see that now."

I couldn't imagine that lurid shade being anyone's color, apart from Raggedy Ann's, but managed to keep the thought to myself. Alex's career was going down the drain. Her big break, making it through the semi-finals in the cut and color competition at New England's annual hair show. She'd worked so hard to get to this point. One round away from winning and now her model was dead.

"They'll say I drove her to it," Alex wailed. "Nobody will let me come near their hair after this. I'll have to move to another country."

I went to comfort her, but she was too jittery for a hug, pacing the room, planning her future career in South America.

"You know, Ashley. It might not be so bad. Have you seen the women's hair in Brazil? They go in for straightening in a big way down there. I could make good money and it wouldn't be too hard to learn the language. I had Spanish in high school."

"They speak Portuguese," I said. "And wasn't it you who told me that the chemicals in those Brazilian hair treatments will kill you?

Formaldehyde is like signing your own death warrant. Those were your exact words."

Too late, I realized that I'd put my foot in it. Alex gave a hysterical shriek and collapsed into tears. She was sobbing in my arms when the Convention Center security guard burst in.

"Everybody okay in here?" He froze as he took in the scene.

"Call an ambulance," I shouted over my shoulder. I knew it was too late for Mimi, but the flurry of getting the paramedics in to work on her would buy us time—time we sorely needed. The note and the bottle of hair dye had distracted me. I hadn't noticed the blood against the black sofa, the growing pool of blood that was beginning to seep from the cushions onto the floor. I wasn't about to touch the body, but it didn't look like suicide to me. Protective as a mother bear, I led Alex away from the gory scene.

An emergency team from Roger Williams Medical Center arrived in a matter of minutes. Two medics rolled the body onto a backboard before placing her on the stretcher, revealing the true cause of the esthetician's death. The handle of a pair of scissors protruded from Mimi's back, the blades sunk deep into her flesh.

I'D BEEN GETTING DRESSED for work when Alex called, slurping coffee from my commuter cup as I fumbled with the buttons of my zoo uniform. The Roger Williams Park Zoo opened at ten and we needed to have the animals fed and watered, habitats cleaned and ready, before the public arrived. I liked getting in early, to spend time with the chimps, before the other trainers showed up. Mornings were their best time.

"Ashley?" The panic I heard in my sister's voice when I answered the phone explained the sick feeling I'd noticed in the pit of my stomach earlier, while I was in the shower.

"What is it?" I asked, alarmed. "Talk to me."

After twenty-six years, the bond between us was still as strong as when we'd shared a womb. Our mother likes to tell the story of how I waited for my sister to be born. I came out first, and it was another hour before Mom delivered Alex. Throughout that time, I was inconsolable, squalling in the nurse's arms until she arrived. We were small enough to share a bassinet, and the moment they laid us down, side-by-side, we fell asleep. I wasn't surprised that she'd called me before she called 911. I'd always been there for her.

Alex was blubbering into the phone and I couldn't make sense of what she was saying. "Dye job. Killed her. She's dead, Ashley."

"Who's dead?"

"Mimi."

"Who's Mimi?"

"My new partner. It's too awful," she sobbed.

"Where are you?"

"The Convention Center on Sabin Street."

"Hang on," I said. "I'm on my way."

Fortunately, my apartment is in Federal Hill. It's not even a mile down Broadway to the corner of Sabin, faster to run the distance than to get the car and deal with parking on the other end. I made it in a matter of minutes, even in my clunky work boots.

Alex was peeking out anxiously from the rotunda entrance as I approached the vast building at a jog. She'd flung herself at me and led me inside, clinging to my hand all the way down the carpeted corridor to the Hospitality Lounge.

Now she clung to me again as the security guard led us back along the corridor to an empty meeting room. Belatedly, he realized that we were in need of attention. He was a young guy with a weightlifter's physique, an adrenaline junkie eager to get back to the excitement at the crime scene, but he knew how to do his job.

"Will you two ladies be okay for now?" he asked, handing Alex and me each a bottle of water and edging toward the door.

I figured we had five minutes before the cops showed up. "We'll be fine, thank you," I assured him.

Alex opened her bottle of water, tipped her head back and poured a thin stream into her open mouth. I saw her swallow, so I know that some water was getting in, but not a drop escaped to mar the smooth foundation on her chin.

"You know, Ashley," she said, capping the bottle. "I'm inclined to agree with you. Mimi totally overreacted. I could have toned down the color, put on a semi-permanent gloss. Suicide is pretty extreme…"

"She didn't commit suicide. She was stabbed."

"Stabbed?" My sister gasped.

I pushed on. Five minutes didn't allow time for beating around the bush. "You need to tell me everything that happened, from the moment you entered the Hospitality Lounge."

"She was like that when I found her," Alex said.

"Like what?"

"Dead."

"When did you find her?"

"Like, a second before I called you." My sister picked up her phone and tapped the screen with a varnished nail. "The call log says 6:02."

"Did you see anyone in the corridor?"

She shook her pretty blonde head. "The building was deserted. There's supposed to be a security guard in the lobby, checking people's I.D., but I guess it was too early."

"What were you doing at the Convention Center at this hour of the morning?" Anyone listening would have thought I was heartless, but Alex and I were alike in one way. Beneath her polished surface and the soft layer of femininity was a core of steel. And she was savvy, my twin, instantly perceiving the reason I was grilling her.

"I know it looks suspicious, but I had a good reason for being in the building this early in the morning. I'm missing a pair of shears. I thought I'd brought them home last night—they're really expensive —but they weren't in my bag. I thought I'd left them in my traveling kit. The organizers let us keep our supplies in the Hospitality Lounge overnight, those of us who were going on to the final round today." A note of pride crept into her voice.

"Did you find them?" *Please*, I was thinking. *Tell me they were where you left them.*

"No, I didn't, and I'm going to have a word with those organizers. They promised the room would be locked. Only the stylists and our models would have key cards to get in. Well, the door wasn't locked when I got there. It was partly open, and my traveling kit was unzipped. Ashley, I never leave it unzipped. I've got hundreds of dollars of equipment in there."

"What about the shears?"

Alex stamped her sandal-clad foot. "Someone swiped them."

A small ray of sunshine. "Be sure to tell that to the police."

⧗

CRAIG GLUCK's office was on Pleasant View, in the same Smithfield strip mall where my sister had her salon. Convenience must have been the reason she'd chosen him to be her lawyer. It couldn't have been his credentials.

"Where is the Thin Mint Legal Studies Institute?" I said, squinting at the blurry photocopied degree that hung behind Craig's desk.

"Thirment," Craig corrected. "California, I think. It's an accredited online program."

I tried to suppress my incredulity, for Alex's sake. She'd insisted on dragging me out to see her lawyer the minute the detectives told us we were free to leave. Any hope I had of seeing the chimps that morning was gone; reluctantly, I'd called my supervisor and asked for time off. Family emergency.

The three of us were sitting around Craig's conference table, one of those folding metal tables with a vinyl top in simulated wood grain. Our mother kept one just like it in the garage, to haul out every spring for her annual yard sale. Come to think of it, Craig's entire office looked as if it had been furnished from yard sales, lending his practice a fly-by-night appearance. His suit looked like a hand-me-down, too, the baggy jacket dwarfing his small frame, and he blinked a lot behind his owlish eyeglasses. Everything about him proclaimed his inexperience: hardly reassuring, even for mundane transactions, and positively alarming when Alex was a "person of interest" in a murder investigation.

"Craig knows that I'm the last person in the world who'd have wanted Mimi dead," my sister was explaining. "Mimi and I were going into business together. Doing the show was part of the build-up. That's why she agreed to be my model. Her customers would see how gorgeous I made her look and they'd sign on for the full package: facials, waxing, make-up—the stuff she does. Cuts and color—the stuff I do. We had a name picked out and everything. We were going to announce it today, after they named the winners."

The final round had been postponed until evening. Several of the contestants were still being questioned in an effort to establish who'd seen the victim last, and the police were reviewing footage from various security cameras throughout the Convention Center, looking for the culprit. Needless to say, the press was all over the story. Alex was not an official suspect, although the police had made her promise she'd stay in the area, readily available for further questioning. When they brought her in again, she intended to be prepared with documentary evidence.

"Craig negotiated the contract with Mimi's attorney and we both signed it in the presence of a notary," she said. "We'd played with the idea of calling it 'Courvoisier and After,' but we both decided that sounded like someone who had too much to drink. Mimi came up with 'Happily Ever After.'"

"That was generous of her," I said, "giving you top billing." After was our last name.

"Mimi was incredibly generous. I think I was in shock this morning, when I found her...the way she was."

Alex, I realized, was genuinely upset. In the course of the morning, she hadn't bothered to touch up her face, and her mascara was flaking, the liner smeared. I'd never once seen her with raccoon eyes.

"I can't stop thinking about her being stabbed in the back," she said. "Who would want to kill Mimi?"

Craig cleared his throat. "Erm, I'm afraid you've got a pretty good motive."

"Why would I have wanted to kill my business partner?"

"Erm, she wasn't your business partner. Not legally. Not anymore, I mean. She, erm, backed out of the contract."

"She what?"

The attorney (if that's what he was) had a fit of coughing. "I got a call yesterday afternoon from her lawyer. He was overnighting the paperwork. I left a message in your voicemail. You must have gotten it."

"I checked my messages when I got home last night."

"I left it on your business number."

My sister flipped her hair, a key sign of irritation. "The shop was closed yesterday. I was at the hair show."

"Oops," said Craig.

I chose that moment to step in. "Who else would have had a motive to kill Mimi?"

"Who besides me, you mean? If I'd known—which I didn't—that Mimi welched on our agreement." Here Alex glared at her attorney, who withered, looking even smaller inside his hand-me-down suit.

"I think that's a very good question," said Craig. "Who else in Ms. Courvoisier's circle of associates would have liked to see her dead?" His words came out in a rush, as if he were attempting to get the sentence out before he was felled by another fit of coughing. Or by my sister.

"Her boss, maybe. At Spa Europa. Signora Carla." Alex grew pensive. "If she found out."

"Found what out?" I asked.

"Mimi hadn't told her she was quitting to go into business with me. She made me promise to keep it quiet until the show. I would've told you, Ashley, but you're always at the zoo."

"I'm sorry." As a rule, Alex and I told one another everything, but it had been a while since we'd really talked. Maybe I was spending too much time with the chimps.

Craig raised his hand, as if he needed one of us to call on him before he dared to speak again.

"Yes?" I prompted.

"Ms. Courvoisier's attorney made it clear, when he phoned to say that his client had voided the agreement, that we could not disclose the, erm, prior contract. They did offer an incentive for holding up your end of the bargain. A pretty healthy incentive, if you want my opinion. Off the record," he added hastily. "It's all in the documents that came in this morning. I've only given them a cursory glance, but the terms are more than fair."

This was the longest speech I'd heard him make, and he did sound more lawyerly, when he used words like incentive and cursory and insisted on speaking off the record. But I still didn't understand why Mimi had been so hush-hush.

"Spa Europa is a very upscale place, very expensive," Alex explained. "Their treatments start at a hundred and twenty-five dollars, and that's for a fifty-minute facial. Massages are two hundred. That includes the use of the sauna, and they've got these posh robes and slippers. A class joint. With those prices, you'd think the staff would be doing okay, but they're not."

"Why not?" I asked.

"Because Signora Carla pays them peanuts. Mimi said she wouldn't give them more than thirty-four hours a week so she doesn't have to provide benefits. Well, the schedule says they're part-time workers, but most of them end up working extra shifts because Signora Carla overbooks."

Craig slammed his hand down on the table. "That's illegal!"

We both looked at him, startled less by the noise than by the assertiveness of the outburst. Craig seemed startled too.

"Erm, I got an 'A' in labor law," he said, shrinking back inside his suit.

"Mimi said it was practically a sweat shop, and she was positive that some of the manicurists are undocumented. She was totally fed up, but she kept putting off telling Signora Carla that she was leaving." My twin shivered involuntarily. "The woman's a terror."

"You mean the employees are afraid of her?" Craig was getting worked up again.

Alex didn't dispute this. "There's only one person at Spa Europa who's not afraid of Signora Carla. Her head esthetician, Daniél, does pretty much as he pleases—not that he isn't good at his job. He's brilliant, and that's why he's untouchable. He's got such a following, the place would fold if he left and Signora Carla knows it."

"I want to talk to this man," I told her. "How do I get to him?"

⧗

DANIÉL'S TREATMENT room was a shrine for Liz Taylor. Framed stills from every phase of the actress's career covered the walls. Liz as Cleopatra: black hair bobbed, violet eyes rimmed with kohl, she stared out exotically from beneath a beaded headdress. Liz in *National Velvet*, clear-eyed innocent and so young. The ripe Liz of *BUtterfield 8*, luscious in a close-fitting sheath. By then she'd become a home-wrecker, but who could blame Eddie Fisher for succumbing to those succulent charms? I guess I was used to the blown-out Liz whose face used to adorn the tabloids I saw in the supermarket checkout line. Padding in my spa slippers from one photograph to the next, I was awestruck by the woman's beauty.

"She must taste like butter," Daniél said, coming in to find me standing in front of *Cat on a Hot Tin Roof*. I wasn't sure what I'd expected from a black male esthetician named Daniél, but it certainly wasn't the person who was now helping me onto the bed in the center of the room and getting me settled under the covers.

"You're a client of Mimi's?" he said dubiously.

My sister had wangled a favor out of the spa's receptionist, a girl she'd known from beauty school, and managed to get me slotted into Daniél's schedule that same afternoon. We decided it would be the best way to get him alone without putting him on his guard. I hadn't been keen on subjecting myself to a facial. The chimps were very sensitive and found most fragrances off-putting although Bart, the bonobo, was fond of my coconut shampoo.

"When are you going to stop playing with monkeys and get a real job?" Alex had said when I complained about the scents I'd be subjecting myself to at the spa.

"I have a real job."

"I mean a job where you don't play in monkey poop all day long."

Although I was wearing the same robe and slippers as everyone else in the salon, I must not have looked like someone who was a regular client at Spa Europa.

"A friend recommended Mimi, but this is actually my first facial," I admitted.

Daniél closed his eyes and it took a moment for him to answer. "Mimi passed away this morning. A terrible tragedy."

"I'm sorry," I said. "My friend thought the world of her."

"Most people did." Brushing the hair off my forehead, he wound a powder blue turban around my head. His touch was remarkably gentle. "The first thing I'm going to do is clean your face. Then I'll analyze your skin." He squirted some pale green lotion into the palm of his hand and began to massage my face, fingers dancing in small circles from my forehead to my temples, inwards from my cheekbones to the bridge of my nose, down around my mouth to the point of my chin, then up and outwards along my jaw. I closed my eyes and let myself be soothed by the new age music they'd piped into the salon, whales singing amidst the splashing of waves. Not my thing ordinarily, but here it was exactly right.

"This is our chamomile cleanser," Daniél said. "It contains the essence of eleven herbs and flowers." He moved away and I heard the sound of water running in the sink. "Tell me if this is too hot." He placed a warm towel over my face and blotted the lotion from my skin. I felt my pores opening to the heat.

"No, that feels good," I murmured from under the towel. I would have liked to forget everything and enjoy the treatment, but my twin was a "person of interest" in a murder investigation. I opened my eyes when he lifted the towel off my face and got right to the point. "What was Mimi like?"

Daniél moved to sit on the stool beside me and tucked a stray hair back inside the turban. "Please close your eyes," he said. He placed a moist cotton pad on each of my eyelids, pressed lightly around the edges, then directed a high-intensity light on my face. Even through my closed eyelids, I sensed its harsh glare. The esthetician's fingertips moved briskly over my skin, feeling the wrinkles beginning to form in the corners of my eyes and the blackheads embedded around my nostrils. I wondered if he was going to ignore my question.

"Mimi?" I asked, again.

"You're very yin," he said, squeezing a blackhead. "She was too."

Ouch, I thought. But he'd given me an opening. "Really? I had the impression she was a yang. My friend described her as nurturing, an earth-mother type." Considering the way she'd looked that morning, this was a stretch.

"She came on like a yang," acknowledged Daniél, squeezing a spot on my forehead. "But she was a lot shrewder than she looked. Most people didn't look. They thought they could trust her because she smiled a lot and told them personal things about herself."

"You didn't trust her."

"It's not wise to trust anyone," he said, "particularly on a first acquaintance."

Daniél switched off the light and I was relieved to be back in darkness. I heard the sound of glass clinking and imagined him rooting among the bottles on the counter. He returned to my side and began spreading a thickish substance over my face.

"What's that?" The goo smelled like peppermint and made my skin tingle. Bart liked the taste of peppermint. We'd trained him to brush his teeth and zoo patrons got a kick of watching him lick the toothpaste off the brush. Sometimes he'd try to eat the brush.

"This is our exfoliating masque. It penetrates your pores and removes the dead layer of skin. While it dries, I'm going to massage your hands. You might feel a little tightness as the masque hardens." I heard the squeak of a pump bottle followed by the sound of him rubbing his palms together. He took my right hand and began to knead it, starting with the fleshy place at the base of my thumb and working outwards along my fingers. I was suddenly aware of how much tension I'd been carrying around for the past several hours. I took a deep breath and let it out slowly, making a conscious effort to relax.

"That's better," Daniél said. "Now why don't you tell me why you're really here?"

With my eyes closed, I told him everything. How Alex had found Mimi's body in the Hospitality Lounge, the red herring of the bottle of dye and the suicide note. The scissors in Mimi's back. How the two of them were planning to open their own shop, only Mimi'd had second thoughts. Daniél had warned against trusting people on a first acquaintance, but I trusted him completely. It comes from hanging around with the chimps, I think. My instincts about humans are rarely wrong.

"At least she had the decency to compensate my sister when she decided to back out," I concluded. Craig had mentioned a figure. Twenty-five thousand dollars was a very healthy incentive for keeping silent.

As I talked, Daniél finished massaging my hands, much to my regret. He cleaned the masque off my face and applied a soothing moisturizer, all without saying a word. Now, as he helped me sit up and removed the turban to release my hair, he offered a single sentence of advice.

"You and your sister might want to investigate how Mimi managed to come up with that kind of money, working in a job that pays minimum wage, plus tips."

⌛

"BLACKMAIL," said Craig. "That explains this." He held up a handwritten list of Asian names for Alex and me to see. "I found it in the documents Ms. Courvoisier's lawyer FedExed over, sandwiched between the pages."

Alex and I scrutinized the list, but neither one of us could figure out what it meant. Each name had a date beside it, a number in a column marked "hours," followed by an amount of money in a column marked "earnings." All totaled, the sums didn't amount to very much.

"It's nowhere near twenty-five thousand dollars," Alex pointed out. She was nervous because the final round of the competition would be taking place in less than an hour and she still hadn't met her model. Craig and I were sitting with her in the food court of

Providence Place, the fancy mall across the skybridge from the Convention Center. Craig and I had plates of Chinese take-out in front of us. Alex wasn't eating, having recently reapplied her make-up, but her attorney and I were both ravenous. Apart from the herbal infusion Daniél had handed me at the end of my treatment, to clear out any toxins that remained in my system, I hadn't eaten since breakfast.

"No," Craig agreed. "This is a list of undocumented employees and what they earned. Your sister's boss was paying them under the table. Paying them pennies. Just look at these numbers. Twelve hours of work for forty-eight dollars to Lin Yee on November 12th. Ten hours for forty dollars, and she was docked three dollars for lateness, according to this notation."

"So you think Signora Carla killed Mimi to keep word from getting out?" I had to admit, I was impressed by his deductive abilities.

He nodded. "I can take this evidence to the police and your sister will be cleared of all suspicion of wrongdoing."

"Not totally cleared," Alex interrupted. "The news picked up on the hair dye and the note. It makes me look bad." Not only did it make her look bad, I realized, it had shaken her belief in her own abilities. She needed to go into the final round with her confidence intact.

Craig removed his glasses. He straightened his shoulders and somehow seemed to fill out his suit jacket. When he smiled, I noticed that he had dimples. My sister noticed too.

"I talked to Mimi's lawyer. Mimi was planning to fake her suicide and skip out of town with the money. The new business was just a front, so she could open a bank account in the name of Happily Ever After and transfer the money without attracting suspicion. She was using you, but she thought if she paid you off, you wouldn't be sore."

"How'd you get the lawyer to admit to everything?" Alex wanted to know.

"I, erm, threatened him."

My sister and I spoke in unison. "You did?"

"Just a little. Hiring undocumented workers is a big-time no-no. If he knew about it—and this list suggests that he did—then he was obligated to report it to ICE."

"Could you get Mimi's lawyer to explain about the fake suicide on camera?" I asked.

Craig smiled. "That shouldn't be a problem."

My sister leaned across the table and planted a kiss on her attorney's cheek. She left a big smear, and she didn't even care that she'd marred her perfectly glossed mouth. "You know, Craig. With the right haircut, you could attract a better class of client."

"Erm, thanks," he said, making no move to wipe off the lipstick. "I happen to like the class of client I've attracted, but I wouldn't mind a haircut."

Occasionally, among chimps, a low-ranking male will surprise everyone by making off with an attractive female. I speared a cube of eggplant with spicy garlic sauce on the end of my chopsticks and put it into my mouth. I hope it worked out for the two of them.

V.S. KEMANIS

V.S. Kemanis has enjoyed a varied career in the law and the arts. As an attorney, she has worked for the Manhattan District Attorney, the NYS Organized Crime Task Force, state appellate courts, and judges. Publishing credits include the Dana Hargrove legal suspense series, five collections of short fiction on wide-ranging themes, and stories appearing in *Ellery Queen's Mystery Magazine* and *EQMM's Crooked Road, Vol. 3*, anthology, among others. She is a member of the Short Mystery Fiction Society and Mystery Writers of America, New York Chapter, where she serves on the Board of Directors. Find her at vskemanis.com.

SUCKER PUNCH

V.S. KEMANIS

THE TELLTALE GLEAM in Zach's eye gives him away. "I've got an idea."

Freddy knows that look, those words. Zach has been coming up with ideas ever since they were kids, scraping their knees on the streets of Oakland. Next-door neighbors, born within a month of each other, they're lifelong buddies. Zach wouldn't think of excluding Freddy from his latest plan.

"This one is a sure thing."

Another familiar claim. Freddy isn't the brightest lightbulb in the attic, but he knows enough to be skeptical. Are they millionaires yet? None of Zach's get-rich-quick schemes have ever gotten them anywhere. There've been a lot of them, a few more memorable than others.

At age five, the lemonade stand. To boost profits, Zach watered the product (supplied by Freddy's mom) to the point of questionable lemon content. Girls and women swarmed, buying many half-full paper cups, not to sip the tasteless liquid but to drink in Zach's charms. Even at that age he was a devilish, charismatic entrepreneur. Freddy, the good-natured sidekick, smiled dumbly and asked his mom for another pitcher. They made five dollars, split two-three, the lion's share to Zach. It was his idea, after all.

At age nine, a backyard carnival. Zach set up a dart game, rope swing, stilt walk, horseshoes, and dime toss. He made up skits for Freddy the Clown ("you already look goofy—just add this wig and nose"). A quarter per show, and a quarter for every ride and game. Zach's parents thought it was a cute idea, unaware of their son's profit motive. As the coffers filled, the plan imploded when irate moms and dads stormed the house, refusing to give their kids any more money for carnival games. Zach's dad made him give it all back. Freddy the Clown suffered lasting damage to his reputation.

At age fifteen, the Earthworm Farm. Memories of the failed carnival inspired Zach to insist on Freddy's backyard for the venture. "Organic earthworm castings. This stuff is black gold, Freddy. Grows tomatoes as big as your head. We'll make a ton selling worm turds to gardeners." Freddy timidly balked, Zach persisted—he needed Freddy's paper route money for the initial investment. "They're hermaphrodites and screw like crazy. We'll have millions before we know it." They set up the earthworm beds and watched the population explode, only to suffer a devastating plague. An infestation of red mites—all Freddy's fault, if you asked Zach. Weren't the worm beds in Freddy's backyard? He should have taken better care.

At age twenty, card counting. Despite his innate brilliance, Zach barely survived high school, flunked out of community college, and couldn't hold down a job. Minutes after losing a job at the multiplex, he came up with a Hollywood-worthy plan to use his photographic memory for lucre. "I'll cut you in, Freddy. Twenty percent, and *I'll* do all the work." They practiced, Freddy the blackjack dealer. As soon as they both turned twenty-one, they were off to Vegas to rake in the coin. "Just watch out for the bouncers," Zach instructed, coming up with an elaborate system of signals. When the day was done, they were down five hundred—their joint investment—and Freddy was out on his tail. The casino bouncers didn't like the looks of that sweaty youth pacing, twitching, saluting, and winking around the blackjack tables.

Barely a year has passed since that one, and now Zach shows up at Freddy's apartment with his laptop, spouting, "I have an idea," again. Another "sure thing." These words always trigger a flash-bang mind-collage of all their ventures, from lemonade stand to carnival to earthworm farm to card counting and many, many more in between. Zach has a way of convincing the world that he's better than his circumstances, destined to be rich and famous or, at least, rich. Freddy always listens. Freddy always gives in. But maybe it's time for a change.

"I don't know, Zach. None of our businesses ever work out."

"Is it *my* fault you were dropped on your head at birth?" One of Zach's favorite jokes. Freddy is getting a little tired of it, but he lets it go. Zach always follows up—as he does now—with a brotherly punch on the shoulder and a huge, toothy smile, just to show it's all in fun. The gleam in his dark eyes and his magnetic good looks are irresistible to everyone in the world, Freddy included. Zach knows this about himself. His life plan is to find a lonely, rich, older lady and rope her in with his fawning sex appeal. It's his best idea yet, a potentially huge moneymaker. He imagines the sunny days under his lady's admiring gaze, floating on her yacht in the Caribbean, showing off his tanned bod in a Speedo, butter dripping onto his chest from mouthfuls of succulent lobster tail. So far, that brilliant idea hasn't worked out either.

"Ha ha." For the umpteenth time, Freddy laughs along about being dropped on his head. "So, tell me. What's the new idea?"

"Crowdfunding. It's ridiculously easy. Just ask people for money *and they give it to you.*"

"Don't you need a good cause for that? Like, you can't pay the chemo bill for your two-year-old with cancer. You know, with photos of the kid's bald head."

"It doesn't have to be a cause or a charity. Have you ever looked at these sites? People are suckers for *anything.*" Zach powers up his laptop and enters a search. "Look at this one. She needs five thousand to remove the tattoos she willingly allowed someone to fry all over her body." The top photo on the page shows a scorpion on the young woman's nose, a snake slithering from jaw to jaw along her hairline. "Do I feel sorry for this girl? Am I going to give her money to fix her mistakes? *Noooo*. But ten people already did."

Zach laughs heartily, an infectious mirth. Before he leaves the tattooed lady, Freddy notices an updated photo, posted midway into her campaign, meant to demonstrate her serious intentions. Half of the snake is gone, replaced with raw-looking skin. "I'm using every penny I earn, but it isn't enough," she writes. "I desperately need your help!" The ten contributors aren't overly impressed, pledging only five or ten dollars each. One of them comments, "Burn, baby! I hope it hurts!"

Freddy looks on as Zach scrolls through the listings. Many of them, he would agree, are laughable. Interspersed among the truly needy cases—the cancer sufferers and accident victims—are bizarre tech startups, wacky inventors, starving artists, and spiritual messengers begging for attention and, more to the point, begging for big bucks. Few are making their goals.

"Looks like only the charities and horrible diseases are getting any money," Freddy points out. "Besides, I don't see why you need *me* for this. You can do it on your own. I'm making out okay. Just got a raise at Food Super." Freddy's bloody white apron attests to his dedication behind the counter in meats, poultry, and fish, a job he's held since graduating from high school. He never went to college, sure that he wouldn't make it through anyway. At twenty-two, he's okay with his life and looks forward to the possibilities—promotion to head of the meat department, or manager of his own store one day. Who needs Zach and his crazy ideas?

"How could I cut you out, man?" Zach dons a rueful expression. "Sometimes I feel bad about a couple of those old projects."

Really? Freddy is taken aback.

But then Zach's face lights up, and he gives Freddy the standard brotherly punch on the shoulder. "Seriously, dude, I've figured it out. I think it'll look better with a team. A few photos of the two of us. Blood brothers, lifelong friends. What could be a better hook?"

"What exactly do the 'brothers' need money for?"

"Our passion, our dream. What we've been saving up for. A trip to the Himalayas, climbing Mount Everest."

"Really. Okay. Yeah. Our dream."

"We've got the photos to prove it." Zach opens his photo library and comes up with a picture of the two of them wearing muscle shirts and shorts, Zach's arm slung around Freddy's shoulder, at the top of Mount Diablo.

"That was a long time ago."

"Yeah, we were seniors. You remember, we cut that day."

Freddy remembers it well, the way Zach strong-armed him into going on a hike, missing a crucial English test, with serious consequences to his grade. But it was fun, he remembers that too, and he misses all the many good times they've had together. Lately, they've been drifting apart. Zach always inspired zaniness, spontaneity, and manic fun, and the Diablo trip was one of the best. No moneymaking schemes, just a day with perfect weather, hiking up a mountain. A short one. Someone at the top took that picture.

Everest might be taking this adventure too far. "To follow our dream?"

"Yeah," Zach confirms, reinventing history. "Here we are, in training. My leg muscles are killer in this pic."

Besides the leg muscles, Zach's face has a winning smile under the cool sunglasses, adding to his overall hunk image. Freddy doesn't look too bad himself, his scrawny calves partly in shadow. In the photo, as in real life, Zach is the center of attention, Freddy the appendage, fulfilling his role as sidekick, conveying their status as "bros."

"But…" Freddy begins his usual, timid objections while googling on his smartphone. "You can see we're on Mount Diablo and," he finds it, "the elevation is only 3,848 feet."

"Not the point, Fred. This is obviously a training photo. I'll beef up the pitch and throw in some facts about our grueling climbing regimen." Zach starts drafting the text.

"Facts?"

Zach is typing, not listening. "I researched the whole thing. The best time to summit Everest is either the spring or the fall, so we'll cut the campaign off two months from today, in time for a spring trek. Perfect. That's April Fool's Day, the day for suckers. I figure it costs at least twenty grand each for the trip, so I'll ask for forty. I found this site that doesn't dock you for not making your goal, so anything we get is ours, eighty-twenty." He flicks a look at Freddy. "Only because it's my idea."

When Zach finishes the pitch, Freddy looks it over. He isn't quite sure about the spelling of "shurpa," "Himolayas," and "trecking," and has even bigger concerns about Zach's use of the crowdfunding site. "If we get any money from this, we have to use it for what you wrote here. No way are you going to Everest. I know I'm not."

Zach breaks into a confident smile. "No way can they get inside our heads. It's *fine* as long as we're *planning* the trip. We'll make a lot of cash, but it isn't going to be forty. Maybe twenty or thirty, so, you know, uh-oh. Too bad, not enough to go *this* spring. We'll have to keep training and fundraising."

"You won't get thirty or even twenty. Who's going to help two bros take a hike?"

Zach's face registers a glimmer of doubt. Maybe he sees Freddy's point. "I'll throw in a few more hooks." He types madly. The trip is a "spiritual journey" ("chicks love that stuff," he tells Freddy), and the money they spend in "Nepaul" will help boost the impoverished economy. Freddy takes a look and puzzles over another one of Zach's "facts."

"When were we 'tragically robbed of our *life savings* for our spiritual journey?'"

"Last year. In Vegas. At the blackjack tables. I know that was every penny I had. Yours too."

Freddy shakes his head. "Whatever." He gives up. When Zach is on a roll, he can't be stopped. He's bound to fail, of course, but it's no skin off Freddy's back. His only investment for this one is the use of his first name, "Freddy, Zach's bro," and his smile on a photo, taken on a nice afternoon, five years ago.

⏳

ONCE THE CAMPAIGN IS UP, Zach disappears. Typical. In the old days, depending on the project, his temporary disappearance usually meant he was abandoning any further efforts until it was time to reappear and blame Freddy for botching the ingenious plan.

This one is different. Zach demands nothing of Freddy and will have nothing to pin on him. And Zach hasn't been around much in the past year anyway, so his absence now isn't very different. Freddy is left with nothing but his mild curiosity. In the first week, he takes a quick look at the crowdfunding site during his break from the meat counter, just to see what's happening. It's day four, and "Send Two Bros to Everest!" has garnered only three donations of five dollars each, one contributor commenting, "Nice gams!"

Back on the job, thinking about it, Freddy brings the cleaver down "thwack" on a leg of lamb. *Yeah, Zach, dream on.* It's not Freddy's dream, so he pushes the scheme entirely out of his mind.

⏳

FREDDY HASN'T SEEN Zach for almost two months when a few strange things happen.

First, an odd encounter with two young women at Food Super. They're friends or sisters maybe, about Freddy's age, and they're planning a dinner party. Giggling, they ask Freddy's advice on the tenderest cut of beef. He recommends the top sirloin. They stare at him openly, in awe (something Freddy dreams of, but never seems to get from the opposite sex). They laugh and look at each other, sending a silent message. Then, the prettier one turns to stare at him again and says, "*That* was quick." Her eyes descend to Freddy's hands, holding that nice chunk of top sirloin. She asks him to wrap it up for her.

Days later, two city health inspectors make an unannounced visit to the meat department. They spend a long time testing the meat and bone saw. Freddy's boss, Albert, is completely thrown by the inspector's question, "When did you fix the safety on this?" The safety has always been in place, Al tells them—why are they asking? "There's been a complaint." Al is mystified at this news but maintains his respectful demeanor until the inspectors are gone. He turns to Freddy with narrowed eyes and pain on his face. "You made a complaint?" Freddy is mortified, but what is Al to think? For such a long time, it's been just the two of them together, Al and Freddy, the team in meats.

Finally, it's April Fool's Day. During his lunch break, sitting outside the meat locker, Freddy gets a text from Zach. "How's a cool 5 grand, your cut! $$$ here soon!" Unbelievable. Freddy uses the calculator on his phone. It's an eighty-twenty split, so that means... Zach pulled in twenty-five grand? How is that possible?

Freddy opens "Send Two Bros to Everest!" and finds, splashed in the middle of the webpage, an "Update! Urgent Appeal!" posted a week ago. The three photos say it all. Freddy needs a moment to remember the first two. A couple of years ago, Zach visited Food Super, in the mood to entertain Freddy. Butcher jokes were flying. In the first photo, Freddy stands behind the cutting table in his soiled apron, his face snarled in blood lust as he holds the cleaver high in the air, about to fall on a pile of red muscle and ribs. The second photo shows the meat and bone saw, spattered with bloody remains. The third photo is a close up of...well, where did Zach get that one? A horror movie? It's a hand, or rather, part of a hand.

Freddy's jaw drops to his knees as he reads the update. Sadly, a tragic work accident at Food Super has cut short their hopes for a spring trek. The bros are now planning for the fall, but money is desperately needed for Freddy's new, mechanical prosthesis and intense physical therapy, so he can master its use on the treacherous snow-covered, oxygen-thin slopes. "Be generous, give now and help the first handless climber to summit Everest!"

Before Freddy gets his head around this, Al marches up, red-eyed and fuming, flanked by two police officers.

"Frederick Measleton?" says one of them.

Freddy stares back in stunned silence.

Al is practically crying. "After all these years, Freddy, I don't understand how you could do this to me. How could you do this to Food Super?"

Al is like a father to Freddy, the last person he would ever want to hurt. His heart is beating fast, his voice lost to him. Can't they see this is all Zach's doing? But...nothing is ever Zach's fault.

"You're coming with us," the officer says.

⧖

WHEN FREDDY WALKS into the police station, Zach is handcuffed to a wooden bench. He's a new Zach, contrite and unrecognizable in these words: "Don't worry about a thing, man. I told them already. It's all on me."

A surprising sound to Freddy, a person who's been the fall guy for so many of Zach's failures. A person who has heard about a fictional fall on his head at birth, over and over and over again.

But, on further thought, maybe it isn't so surprising. They've had some great times together. Didn't Zach always include Freddy in everything he did, the good and the bad? That's what lifelong buddies do.

When all is said and done, Freddy is cleared, Al forgives him, and Zach gets a fair deal for his first entanglement with the law. The judge goes light. Community service and restitution. Zach is ordered to stay away from Food Super. More important, lesson learned. There will be no more moneymaking schemes.

Not long after that, the bros get together in the park and talk about doing a hike up Mount Tamalpais. A very doable 2,572 feet.

"It's funny, man, but you were right," Zach says.

Another first. Freddy has never heard Zach say he was right. "About what?"

"No one was gonna help two bros take a hike."

"Yeah, I told you. People fall for those medical emergencies. That was some photo you posted on the update. Where did you find it? That sliced hand."

"Sliced ham? Oh, sorry. *Hand.*" Zach lets loose a raucous laugh.

Freddy laughs along. When they stop laughing, Zach says, "They have all kinds of bloody photos on these medical websites."

"Well, that was some photo you found." Freddy shakes his head and falls silent for a moment. Then he says, "You were right too."

"About what?"

"No way can they get inside your head to know if you're actually going to do what you *say* you're going to do."

"Then why did they arrest me for fraud?"

"Because you forgot something. They don't *have* to get inside your head if the thing you're planning is obviously impossible. A lie. Fake news."

"Fake news, eh?"

"No facts to back it up. No sliced hand."

"You need facts?" A devilish grin curls Zach's lips. He snatches Freddy's hand and pushes it through an imaginary blade, making a high-pitched, metallic squeal.

"Argh," Freddy yells. He can almost feel it.

Zach lets go, stops the squeal, and gives another hearty laugh. Freddy shudders. For a month now, he's been wary of the meat and bone saw at Food Super. Zach's little joke is no help.

But, a minute later, all is forgiven and forgotten. It's a bright, sunny day, a good day for a hike. Zach breaks out in a big, toothy smile and delivers the old brotherly punch to the shoulder.

JUDY PENZ SHELUK

Judy Penz Sheluk (editor/author) is the author of two mystery series: the Glass Dolphin Mysteries and the Marketville Mysteries. Her short stories appear in several collections, including *Live Free or Tri* and *Unhappy Endings*. Judy is a member of Sisters in Crime National, Toronto, and Guppy Chapters, the Short Mystery Fiction Society, International Thriller Writers, South Simcoe Arts Council, and Crime Writers of Canada, where she serves on the Board of Directors. Find her at judypenzsheluk.com.

PLAN D

JUDY PENZ SHELUK

JENNY WASN'T sure when she first got the idea. Maybe it was the big ice storm back in the winter of 2012. One day there were icicles hanging from the eaves, glistening in the pale moonlit night like giant teardrops. The next day, as the temperature soared and the sun shone, the icicles had slowly melted, drip by drip, until they had vanished without a trace.

"TED GOT LAID OFF AGAIN," Jenny said. She was sitting in the Coffee Klatch Café with her sister, Stephanie.

Stephanie raised a well-groomed eyebrow, then shrugged. "I'm not surprised. Can't be a lot of demand for an appliance repairman's helper these days. We live in such a disposable society."

Jenny concentrated on her vanilla bean non-fat latte, extra foam, took a sip, grimacing slightly at the too sweet taste. She'd have to remember to order half the syrup next time. They always overdid the syrup.

"So is Ted finally willing to admit it's time to get some

retraining?" Stephanie asked. "Or would that take too much initiative on his part?"

"Ted has initiative, he's just had a string of bad luck," Jenny said, although she knew it wasn't true. She could picture her husband sprawled out on the battered brown sofa, a TV remote in his left hand, a scotch on the rocks in the other. When it came to watching television, Ted was ambidextrous. And ambitious. He could channel surf with the best of them.

"Maybe it's time for you to stop making excuses for him, Jenny, and start making him accountable. Lord knows he's been dead weight since the day you two got married. Retraining just might be the answer. Unless you have another plan."

Dead weight. That had to be a sign to confide in her sister.

"As a matter of fact," Jenny said, "I do."

☒

NATURALLY JENNY DIDN'T IMPLEMENT her plan straight away. She was cautious if nothing else, and besides, part of her still loved Ted. Still remembered the way things had been, in the beginning. Before the endless stream of minimum wage jobs and broken promises. There might even be a chance to save him, save their marriage, save her sanity.

There was also the added complication of Stephanie. Jenny had made the mistake of confiding in her that day at the Coffee Klatch Café, had misread the sign. She thought her sister would understand.

She hadn't. Instead she'd gotten all holier than thou on her. In the end, Jenny had assured Stephanie that she'd just been kidding around. "Icicles," she had said, forcing a laugh. "C'mon, Steph, what do you take me for?"

And yet, despite all of that, the idea continued to niggle at her. Niggled through the first daffodils of spring, and two more lost jobs, one "too junior," the other "too senior" for Ted's skill set. It niggled through the hot, sticky nights of summer—the air conditioning turned off to save on hydro—Ted lying snoring and slack-jawed by her side, a thin stream of drool finding its way down his stubbly chin and onto the freshly washed cotton sheets.

It kept on niggling right through the cool, crisp days of autumn, especially when Jenny found herself doing ninety-nine point nine percent of the leaf raking while an apparently "allergic to leaf mould" Ted stayed indoors to watch football. *What if,* she thought, cramming another mound of leaves into the oversized paper yard waste bag, *what if the icicle became an ice pick?*

For the first time since she was a kid, Jenny looked forward to winter.

⏳

IT TURNED out the icicle wouldn't cut it. All those months of thinking and waiting and the idea turned out to be a big, fat, watery bust. Repeated attempts on Teddy—a stuffed bear, not her husband —had only served to prove it over and over and over again. The tip either broke or melted before it could do the job, leaving Teddy wet and wounded, but decidedly alive. Well, as alive as a stuffed bear could be, although Jenny was convinced that at one point his big black button eyes had begged her to stop.

Jenny could have taken it as a sign to give up. She believed in signs, in omens. Like the time she couldn't find her car keys. As it turned out, she'd put the keys in the mailbox by mistake, and a good thing, too. She'd managed to avoid getting into a major league pile-up on the highway. Folks had been stuck on there for hours while the emergency responders and tow trucks tried to clean up the mess.

But she couldn't let it go. The thought of another ten years of marriage, of another decade of defending Ted to Stephanie, left her feeling sucked dry and semi-suicidal.

She'd checked with a lawyer—under an assumed name, of course—and a divorce meant splitting everything with Ted, right down the middle. Well screw that. She'd already given Ted the better part of her adult life, the part where she'd had cellulite-free thighs and size zero jeans. She'd be damned if she'd give him half the house and half the money too. It was her that made sure the mortgage got paid, her that kept the refrigerator stocked with food, her that had managed to save a few measly dollars for retirement.

Her, her, her. It was always all on her.

What Jenny needed was a Plan B. Only this time, she wouldn't share it with Stephanie.

She wouldn't share it with anyone.

⏳

THE IDEA CAME to Jenny when she was filling up the ice cube trays. She rarely used ice, rarely drank cold beverages, her drink of choice being coffee. But today she'd felt like a diet cola, and as usual Ted had used up all the ice for his after dinner cocktails.

Recently, coming off a two-day marathon of back-to-back episodes of *Mad Men*, he'd switched from scotch to Manhattans, which turned out to be a blend of whiskey, sweet vermouth, bitters, and a maraschino cherry.

As if they had money for such nonsense. Always a dreamer, Ted was, as if an alcoholic beverage would transform him from an unemployed loser into a bigwig in the advertising business.

Nevertheless, for once Ted had managed to make her life easier. Jenny had read about a Georgia woman who'd killed off two men by poisoning them with antifreeze. Apparently antifreeze had two distinct advantages as a murder weapon: it was odorless, and the sweet taste was easily disguised in liquids. Not that Jenny was about to try any herself.

Further research revealed that the ethylene glycol in antifreeze was deadly when consumed and absorbed into the bloodstream. Even better, it could take a few days to bring on death by a combination of kidney failure, heart attack, and coma.

In the case of the Georgia woman's husband, and a few years later, her boyfriend, the men had exhibited severe flulike symptoms before being taken to the emergency room. Both died less than twenty-four hours after they left the hospital, with heart failure initially being identified as the cause.

Where the Georgia woman had made her mistake, Jenny

decided after reading everything she could about the case, was that she'd used the same method for both men. It was only after the boyfriend had died that the police decided to exhume the body of her first husband. Which meant the Georgia woman would have gotten away with murder, if she had thought things out a little bit better.

Jenny acknowledged that her own plan was not without its faults. It seemed antifreeze didn't freeze until -40 or so, far colder than a typical freezer. Which made sense, when you thought about the name. Why else call it antifreeze?

Then there was the problem of the color, which manufacturers added so it was instantly recognizable. She'd found green, pink, reddish-orange, and blue at the automotive supply store, and bought all four, but even diluted with water, the color remained problematic, at least until all that was left was a mere drop. By that point, it might have looked clear-ish, and it just might have frozen, but Jenny doubted there'd be enough poison left to do the job— unless she continued to make the ice cube concoction for weeks on end.

As much as she was tired of Ted, Jenny didn't think she had the stomach to poison him in dribs and drabs. And the last thing she needed was Ted getting sick enough to see a doctor, but not sick enough to die. With her luck, he'd be an invalid, and she'd be at his beck and call for the rest of her days.

Simply put, making ice cubes out of antifreeze just wouldn't work. Jenny toyed with the idea of adding antifreeze to the sweet vermouth, which had a brownish-red color, but by the time she thought of it Ted had abandoned Manhattans and gone back to his scotch on the rocks. It was just like him not to stick with something. Even an imaginary work cocktail was too much of a commitment.

What Jenny needed was a Plan C.

The next-door neighbor was always filling his front yard skating rink, eyesore that it was.

What if that water somehow flooded their driveway one night?

And what if she sent Ted out to go get milk, if he slipped and fell on the ice, hit his head…

It was a plan worth considering.

☒

"I'M JUST glad that Ted's found a job," Jenny said, trying to insert a note of pride in her voice. She was sitting in the Coffee Klatch Café with her sister, Stephanie. Ted waved at them from behind the counter. He was wearing the brown-and-white striped apron that all the baristas wore, though admittedly the rest of the staff was a few years younger than he was.

"Ted does seem pleased with himself," Stephanie said. "But a barista, Jenny. Seriously, what sort of career is that for a forty-five-year-old man?"

"So maybe this isn't his dream job, but after his fall in the driveway a couple of weeks ago, I'm just glad he's able to work at all."

"You've got a point there. He was lucky that the fur-lined hood of his parka softened his fall."

"Yes, that *was* lucky," Jenny said, staring down at her latte. "Actually I'm impressed with how seriously Ted seems to be taking this. He even managed to get the foam on my latte just right."

"Well, as long as you're happy, I'm happy," Stephanie said. "You are happy, aren't you? I mean you've abandoned that ridiculous idea with the icicles. Because Ted mentioned that he found you stabbing a stuffed teddy bear, and I have to admit I was more than a little bit worried."

Now that was news to Jenny. She had no idea Ted had known about her experiments with Teddy, never mind that he had mentioned it to Stephanie.

"I was just releasing some frustrations. It was all perfectly harmless. Even the bear came out unscathed. A gentle wash in the laundry and he was as good as new."

"It's just that we both know how obsessive you can be when you get an idea in your head."

Jenny thought about the half empty jugs of antifreeze in the garage. She probably should have thrown them out, instead of keeping them. Looked at in the wrong light, folks might consider an antifreeze collection as obsessive. And flooding the driveway only around Ted's car had been a bit sloppy.

"What are you trying to say, Stephanie?"

"Just be careful, that's all I'm saying, Jenny. Just be careful. Who knows what Ted will do if he suspects——"

"There's nothing to suspect," Jenny said, "and even if there were, Ted would be the last guy on the block to figure it out." She took a sip of her vanilla bean non-fat latte, grimaced at the too sweet taste. She'd made of point of telling Ted to give her half the syrup, and instead, he must have given her double. It was just like him to screw up the simplest of jobs. Before long, he'd be fired from this one too. She was about to take it back when she saw the look on his face.

"Made it especially for you, baby," Ted said, smiling. The way he used to smile at her, back when things were good between them. Before the minimum wage jobs and all the broken promises.

Jenny took another sip of her vanilla bean latte and decided to finish it, for Ted's sake.

After all, a little bit of extra syrup wouldn't kill her.

THE LINEUP

Tom Barlow
tjbarlow.com

Susan Daly
susandaly.com

Lisa de Nikolits
lisadenikolitswriter.com

P.A. De Voe
padevoe.com

Peter DiChellis
shortwalkdarkstreet.wordpress.com

Lesley A. Diehl
lesleyadiehl.com

Mary Dutta
Twitter: @Mary_Dutta

C.C. Guthrie
Goodreads: C.C.Guthrie

William Kamowski
williamkamowski.com

V.S. Kemanis
vskemanis.com

Lisa Lieberman
DeathlessProse.com.

Edward Lodi
Facebook: Rock Village Publishing

Rosemary McCracken
rosemarymccracken.com

LD Masterson
ldmasterson-author.blogspot.com

Edith Maxwell
edithmaxwell.com

Judy Penz Sheluk
judypenzsheluk.com

KM Rockwood
kmrockwood.com

Peggy Rothschild
peggyrothschild.net

Johanna Beate Stumpf
johannawritesstuff.wordpress.com

Vicki Weisfeld
vweisfeld.com

Chris Wheatley
silverpilgrim.com

Made in the USA
Middletown, DE
03 June 2020